EDITED BY

DANIELLE ACKLEY-MCPHAIL
JOHN L. FRENCH

PUBLISHED BY
eSpec Books LLC
Danielle McPhail, Publisher
PO Box 242,
Pennsville, New Jersey 08070
www.especbooks.com

ISBN: 978-1-956463-27-9
ISBN (ebook): 978-1-956463-26-2

All persons, places, and events in this book are fictitious
and any resemblance to actual persons, places, or events is purely
coincidental.

Cover Art, Design, and Interior Graphics:
Mike McPhail, McP Digital Graphics
Interior Design: Danielle McPhail, McP Digital Graphics

Our Word Mechanics

Danielle Ackley-McPhail

Derek Tyler Attico

James Chambers

John L. French

Heather E. Hutsell

Misty Massey

Bernie Mojzes

Aaron Rosenberg

Ken Schrader

Maria V. Snyder

David Lee Summers

Steampunk Titles by Espec Books

The Clockwork Chronicles
The Clockwork Witch
The Clockwork Solution
(Michelle D. Sonnier)

Baba Ali and the Clockwork Djinn
(Danielle Ackley-McPhail
and Day Al-Mohamed)

A Curse of Ash and Iron
(Christine Norris)

Spirit Seeker
(Jeff Young)

Esprit De Corpse
(Ef Deal)

Crimson Whisper
(Ken Schrader)

Steampunk Anthologies by Espec Books

After Punk:
Steampowered tales of the Afterlife

Gaslight & Grimm
Grimm Machinations

A Cast of Crows

The Weird Wild West

FOR THOSE KIDS
—PAST, PRESENT, AND FUTURE—
TAKING THEIR TOYS APART
TO FIGURE OUT HOW THEY WORKED

Contents

The Falcon and the Goose

David Lee Summers

JACK FLOYD, LEAD MECHANIC OF THE RIO GRANDE SOUTHERN RAILROAD, rode in the wrecker car with a work crew on the narrow-gauge, winding its way through Southern Colorado's San Juan Mountains. He had a mess to clean up—a steam locomotive's boiler had exploded. He looked out the window and noticed a gray peak with a rock that resembled a lizard's head looking skyward as though imploring the heavens for patience. The rock reflected Floyd's mood. The wrecker train slowed as it approached the passenger train, dead on the tracks.

Once the train came to a stop, Floyd climbed down from the wrecker car and strode forward. Number Five, one of the most reliable locomotives on the line, looked as though it had sprouted tentacles through the front, ready to grab someone. When the boiler burst, it shoved pipes and rods through the locomotive's smokebox bulkhead. Fortunately, the engineer and fireman were able to jump clear and only sustained minor injuries. There were just a handful of passengers, and the conductor had led all the people back to a nearby town, Ophir.

The crew set to work laying a temporary track so the wrecker car could get in position to disassemble Number Five and clear the rails. While they worked, the thrum of diesel engines echoed through the mountain valley. Floyd looked up as a small, sleek airship passed overhead. Gold filagree decorated the gondola and a painted falcon—proclaiming the airship's name—adorned the superstructure's side. The *Falcon* had clearly started life as an airyacht, but Clint Barstow and Annie Patton had pressed it into service, competing with the railroad. They said they could transport goods and people to the mountain towns faster and in more style than the trains. After all, they didn't have to follow the rough terrain.

Mechanic Bob Lane sneered at the airyacht. "They say Clint and Annie stole that ship from some cattle baron in Kansas City."

The engineer who pulled the wrecker car, Art Scott, jumped to their defense. "No one's been able to prove anything."

Floyd snorted. He suspected the falcon on the craft's side not only announced the ship's name but obscured the craft's original markings.

Once the temporary track neared completion, Floyd began examining the locomotive's remains. He knelt down and picked up a pressure release valve blown clear in the explosion. He frowned as he tried to turn it, but it wouldn't budge. Careful study revealed a small spot weld, too precise to have been caused by the explosion's heat. He stood, pushed his glasses up his nose, and glared in the direction the *Falcon* had flown.

Pete Jameson, the wrecker crew's fireman, approached and touched his hat brim. "Mr. Floyd, we're ready to move the wrecker into place."

"Then get to it," Floyd snapped. When he saw the shocked look on Jameson's face, he took a deep breath and calmed himself. "Sorry, I'm irritated. Number Five is beyond repair, and we already have too few locomotives on the line." He held up the valve. "If someone wants to compete, they don't have to resort to sabotage. Someone coulda got hurt."

Jameson's brow furrowed. "Who do you think did it?"

"Who would benefit from us losing a locomotive?"

"You think it was Clint and Annie?"

"Who else?"

Jameson removed his hat and wrung it in his hands. "I can't believe they're responsible. They always seem friendly when I see them, ready with a smile and a laugh."

Floyd sneered and thrust the valve into his pocket. "Yeah, I bet they're laughing all right."

Jameson scrambled off to help the engineer get the wrecker in position, and Floyd shook his head at Number Five's remains. This was 1933 and no one was building new steam locomotives now that diesels were coming into service. What's more, none of the companies building diesel locomotives wanted to support narrow-gauge rail. Even if they did, the Rio Grande Southern couldn't afford to buy one. Somehow, some way, he'd need to solve the problem, or the railroad would lose its postal contract to Clint Barstow and Annie Patton.

It took two days of backbreaking labor to clear the tracks. Jack Floyd caught sight of the *Falcon* each day. Whether they committed the sabotage or not, they took advantage of the railroad's downtime to build their business.

At last, Number Five's component parts sat on the flat car or beside the track. The crew coupled the empty box car and passenger coach to the wrecker train, then rode into Durango. Once there, Floyd approached Pete. "Look, I'm sorry I snapped at you back at the pass. Would you let me make it up to you? I'll buy you a drink at the Diamond Belle."

Although Prohibition was on its way out, it was still the law of the land and alcohol couldn't be served openly. Even so, the Diamond Belle's owner made excellent beer and sold it in the back room, out of the sheriff's sight.

"That sounds like a great idea, Mr. Floyd. Let's invite Art along as well."

Once they finished their work, the mechanic, the engineer, and the fireman walked over and passed through the café to a door connecting it to the Strater Hotel. The door opened, and the hotel's owner, Earl Barker, stepped through, smiling apologetically. "You're welcome as always, gentlemen, but I thought you should know we have some guests from a rival company tonight. I don't want any trouble."

"You mean a crew from the Denver and Rio Grande Railroad?" Floyd narrowed his gaze.

Barker shook his head. "No, the crew from the *Falcon*."

Floyd pushed his way past Mr. Barker and found three men in coveralls sitting at the bar—the *Falcon's* crew. A woman and a man danced to jazz playing on an audiophone. She wore a tight sweater dress that revealed her curves. The man wore a suit and tie. Both were young, trim, and good-looking. Floyd immediately recognized them as Clint Barstow and Annie Patton.

Before Floyd could say anything, Patton turned around and smiled. "Well, if it isn't our intrepid railroad men. Welcome in and join us! The more, the merrier." She then flung her arms around Floyd, who fought to remember this woman likely ordered the destruction of one of his locomotives. Meeting a cold reception, she turned her attention to Jameson and Scott. The two men returned her embrace far too eagerly for Floyd's liking.

Floyd turned and found himself facing Barstow, who held out his hand. Floyd reached into his pocket and took out the sabotaged valve. "Do you know anything about this?"

Barstow shrugged. "Looks like a valve."

"It's a pressure release valve someone welded shut."

Barstow's eyes widened in feigned astonishment. "Who would do something like that?"

Before Floyd could respond, Barker stepped up and cleared his throat. Floyd looked around and noticed the airship men's eyes on him. He realized this would be a bad time for a confrontation. He shook his head and returned the valve to his pocket. "Whoever did it had better hope I don't catch them doing it again."

Barstow flashed a wicked smile. "Well, if you ever decide the railroad's no longer a growing concern, we could always use a good mechanic."

Floyd looked around. Jameson and Scott stood in the corner talking with Annie Patton. The fireman's eyes roved along her tight dress while the engineer listened with rapt attention. Floyd placed a dollar coin on the bar. "I promised to buy Pete a beer. Keep the change."

The bartender swept up the coin and nodded. "Yes, sir. Thank you."

Floyd turned around and went outside. Tired, thirsty, and hungry, he really wanted something to eat and drink, but he couldn't stand spending more time with Barstow, Patton, and their crew. As he reached the street, thoughts of food and drink slipped his mind. A Packard delivery truck sat in front of the hotel.

He walked up to it and performed some mental calculations. There were no roads aside from the rail up to the remote mining towns of the San Juan Mountains between Durango and Ridgway. He wondered if he could refit the truck to roll on train wheelsets instead of tires. He dropped to the ground and looked underneath the truck.

"What are you doing there?" came a voice.

Floyd sat up too quickly and bonked his head on the truck's bumper. Rubbing his head, he slid out and faced an irate man wearing a work shirt and suspenders. Floyd guessed this must be the truck driver. "How much horsepower does this thing have?"

The driver scratched his head and rattled off a number.

Floyd nodded, satisfied. "Suspension looks solid."

"It is," affirmed the driver. "Not bad on these mountain roads."

About that time, Jameson appeared. "So, this is where you got off to. Clint and Annie say there's no hard feelings. You're welcome to come back in. Heck, they even offered Art and me jobs with their airship line."

Floyd narrowed his gaze and considered Barstow's off-hand offer. "I bet they did." Hiring men away from the railroad might sabotage the line just as much as destroying trains, and it was less likely to arouse the law's suspicion. "I won't stop you from going back, but I think I'm going to grab some dinner elsewhere." With that, Floyd thanked the truck driver for his time and sought another dining establishment. He wanted to sketch some plans on his notepad while they were fresh in his mind.

After a night in Durango, the wrecker crew returned home to Ridgway. Scott and Jameson didn't leave the railroad but continued discussing the possibilities of flying aboard the *Falcon* as they left the next day on a freight run. Floyd spent the next week redrafting the plans he'd hastily penciled into his notebook at dinner. Once he knew what he needed, he went to the telegraph office and sent a few wires to nearby towns.

Floyd entered the break room and found Jameson sipping a cup of coffee after returning from the run. "Quiet run?" Floyd asked.

"Mostly." Jameson removed his hat and ran his hands through his hair. "When we stopped for water in Pandora, I returned to the cab and found all the valves turned. If I'd started stoking the firebox without checking, we would surely have blown the boiler."

"Was the *Falcon* nearby at the time?"

"Yeah, I saw it take off a little before our departure time."

"Still thinking about working for those people?"

Jameson sipped his coffee, then shook his head. "Could have been anyone who did that, and it was just mischief. After they destroyed Number Five, they haven't done anything else that would hurt people... and I fear locomotives may go the way of the Dodo Bird."

Floyd left the fireman to his coffee and went to the telegraph office. Receiving the desired response, the next day, he carried a set of rolled-up schematics into the rail shop superintendent's office and unfurled his plans on the desk. "Our locomotives are almost fifty years old. We need a way to keep freight and passengers moving if we want to keep our mail contract. Also, Barstow and Patton's gang attempted to sabotage another one of our trains. One of these days, they're going to succeed again."

Caleb Gordon grunted. "They're already succeeding. Art Scott turned in his resignation this morning. Not sure if the attempted sabotage spooked him or if he decided to go work for the airship crew."

Floyd shrugged. "Could have been both."

The superintendent turned his attention to the plans, one eyebrow lifted.

"It's a way to bring diesel power to the narrow gauge," Floyd explained.

"You want to put *this* on the line?" Gordon struggled to find words. "Can a truck even pull rail cars?"

Floyd made a show of cleaning his glasses. "I've done the math. It should work."

"How much will this cost?"

"There's a used Packard diesel down in Ouray that I can get for $500. I can use spare parts here at the shop for the rest." He refrained from mentioning there were plenty after they'd had to scrap Number Five, but the fact hung heavy in the air anyway.

Gordon tapped his fingers on the desk. At last, he turned around, opened a safe, and counted out the money. "You know the trainmen are going to laugh at this thing. I don't want to lose any more to Clint and Annie's shenanigans."

Floyd settled his glasses on his nose. "If it gets the job done, they won't laugh."

That afternoon, Floyd took a bus down to Ouray. The next day, he returned with a three-year-old Packard truck. He pulled it into the machine shop, rolled up his sleeves, and set to work.

At first, the other shop mechanics scoffed at Floyd's project. Most had grown comfortable in their role maintaining steam locomotives and expected to do that for the rest of their careers. However, they were also smart enough to recognize that even without Barstow and Patton's sabotage, their careers might end earlier than expected as the steam engines aged out of service. That alone held back their jibes. The Depression was not a good time to be without a paycheck.

Little by little, the mechanics rolled up their sleeves and helped Floyd to convert the Packard diesel truck to roll on rails. They converted the truck's drive train to work with steel wheelsets. Bob Lane set to adapting the brakes. "You know, this thing's no locomotive. It's just a motor for a boxcar."

"Right now, that's all we need," Floyd said as he modified the truck's trailer hitch to take a boxcar's weight.

"You may be onto something. If this crazy idea works, we could build a fleet of these." Shawnee Miller, the shop's lone woman mechanic, mounted the sandbox assembly from the destroyed Number Five to the Packard and tested it to make sure it would provide needed traction on the steel rails.

Floyd stood back and wiped his hands on a rag, hopeful that his idea would actually work.

On the first of November, they were ready to test the motor. Lane ran the crane and lifted the modified truck onto the track. Floyd drove it outside into the clear, crisp air, where a team coupled a modified boxcar to the back. The boxcar contained both passenger seating and cargo space. The motor wouldn't pull as much weight as a steam locomotive, but it would keep the mail going, and trains were rarely full during these hard times anyway.

Cautiously, Floyd accelerated up the tracks. As he did, he watched the gauges on the Packard's dashboard. Despite the cold November air, the engine began to heat up, pulling the boxcar's weight. He stopped the motor, hopped out, and propped up the engine cowling. As he hoped, the motor ran cooler. He drove up to the roundhouse and had the foreman turn him around so he could drive back down the track.

As he returned to the shops, he honked the horn, then hopped out.

Miller and Lane laughed, slapping each other on the back.

"What's so funny?" Floyd asked.

"It honks just like a goose." Miller wiped tears from her eyes.

Lane shook his head. "The way it sways from side to side, it waddles like one too."

Floyd adjusted his glasses. "Didn't feel *that* bad."

Lane patted him on the back. "Geese may waddle, but they don't topple. Should be fine." He then pointed at the engine cowling. "It's even got wings. Mr. Floyd, what you've got there is no motor. It's a goose. It's a goddamned galloping goose."

At that point, Floyd knew the motor had acquired a nickname that would stick.

Caleb Gordon didn't laugh when he saw the *Goose*. He dubbed it Number Nine to replace the destroyed locomotive, then assigned it to the train schedule in two days.

"I'd like to take the motor on its first run," Floyd said.

"The motor?" Gordon's eyebrows came together.

"The *Goose*."

Gordon nodded. "That's fine. You can go as engineer. We'll send Ed Hamblin as conductor." He cocked his head as though considering something. "I don't see a firebox on that thing. I presume you don't need a fireman." He rubbed his hands together as though considering the money he might save in the budget.

Floyd's gut twisted, but an idea came to him. "I'd like to take Pete Jameson with me. There's still fuel flow and temperature to monitor. Besides, he's been good at spotting attempted sabotage and preventing it. Just because this is a new type of transport doesn't mean Clint and Annie won't stop their attempts at hurting our business."

Gordon frowned but nodded. "All right, you can take Jameson along."

Two days later, Jameson shook his head while contemplating the *Goose*.

Floyd motioned for Jameson to join him at the engine. He pointed to the boxcar at the tail. "That's more load than this engine was designed to pull, and we'll be pulling it uphill. The engine's prone to overheating. Keep an eye on the coolant and top off the radiator at any water towers if needed." Floyd showed Jameson how to do that. He then showed Jameson the glow plugs, the fuel lines, and how to check the oil. Floyd's big smile as he rattled off details betrayed his pride in creating a narrow-gauge diesel engine.

"Will we be able to make the run on one tank of fuel?" Ed Hamblin, the conductor, asked. Conductors served as a train's manager. Fuel budget was part of his job.

"The tank holds sixteen gallons of diesel fuel, and I've welded in a spare tank. There's a switch in the cab to go between the two. That should be enough for two round trips," Floyd said.

Hamblin checked his pocket watch. "All set to leave in an hour?"

Floyd nodded. "We already have some rock drills for Pandora and a delivery of goods for the mercantile store in Ophir. We won't be taking any passengers from here in Ridgway, but Number Four took some Girl Scouts on a trip yesterday. They may want to continue further up the line with us."

Jameson sighed and walked to a place where he could see the Falcon tethered to a nearby building, preparing to make a run. Floyd followed and wondered what Jameson thought. The fireman had witnessed at least two sabotage attempts, but Clint and Annie's outlaw lifestyle seemed to appeal to him. "I know the motor is small compared to a normal train, but even it has more cargo capacity than that airyacht."

Jameson shrugged. "The question is, do you really need me?" He turned and looked Floyd in the eye. "Sure, maybe this run, when you're just testing things out for the first time, but what happens when you've trained the engineers? There's nothing you showed me one man couldn't handle in the cab alone."

Floyd looked from Jameson to the airship. "I know flying through the sky seems like a new adventure, but those people don't care about the folks in these mining towns or the men running the rails. They showed us that when they destroyed Number Five. Can you imagine Barstow and Patton hauling Girl Scouts? Sure, they'll take rock drills to the mines for cash, but do they care if the miners strike paydirt? No. If the towns go bust, they'll just move on somewhere else. Besides… one engineer alone in the cab is just asking for trouble. The conductor can't make it forward in time if something goes wrong."

Jameson swallowed, then nodded. Floyd could see the adventure and danger of flying with the airyacht's crew captivated the fireman more than driving the *Goose*. Jameson looked to the ground for a moment, then met Floyd's eye. "Promise me there'll always be a fireman on one of your motors."

Floyd grinned. "We'll make it work." He patted Jameson on the shoulder. "Take a break, and we'll see you back here in an hour."

Jameson started toward the break room, then turned. "You know, last night, I had the craziest dream. I dreamt of a falcon and a goose battling it out. The falcon dove at the goose, talons extended, but the goose struck at the falcon's tail feathers as it passed. Blood, chunks of flesh, and feathers spewed everywhere. At first, I thought the strong falcon would take out the gangly goose, but them geese are mean and tenacious. I'm not sure a real-life falcon would be stupid enough to attack a goose." With that, the fireman turned and went off to the break room.

Weird as the dream was, pride warmed Floyd's chest. At first, he'd hated the "Goose" nickname, but it now began to grow on him. He checked oil and fuel levels. Made sure there was plenty of water in the radiator and checked the sand level. After he finished his rounds, he climbed into the cab and started the engine.

Ed Hamblin came forward, holding a clipboard. "We're good to go." He checked his pocket watch. "We need to get moving in five minutes."

Floyd nodded, then left the cab for a moment. With autumn, the aspens had started to turn vivid yellow even though the pines were still bright green. High above the mountains in the distance, clouds began to form. Floyd shivered as he realized winter was just around the corner. It wouldn't be long before they had snow. He buttoned up his jacket and climbed into the cab.

Jameson arrived and took his spot in the cab next to Floyd, who released the brake and began accelerating along the track. He glanced to the side and noticed the airship backing away from its mooring post. They were going to make a run as well. A few minutes later, the *Falcon* passed the *Goose* and picked up speed.

"How fast can this thing go?" Jameson asked.

"It ain't a race." Floyd shook his head. "I need to learn the feel of this motor before we go too fast."

"How fast are we going?"

Floyd looked at the speedometer. "About seventeen miles per hour."

Jameson groaned, and Floyd understood. A steam locomotive could make twenty-five miles per hour uphill. Closer to thirty-five on the flats without the danger of jumping the tracks.

It took nearly an hour for the Goose to reach its first stop at Placerville, a little town of brick and wood buildings tucked in among pine trees. Hamblin dropped the mail but discovered the *Falcon* snagged their cargo shipment before they'd arrived. Still, the *Goose* picked up a passenger. The gentleman wore a suit and a tie, which seemed overly nice for a rough mining town like Placerville, but Floyd suspected he may have been a traveling salesman or a preacher. The man only carried a small bag, and though Floyd thought he looked familiar, he couldn't pin him to a specific time or place.

The *Goose* passed through Telluride and continued on to a dead end at Pandora. Rising high to the right were great red needle-like mountains, more majestic than any human-built cathedral. Ed Hamblin unloaded the rock drills at Pandora's roundhouse.

When the *Goose* returned to Telluride, the Girl Scouts all stood on the platform laughing and pointing at the motor. Floyd's cheeks flushed, but when they stopped, he heard their chatter. To them, riding on the *Goose* would be a grand adventure. Their leader, who introduced herself as Darjeeling Philpot, shuffled them into the converted boxcar, and Hamblin showed them to their seats. The man in the fine clothes squirmed, uncomfortable to have so many young girls around.

As the *Goose* continued on to Rico, the clouds thickened and the air chilled. The *Goose* had some issues with overheating on the steeper climbs like Floyd predicted, but as the air cooled, he paused and lowered the cowling.

A silver mining town, Rico had large buildings of red stone lining the main street. A mooring mast had been installed at the top of the old Dey Building, and the *Falcon* was tied to the mast. It seemed to Floyd that the airyacht swayed back and forth more than he'd seen before. His mechanic's brain began to contemplate how the craft would fare in the high winds that whipped through the mountain valleys during winter's full onslaught.

Hamblin learned the passengers the *Goose* had been scheduled to pick up had demanded refunds and taken passage aboard the *Falcon* instead. Floyd cursed under his breath and stormed from the depot to the Dey Building with Jameson on his tail. They found the passengers out front posing with Patton and Barstow. The Dey building's bottom level held a saloon, while Falcon Freight's offices were upstairs. Patton flashed a pistol and chewed on a cigar while Barstow caressed a Browning automatic rifle. They looked like dangerous gangsters, and the passengers loved every minute of it.

Patton caught Floyd's eye and winked. "What's the matter, train man? Feeling a little inadequate?" She cast her glance up toward the airyacht. "There's still time to trade... up."

Barstow and Patton laughed.

"Tell me, Annie, what would you do if you saw a train stranded while flying your route? Would you stop and help?"

"Freight's gotta go through," Barstow said. "We'd pick up passengers if they'd pay to upgrade." He looked around at the passengers. "These good folks did. After all, we're the future."

Patton pointed her pistol at Floyd, and he flinched. *"Bang, bang, train man."* She laughed, then hustled the passengers into the building. They were on the rooftop a few minutes later, climbing into the airship. Even the man the *Goose* had picked up in Placerville left to ride on the airship.

Floyd, Jameson, and Hamblin returned to the *Goose*, but the engine wouldn't turn over. While Floyd contemplated the problem, the *Falcon* took off and continued down the Dolores River valley as snowflakes began to fall. Floyd hopped out and opened the engine cowling. Jameson followed and pointed. "Those cables are supposed to be connected to the glow plugs, aren't they?"

Floyd swore under his breath as he reconnected the cables. "I thought I recognized our passenger. Last time I saw him was at the speakeasy in Durango."

"That's right!" Jameson snapped his fingers. "He had a mustache and sat at the bar."

"I guess they could spare him for other *duties* now that Art's aboard the *Falcon*."

With the glow plugs reconnected, Floyd fired up the engine, and the Goose continued on. As they progressed, the wind kicked up, and the snow began to fall harder. The tracks turned slick. In one place, the *Goose* bucked, and the Girl Scouts screamed so loud Floyd could hear them from his seat. He looked back through the door that connected the truck to the boxcar and saw Ed wave a reassuring hand. Soon, the girls were laughing and joking again.

Near a bend in the Dolores River, Floyd caught sight of the *Falcon*. It hung in the air, not making headway against the wind and the snow. A moment later, it tipped forward. Floyd's stomach lurched, just imagining what it must be like as one of the passengers aboard. The airship tumbled sideways and impaled itself on the trees a moment later.

Floyd stopped the *Goose* and jumped out, followed by Jameson. Three of the Girl Scouts grabbed Miss Philpot's arms and begged to join the train crew on their adventure. The leader considered a moment, Then gave a sharp nod and led them out into the swirling snow. Ed lingered by the door, watching the Goose but keeping an eye on the passengers. The crack of a bullet sounded from the airship. Jameson ducked low and hustled the Girl Scouts and Miss Philpot to safety. Floyd stood his ground and thrust his hands skyward. "We're unarmed," he shouted. "We're here to help. We don't have to do anything if you don't want, but if we just leave, the storm that's brewing will kill you. At least let your passengers come with us. You're welcome to come too if you leave your weapons behind."

Floyd waited a few minutes. He thought he could make out shouting from within the ship, but it was hard to tell over the wind. He turned to leave.

Just as he did, a ladder dropped from the *Falcon's* gondola, and the passengers began to climb down. As the ladder swayed dangerously in the wind, Floyd rushed to the bottom and stabilized it. Jameson and the Girl Scouts reappeared and helped the passengers down. The conductor settled them all safely inside the *Goose's* passenger compartment, a little tight but doable.

Barstow, Patton, and the airyacht's crew, including Art Scott, followed. Scott's face flushed bright red, and he didn't meet Floyd's gaze. When they were all aboard the *Goose*, Miss Philpot passed around mugs of tea from her Thermos. For a moment, it looked as though she wanted to hurl the tea at Patton and Barstow rather than serve them, but she cast a glance at her charges and seemed to decide she should set a good example. The people from the airship shivered and sipped gratefully. Meanwhile, the storm ripped into the *Falcon*, taking great swaths of painted fabric from its side. Floyd was reminded of Jameson's dream about the goose and the falcon.

Patton approached Floyd, steaming coffee cup in hand. "Well, train man, I guess you got the last laugh after all."

Floyd shrugged. "I'm not laughing. Whether it's storms or technology, it's hard to predict the future. You gotta try out different options and see what works. In the meantime, we've gotta be prepared to help each other out. Otherwise, everyone loses." Floyd's gaze wandered along the tracks. "Time for this goose to fly south for the winter."

With that, he climbed in the front seat and continued the southward journey into Dolores, where the *Goose* would wait out the storm.

Nobody's Hero

Aaron Rosenberg

Lily Jeffries was debating between two boxes of pre-packaged donuts when she heard the bell *ding* on the convenience store's front door. She went back to her contemplation, boxes in her hands—powdered versus chocolate—but glanced up, startled, when she heard:

"Hand over the money from the till! Now!"

Rising to her feet, she pushed up on her tiptoes to see over the aisle—curse being so short!—and saw a pair of figures by the checkout. Both wore nondescript clothing and ski masks. Both had pistols. One pointed his weapon at the poor store employee, who was trying not to cower. But the other had his back to all that, scanning the rest of the store. He stiffened when he caught sight of Lily.

"You!" he shouted. "Hands up and come here! No funny business!"

Feeling silly because she still held both donut boxes, Lily raised them and carefully made her way down the aisle and toward the front. The clerk had emptied the register, but the second robber only had eyes for her.

"Money!" he barked. "Now!" He held out one hand, but the other was still steady on the gun.

"Okay," Lily agreed slowly. Of course, this was made difficult by her potential purchases, so she angled to the side. "I'm just setting these down here," she explained loudly, resting the donut boxes atop a stack of paper-wrapped toilet paper. Then with one hand, she reached into the front right pocket of her coverall and extracted her wallet. The robber looked wary but not worried, and why should he be? Lily knew what he saw—a short, stocky woman in that nebulous "not young but not old" range, with dark hair already streaked with gray where it was escaping her ponytail, wearing oil-smeared coveralls, a heavy leather toolbelt, and worn but still sturdy work boots. Not exactly a threat.

The man edged forward and snatched the wallet from her, flipping it open and yanking out the cash before tossing the rest back in an impressive display of agility. Lily was sure she'd have fumbled it if she'd tried that. She barely managed to catch the wallet as it was!

Then the men headed toward the door, pushing through it and taking off into the night. Lily slumped, her heart racing as she and the employee eyed each other in the silent aftermath.

"I'll have to buy them some other time," she told him. "Sorry."

The police arrived promptly, at least, and took her statement quickly and efficiently before releasing her. Which was good. If Lily'd had to wait any longer, she wasn't sure her legs would have been able to carry her home.

"You did the right thing, babe," Dee assured her for the tenth time, rubbing Lily's shoulders. They were on the couch together, and Dee had twisted sideways to give hugs, backrubs, and support. "What good would it have done if you'd tried being a hero?"

Lily nodded, staring at her hands. "I know. You're right. I know you're right. It's just—do you know what I've got here?" She gestured at the toolbelt she'd taken off and set atop the coffee table—something Dee hated but was willing to forgive right now. Scooting forward, Lily rummaged in a few of the larger compartments and pulled out several pieces of metal, circuitry, and wiring. One of them was recognizably a handle, while another was wide and bell-shaped.

Her wife gaped at the collection. "Is that—?"

Lily sighed. "Yeah. Betty Baffle's Slo-Gun. Something's off. Its range is half what it should be. Couldn't finish it at work, so I brought it home to tinker a bit after I ate." She held up the assorted parts. "You see? I could've reassembled it! Right then and there! Shot them both, slowed them to a crawl, and let the cops come and pick them up. Instead, I did nothing!"

But Dee was already shaking her head. "And what if it hadn't worked?" she asked, always sensible. "What if it had fritzed out on you? Or you weren't quick enough, and they shot you while you were still putting it together?" Cupping the back of Lily's head, she leaned in so their foreheads touched, hers soft and smooth as ever, her jasmine perfume drifting over them both like a soothing cloud. "You did the right thing. Stayed calm and came home in one piece."

"What's in one piece?" The voice was small and sleepy and they parted, turning as one to stare at the small figure in the hall. Alloy PJs covered her skinny body and a bedraggled stuffed turtle dangled from one hand while the other rubbed at her eyes.

"We are," Dee responded quickly, both of them reaching out as their daughter crossed the living room and tumbled into their arms. "Our family. Just like always." Her tone turned serious, her "librarian voice," as Lily liked to call it. "And what are you doing out of bed, young lady? It's late!" Which it was—she'd got caught up in her work again. Like always.

"Thirsty," Ginny replied. "Glass of water." She lifted her head and smiled hopefully at Lily. "Donuts?"

Lily hated that she had to shake her head. "They were out, sweetie," she lied. "I'll bring some home tomorrow." Scooping the little girl up, she stood and headed for the kitchen. "A quick sip of water, then I'm putting you and Mister Halfshell back in bed."

Ginny nodded; her eyes already half-shut again. "Okay. Love you."

"I love you too." But Lily still felt like a failure.

"What ho, Miss Lily Linkage!" the voice boomed through the Flywheel, and Lily didn't have to look up from her workbench to know who stood framed in the arched doorway to the rest of the Manifold.

"Heya, Commander," she replied. Heavy footsteps echoed, drawing closer, and before long, a presence hovered just over her shoulder. The shadow should have felt dreary and depressing, but somehow it was the opposite, warm and energizing like a cozy blanket.

"How goes the work on Miss Betty's Baffle?" he asked, his voice no softer than before.

But then, Commander Nathan Staybolt, leader of the Heroic League, didn't exactly do "quiet."

"Nearly got it," Lily answered. Her attention was still firmly on the odd weapon, which she'd worked on more last night and then again this morning, and was now fully reassembling for testing. "One of the bearings had cracked, so the crankshaft wasn't sitting straight. That threw off the whole assemblage. Should be good now." She finished tightening the last screw, lifted the Slo-Gun with one hand, and glanced at the heroic figure behind her. "Care to do the honors?" She gestured toward a cup of water she'd collected for just this purpose.

He grinned, his gleaming white teeth visible beneath his impressive handlebar mustache. "Of course!" A powerful hand shot out, sending the cup flying off the table—

—and the liquid spilling out of it turned immobile halfway across the cavernous room as Lily aimed and fired, the restored gun shooting a pulsating ray that stopped the water as if it had been flash-frozen.

"Excellent!" Staybolt's hearty slap nearly smashed Lily into the table, but she knew he didn't mean anything by it. He often seemed to forget his own strength. "As always, Miss Lily Linkage, you are a marvel!" He held out his hand. "If you are amenable, I will return the device to Miss Betty forthwith. The League is about to meet in the Cylinder."

"Sure thing." She handed the gun over and watched him stroll away, as always, looking as if he were marching in a parade—or across a battlefield. "And it's not 'Lily Linkage,'" she muttered as he disappeared back through the same doorway. "It's just Lily."

Only hero types needed a clever, often alliterative name like that.

And she was no hero.

"Hey."

Lily glanced up from the device she was tinkering with to see another person emerging from the corridor Staybolt had vanished down an hour or more before.

But this person was a good deal lower to the ground and advanced not with the stomp of feet but with the soft whir of gears and the steady whoosh of tires.

"Hey, Trin." It was funny, really. Of all the League members, Trinity Brakehall—one of the richest women in Chicago, one of the city's most eligible bachelorettes despite her disability, and a brilliant mind in her own right—was the one Lily felt closest to. The only one she was comfortable enough with to call by a nickname. Perhaps it was the difficulties the other woman had overcome all her life. In many, that would have led to arrogance. But in Trin, it had yielded quiet confidence and a warm sympathy for others. After Dee, the heiress was the most empathetic person Lily knew.

"I saw you fixed Betsy's gun," that same scion commented now as she maneuvered her motorized chair up beside the worktable. "Nice. No surprise, of course." Her smile was warm, if tired. But then, when wasn't she tired? The woman managed her own financial empire and the affairs of the League, for while Staybolt was its leader, Trin kept the lights on and the fridges stocked.

Lily nodded, accepting the compliment with a small smile. "Yeah. You guys had that run-in with Prybar last week, right? I bet the gun took a blow somewhere in the melee. No outward damage, but a bearing cracked deep inside."

Trin shook her head. "You've got amazing attention to detail, you know that? Most people would've missed something that minute." She glanced at the project laid out before them. "Isn't that—"

"One of the Mandrel's retractable saws, yeah." Lily grinned, tapping the edge of the wicked-looking disc with its razor-sharp teeth. "Governor snapped it off him, right?"

Her friend laughed. "He did. Sheared clear through the darn thing with his hand, right before it could cut Parallel in two. Of course, that damn fool insisted he'd known all along that Joe would save him."

"Of course he did." They shared a chuckle. Parallel was easily the strangest of the League. He claimed to be from an alternate world and that he could see possible futures branching off from every action, allowing him to choose how to best respond to any threat. Whether it was true or not, he certainly had a knack for being in just the right place at just the right time.

Lilly nudged the disc again. "Mandrel's using some sort of alloy," she explained. "Way tougher than steel, but lighter, too. If I can figure out what it is, how to copy it—"

"You're thinking of Alloy," Trin accused. "I'm fine with the suit the way it is now, Lil." Her alter ego was the armored hero Alloy, who no one outside the League knew was a woman—and disabled.

Lily nodded, looking away. "I know. But if it was even lighter and stronger…" She hated the idea of her friend lugging all that weight around, even if it was the servos doing all the work. And, even more, of that armor not being enough someday.

"I'm fine," Trin assured her again, reaching out and resting a hand on one of Lily's. The contrast was stark—pale and perfectly manicured over dark and dirty and chipped. "Are you?"

Surprised, Lily looked up.

Her friend was watching her closely. "I heard about what happened last night," she explained. "At the store. Are you all right?"

Lily pulled her hand away. "Yeah. Fine. I handed over my cash just like any good little victim."

"Hey. Hey!" That same slender hand caught her chin and forced her gaze back toward Trinity's own. "You're not a costume, Lily. You don't have powers or gadgets or any of that stuff. You're not a frontliner. There's no shame in being smart and staying safe." She scowled. "If I'd been there in that store, I'd have done the same thing. Without my suit, what else could I do?" She rapped her free hand against a wheel. "I can't even run away."

Lily scoffed, if only to lighten the mood. "Oh, please! You'd have lobbed beer cans at their heads and taken them both out. Probably with one shot."

Her friend tilted her perfectly coiffed head, considering. "Maybe. Though getting the perfect angle for the ricochet would've been tough." More laughter between them before she went serious again, though at least she finally let go. "I mean it, Lil. You did the right thing. Dee and Ginny need *you*, not your pride. You made it home safe and sound, and that's what matters."

Lily nodded and plastered a smile on her face. She knew her friend meant well. Of course, she did. And she was right.

But still, there was that little voice inside. The one that said, "You work with heroes every day. So why aren't you one?"

She didn't have an answer for that.

A few days later, Lily was resetting one of Snap Ring's throwing discs — darn things had a tendency to lock up after too many uses, had to be taken apart and oiled and then reassembled and re-calibrated before they'd work right again — when the intercom beside her workbench squawked. "Lily to the Ground!" It was Staybolt. "Lily to the Ground, stat!"

Grabbing her toolbelt — she often took it off and draped it over one of the table grips, where it'd still be easy to reach but didn't jab her in the belly and side — Lily took off across the Flywheel. Reaching the room's far side, she slapped a panel on the wall there, causing it to retract and reveal a cylindrical chamber beyond.

Lily gulped. She hated pneumatics, always had. But the Commander had said stat, and this was far and away the quickest route down. So, taking a deep breath, she stepped inside.

The door slid shut behind her, and for an instant, she just bobbed there, nothing concrete holding her up. Then there was a *whooshing* sound, and Lily was sucked down the tube.

Trying not to scream, tears streaming from her eyes, she endured by counting in her head. *One. Two. Three.*

At five, her feet struck a solid surface. She had just enough time to wipe her eyes before the door here opened onto the Ground.

The Manifold's hangar and garage was enormous, a cavernous space wide enough to accommodate all their vehicles at once and tall enough to fit a decent-sized airship, docking rig and all. But right now, she only had eyes for the handful of human-sized figures emerging from one of the League's flying tanks—and particularly the one being carried out by the others.

One whose skin gleamed metal beneath the hangar lights.

Racing to them, Lily looked Alloy over for a second before turning her glare toward Staybolt. "What happened?" she demanded.

"I'm fine, Lil," Trin assured her, but the armored body hadn't moved. "Just a little... locked up, is all."

Betty Baffle—really Betsy Clark, of Neosho, Kansas—was hefting one of Alloy's arms. "It was Rebore," she explained. "We caught him and Prybar holding up the Second Industrial Bank." She wrinkled her petite nose, even that dismayed expression adorable on her. "Couldn't tell if they were in it together or just picked the same place at the same time, but they sure teamed up on us in a hurry!"

"We had 'em on the run," Governor—Joe DeWalt, without his speed-enhancing gear—picked up from Alloy's other side. "But Rebore got off a lucky shot, and Alloy turned into a statue on the spot."

The zoot-suited man lifting Alloy's feet huffed. "I still say you should've let me go after them," he insisted. "I knew exactly where they were going."

"Quiet, Parallel," Staybolt ordered. He had Alloy's head and shoulders himself—never let it be said the man wasn't willing to shoulder his share of the load! "Our friend was at risk. That takes precedence."

"I'm okay in here," Trin insisted again. "Really."

But her voice sounded strained to Lily. "Set her down," she ordered, and the League obeyed at once. They might be heroes out on the streets of Chicago, but when it came to damaged tech, they all knew to listen to her. As soon as Alloy rested on the ground, Lily knelt beside her friend, pulling out various devices to check this and that. "Can you move anything at all?" she asked.

"Nope. Totally frozen."

Which was bad, even if the rest of them hadn't realized it yet. They didn't know the suit the way Trin and Lily did, the one because she'd built and wore it, the other because she'd helped repair and even upgrade it. All of Alloy's systems were down right now. Every gear, every mechanism, every feature.

And that included the air circulators. Trin was going to suffocate if Lily didn't do something to fix that, and fast.

"Where did he hit her?" she asked next, but then waved off any answers as she spotted a small lump that shouldn't be there, up by the right shoulder. "Got it." It was a different color from the rest of the gleaming chrome suit, more a dull pewter, but as she reached for it, Lily felt the charge in the air around the small projectile. Pulling back, she reached for her trusty ammeter instead. *Aha!*

"It's running a negative charge through your systems," she explained once she saw the readings. "It's countering the normal wavelengths. Basically, your suit's working fine. It just can't hear any of the messages you're sending, so it's awaiting input." Trin had created a masterwork in the Alloy suit, converting her brain's electrical impulses into commands that could move the armored body's arms and legs, activate its weaponry and defenses, engage its jetpack, and more. Had Rebore figured that out? Or had this just been a lucky shot?

That didn't matter right now, of course. Only fixing the problem. The easiest solution was often the best, so Lily grabbed a small, stubby rod from her belt, jammed it against the bullet, and then pressed the button.

There was a muted *zap* as the rod delivered a sharp, quick jolt of electricity into the projectile. Normally, she used it to jumpstart something long enough to force it open or closed or whatever. In this case, as she'd hoped, the extra charge overloaded the bullet, which began to sizzle and smoke. The local ionization returned to normal, and Lily heard a faint whine as Alloy's suit filters began to run again, supplying clean air to its wearer. *Yes!*

"Nice one, Lil." Alloy sat up, flexing her arms like she'd just been taking a nap. "Knew you'd fix it." She hopped to her feet, seemingly none the worse for wear, but Lily wasn't done and followed her up, grabbing at the bullet with pliers and wrenching it from the suit. "Hey, mind the paint job!" Which was a joke since Alloy was all polished metal.

But Lily only had eyes for the now-dead device she held. "He'll try the same trick again," she warned. "But I think... if I can insulate and add a dampener... drain the current before it can breach your systems..."

"Oh, yeah!" Trin sounded excited, and a few of the others laughed and rolled their eyes, though they were clearly relieved as well.

"We'll leave you to it," Governor said, clapping Lily on the shoulder. "Great job, Lily." Then he was off, so fast his afterimage lingered for an instant before fading away.

The others congratulated her as well, including Staybolt. "We can always count on you, Miss Lily Linkage," he told her. "Always."

She smiled and accepted the praise, feeling better than she had since the robbery. She didn't even correct him about her name this time—but part of that was because she and Trin were already discussing the best way to add the new defense feature to the suit and arguing over who got to do it.

A week later, Lily was home with Dee and Ginny, watching some TV after dinner—a rare and pleasant occurrence, her getting home in time to eat with them like a normal family!—when the antics onscreen got interrupted by a "Special Bulletin!"

"Uh oh," Dee muttered, but they all sat forward to watch as the announcement page disappeared, replaced by the familiar face of Pat Adams, Chicago's favorite newscaster.

"Sorry to interrupt your regular viewing, friends," Pat announced in his usual rolling consonants and rich broadcast voice, "but we bring you breaking news! The Heroic League is right now engaged in a battle royale with not one, not two, but three of their nemeses, the villains Major Friction, Prybar, and Rebore! We take you live to the scene!"

Lily tensed, but Dee's gentle hand on her arm kept her from budging. Besides, what could she do?

Pat disappeared, and now they saw the conflict he'd just mentioned. A news crew must have rushed to the spot as soon as they'd gotten word. It looked like another bank, and a second later, the voiceover confirmed it as a woman spoke offscreen:

"This is Annie Grant, coming to you live from Chicago's own First National Savings. As you can see, the Heroic League has its hands full, fending off attacks from three known villains, Major Friction, Prybar, and Rebore! We don't know if this was a concerted effort, but it certainly is now!"

The reporter fell silent, letting them focus in on the skirmish itself. Lily easily recognized the three fighting her friends, both from descriptions and prior footage.

Major Friction was about her size and build, short and stocky, and dressed in an unidentifiable uniform but with massive, armored gauntlets and a full-face gas mask with built-in goggles. In fact, between that and the domed helmet above it, not a single feature was visible, leaving everything about his identity a question, including gender— Lily had always heard the villain referred to as a "he," but now she had to wonder.

The other two were more quantifiable, at least. Prybar was a big, powerfully built woman with broad shoulders and thick arms, both easily visible thanks to the leather bomber jacket she'd torn the sleeves off. Brush-short blonde hair spiked up over strong features without any attempt at concealment. Her gloves were short, simple, and fingerless, made of stiff leather, just enough to improve her grip on her massive namesake, which was oddly notched and segmented and ratcheted throughout, less a simple prybar than a strange mechanical device. Lily knew the thing amplified its wielder's already impressive strength to prodigious levels.

Then came Rebore. In some ways, the man was a throwback, Lily thought, though fashion had never been her strong suit. Still, with his long leather duster, broad-brimmed leather hat, and high, battered leather boots, not to mention the dark hair tugged back in a ponytail and the thick mustache over a long chin and red neckerchief, she'd have pegged him for someone from the Wild West, not the modern city. There was nothing old-fashioned about his weaponry, however. His pair of crisscrossed gun belts held heavy pistols of dull iron and steel, their thick bodies extruding into large, faceted chambers that ended in blunt barrels. Rebore's guns housed a variety of ammunition, and he could cycle between them fast enough to fire off several different kinds in rapid succession.

Like now, when Alloy swooped in on him and the gunslinger fired point-blank at his armored assailant. The bullet struck Trin in the chest, sending off a brief blue spark—and nothing happened.

"Yes!" Lily shouted, pumping her fist. It had worked!

Rebore clearly hadn't expected that but he was too close to back up or dive out of the way. Alloy slammed into him full force, sending him flying across the bank's lobby to crash into one of the far walls. He slid down it, stunned and out of the fight, his guns falling from his hands.

Major Friction, meanwhile, had aimed his gauntlets at Governor, glowing green rays lancing from them to strike the speedster mid-charge. They could hear Joe's yelp as his feet slid out from under him, the Major's weapon stealing the friction that kept Governor on the ground. But Joe was no amateur. He turned his fall into a smooth, fast slide, barreling into his foe and sending them both crashing into the heavy oak information desk. Joe stood up a second later, wobbly but still conscious. Major Friction did not. The baddie had taken the brunt of the impact.

That left Prybar. She was trading blows with Staybolt at the moment, the League's leader deflecting her powerful strikes with the reinforced barrels of his armored shotgun. He was unable to retreat enough to get a clear shot, however, meaning he couldn't use his patented knockout shells.

Then, in the act of bringing her weapon down directly toward his head, Prybar froze. Courtesy of the attractive, aviatrix-style adventuress behind her. Betty Baffle to the rescue!

Prybar scowled, well aware of what had happened but unable to free her weapon from the effects of Betty's Slo-Gun. Good thing Lily had fixed that! That gave Staybolt all the time he needed to step back, take aim, and fire. The shell exploded right in front of Prybar's face, showering her with knockout gas. Her eyes fluttered closed, one last curse slipping from her lips as she tumbled to the ground, her prybar released from immobility just in time to fall beside her.

It was over. The Heroic League had triumphed again.

Lily was still trying to slow her own racing heartbeat when she felt a soft shoulder bump her own. "Looks like you did good work there, huh?" her wife said softly.

"That was all them," Lily replied, but she was smiling as she said it. Because, yeah, she had contributed some to that, sure.

She was reminded of it even more—and grinned so hard she thought her cheeks might burst—when she got in the next morning. There, sitting atop her workbench in the Flywheel, was a fresh box of donuts from some fancy French bakery. And tucked under the elaborate blue bow across the top was a piece of thick ivory-colored pasteboard on which, in Trin's elegant high-society hand, had been written two words:

"My Hero."

Lily started when she heard the screams. "What now?" she asked, looking around. At least it wasn't a convenience store—she was at a proper market this time, the Main Street Mercantile, picking up some much-needed groceries. And with its block-wide shopping area, rows of entrances across the front, and multiple lanes of checkouts, not to mention all the cashiers, stockboys, and security guards, she couldn't imagine a pair of no-name hooligans being stupid enough to try robbing this one!

So why were people screaming?

She found out soon enough, as she stepped out from behind a pallet of flour packets and saw people running for the exits, and just as many pushing away from there, scrambling back into the store.

"What's going on?" she asked a man hurrying past her.

"Bomb!" he shouted, not slowing down. "Run!"

Lily's first impulse was to do just that. But it didn't look like running was helping much. "Always stop and assess the situation, even if only for a second," she'd heard Staybolt counsel the others time and again during training, and now she did just that, putting her back to the pallet and taking a moment to look around fully.

Which is when she saw that the front entrances had all been shut, their iron storm doors dropped and presumably sealed in place.

Alarms were going off, she now realized. Blaring sirens she hadn't initially noticed behind the screams and shouts of panicked fellow customers and equally terrified employees. Lights flashed from the ceiling and at the corner of every aisle. Those were triggered by an emergency, like a storm, to warn people to evacuate.

But they should have gone off *before* the doors closed, not after. And there hadn't been a cloud in the sky when she'd left work. What was going on here?

She found out a second later when the loudspeakers crackled to life.

"Your attention, citizens," a cold, electronic voice called out, and Lily felt a chill creep down her spine. She'd heard that voice before, from recordings brought back by Trin and the others. It was the Circuitbreaker.

"Your consumption of this world's natural resources has stretched Mother Earth to her limits and beyond," the villain continued. "Thus, it is necessary to cleanse her of your excess, breaking the circuit and allowing the world to reset properly. Your sacrifice is appreciated." The voice cut out, and the sirens with it, leaving an eerie silence, broken only as screams turned to sobs.

"We're all going to die!" someone cried.

Well, hell, Lily thought. *Not if I have anything to say about it.* Frowning, she turned and, with several grunts of effort, managed to climb up on top of the pallet, the tightly wrapped packets shifting beneath her and releasing occasional puffs of flour into the air but maintaining enough solidity to provide a decent perch.

From up here, she could see the entire store. A few people were still dashing about, some battering on the storm doors, others stumbling out of the back stock area where, presumably, they'd just found the loading bay similarly cut off. The Circuitbreaker was nothing if not thorough. So, if his plan here was to kill everyone in the store and destroy the market's supplies at the same time, what was the best way to go about it? Gas? Acid? Then she remembered what that one man had shouted at her:

Bomb.

Yes, that would do it. An incendiary, nothing fancy but powerful enough to level the place and reduce everything in it to ash.

Fortunately, bombs were a problem Lily could do something about. Maybe. If she could get to it in time. And figure it out.

And get down from this stack of flour first.

The latter took her longer than she'd ever want to admit, but eventually her boots touched the ground once more, and Lily hauled herself, sweating and flour-spattered and out of breath, toward the center of the store. That's where she'd plant a bomb for maximum efficiency, and she knew that was how the Circuitbreaker worked. Cold, methodical, and absolutely determined to rid the world of the "overloaded circuit" that was humankind.

A knot of people stood clustered near the store's middle, and one of them stopped Lily as she approached. "Sorry," the tall, heavyset man said, and she saw he wore the uniform of a store manager. "Need you to keep back. It's not safe."

"I know," she told him. "That's why I'm here." And she showed him her work ID, angling a finger to cover her name but not her photo—or the logo of the League, displayed prominently at the top.

His face changed at once, sagging with relief. "Oh, thank God!" He stepped aside, letting her through and following behind her. "I'm so sorry, I didn't recognize you! You must be—?"

He's trying to figure out which hero I am, Lily realized. *Cute.* "No time for that," she snapped in her best Staybolt impression. "Where's the device?"

"Right, of course. It's here." The manager hurried past and led her to a central support beam. And there, at its base beside a stack of cooking oil cans, was the bomb.

Clever, Lily had to admit. Take out the central support in the explosion, keep anyone from escaping, and maximize damage. Plus, the oil would act as an accelerant.

"Get everyone back," she ordered, dropping to her knees to inspect the device. "Now." She didn't bother to look back, all her attention on the deadly object in front of her.

It was a doozy. For all his crazy notions and utter disdain for humanity, the Circuitbreaker was brilliant. The bomb was a large metallic cube, perhaps three feet to a side, with faceted blue powder-coated faces around thick glass discs. Gleaming chromed hinges linked each side together, and equally shiny steel studs decorated the faces, radiating out from the glass centerpoints. The whole thing hummed with energy, and she could spy lights within. She'd never seen anything like it before.

Which wasn't a good sign.

Well, it was a mechanical device, at least. And that's what she was best at. Tugging a few things from her toolbelt, Lily got started.

First, she checked for external charges, signals, etc. Nothing. Not that she'd expected any. Either it had been equipped with a timer, or it had been triggered by a single quick burst, after which it would be expected to operate independently. Less chance of interference that way.

Next, she checked for access ports. None. The panels appeared to have overlapping edges, so the whole structure was airtight. Probably insulated against signals, too. Which meant a different trigger than she'd first thought.

The object clearly wasn't lightproof, though. Not with those discs. Could she make use of that? The lights within it were going on and off in a pattern, she realized. Two long, two short, pause, then again. Morse code? Or just simple numerics? She was sure it had been three long and one short when she'd first hunkered down here, which meant the shorter ones were becoming more prevalent. Like a countdown—to detonation. Could she convince them to reset?

Taking out her customized high-power flashlight, Lily adjusted its aperture down, reducing it from a wide, diffuse beam to a narrow, incredibly bright one. Then she pointed that right at the closest disc and clicked it on. Off. On. Off. A handful of quick, controlled pulses, three long to one short.

She held her breath.

And let it out slowly as the light within the device changed to match the new rhythm she'd set. A slower one.

Yes!

Lily did it again, this time four longs, no short. Given the pause between each set, it had to be a four-count, nothing more.

The four longs held. The question was, for how long? Did they have an internal counter that would shift it back to three and one after a certain number of beats? How did she shut it off completely?

She could try to crack the thing open. But most likely, there was a failsafe, setting it to detonate immediately if disturbed. What had triggered it to start in the first place?

Rising to her feet, she looked around for the manager, spotting him at once. He had been stealing glances her way the whole time, it seemed, and turned the second she beckoned. "Right before the panic, was there a bright light, a burst of sound, anything?" she asked.

He shook his head. "No, nothing," he insisted. Then he stopped. "Well, there was the tremor." At her quick gesture, he explained, "That's what it felt like. The floor shook. Just for a second. Why?"

But Lily was already trying to remember for herself. She had to have been here already when it happened. Yes, just as she was entering, she'd reached for a cart but had missed because she'd stumbled.

And she'd stumbled because the ground had moved. A strange little shudder, like when an elevator jolted into motion. One, two, three, four—four quick, even little beats.

That was it.

"I need a forklift," she told him. "Brought over here, fast but gentle. Got it?"

Then, without waiting for a reply, she returned to monitoring the device, flashlight at the ready.

By the time they brought the forklift, Lily had had to reset the countdown again. She couldn't keep doing that forever, though. And sooner or later, the League or somebody else would show up and try blowing out the front doors. Which might set this thing off. She had to shut it down completely before then.

She just hoped this worked.

"Ease it under the device," she instructed the scared-looking woman driving the forklift. "Gently, just like you were handling something really fragile. A pallet of eggs. Nice and soft."

The woman nodded, and for all her evident fear, her touch was masterful, the forklift's broad, flat tines slipping under the bomb without even jolting it. "Perfect. Now, listen carefully. I need you to jostle it, just an inch at a time, four times in a row. Perfectly even, a second apiece. Got it?" Another nod. "Great. When I say. Ready? Now!"

The forklift rose, just a *whir* of the motor and the faintest lift to the box resting on it. Then again. Twice more. And Lily watched closely, flashlight ready, body tensed in case she needed to hurl herself to the side. Not that something like that would save her.

Through the glass discs, she saw the lights flare brightly once—and go out.

She waited.

Four seconds. Eight. Twelve. When a full minute had passed, with no lights going back on, she let herself breathe.

It was done.

Resetting the alarms and releasing the emergency lockdown took only a few minutes once they showed her to the right panel. Everyone cheered as the doors retracted, letting sunlight and fresh air in once more.

The Heroic League was massed outside, clearly about to try cutting their way in.

"Li—Lady Linkage?" Alloy stated upon seeing her, correcting herself just in time, and for the first time ever, Lily appreciated Staybolt's silly nickname for her. "Is everything all right?"

"It is now," she answered, smiling at her friend and taking her aside to explain more quietly. "Circuitbreaker set a bomb. It's over there. I've deactivated it, but we need to be careful moving it—he used a seismic trigger. Four beats, a second between each."

"Clever. We'll pad it down, make sure it won't pick anything else up," Trin promised. "You okay?"

Lily nodded. "Yeah, I'm good. Can you guys take it from here?" She felt tears threatening. "I just—I really need to go home."

"Of course. We've got this." Despite the armor's blank face, Lily could hear her friend's smile as she urged, "Go."

Already beginning to step away, Lily thought of something and turned back. "Don't tell them it was me," she asked. "Please?"

Her friend nodded. "Whatever you want. I'll call you later, okay?"

But Lily was already gone.

Dee was waiting by the door when she got home and enveloped her in a huge hug the minute it was shut. "Are you okay?" she cried. "We heard on the news!"

"I'm fine," Lily promised. "Really." She laughed, though it was almost a sob. "Guess I need to go shopping again tomorrow, though."

Her wife laughed with her, tears wetting both their cheeks. "Maybe not back to the Merc for a while, huh?"

The TV was on in the other room, and Lily heard Pat Adams saying, "The crisis at the Main Street Mercantile appears to be over now. The Heroic League is on the scene and confirms that, thanks to the help of an anonymous citizen, the danger is now past."

Ginny had been watching and hurried over as Lily and Dee, arm in arm, entered the room. "Mommy, weren't you just there?" she asked, running to their arms. "Were you the non-y-mouse person? They said you were a hero!"

Lily smiled down at her daughter. "You know, baby, maybe today I was." A part of her had been tempted to take credit for her actions, too. To let the world know that Lily Jeffries had been the one to save them this time.

But she didn't need that, she realized. She did enough good as it was.

Their little girl beamed up at her. "You're *my* hero, Mommy," she declared.

Dee rested her cheek against Lily's. "Mine too."

Lily smiled and smiled. Because, in the end, this was all that mattered.

No Man's Land

John L. French

H E'S IN THE TRENCHES, ONE OF THOUSANDS, MAYBE TENS OF THOUSANDS. He looks to his left, an endless row of men. To his right, there is another endless row. All are like him, soldiers with tin pots on their heads and rifles in their hands. The dead are piled behind, and in front. They have long since run out of sandbags and now their comrades protect them one last time. Across the killing field, a trumpet blows. Drums beat. Men march slowly and steadily toward them.

The order is given. As one, they take aim through the gaps in their dead. On command, they open fire. The front row of the enemy goes down. The second row returns fire, guided by the muzzle flashes in the night. Men on either side of him fall. Some moan in pain, others lie silently and await their deaths.

Those still standing continue to fire. Those approaching shoot back. Men on both sides go down.

He takes a quick break, looks left then right. He thinks he can see the ends of each row. He turns back to the gap in the dead, sees the enemy still advancing. They march and shoot, march and shoot. With each volley, more of his comrades fall.

They should be on top of us by now, he thinks but somehow, they are not. He fires into their midst, over and over and over. He has fired his rifle maybe more than a hundred times. He does not remember reloading.

The number of men on either side of him is lesser and lesser. The number of the enemy is seemingly endless. Until they are not.

He stops firing and looks through the gap. No man's land is filled with the enemy. None are standing. A ragged cheer runs through the trench, as if they had won a great victory. Well, they survived another night, which is victory enough.

Then the cheers turn to cries of horror. He looks out on the field. Through the fog of night and the mist of blood, he sees the bodies of the enemy rise. The endless number that has fallen stands up. After a minute, their lines reform and they resume their march.

He again starts firing, knowing what he does is pointless. You can't kill what is already dead. Having fallen once, they will never go down.

Again, he looks to either side. There is no one left, no one but him. Still, he fires and fires and fires, and the dead come closer and closer and closer.

In the early morning just before sunrise, Victor wakes up screaming. His cries disturb the sleep of some of the patients on the ward. Others find them a relief, for his shouts have woken them from their own nightmares. The sisters go from bed to bed, doing what they can to ease their pain and calm their terror. There are too few to quickly attend to them all but still they try, and their very presence is a comfort.

In the distance comes the thunder of long-range guns. Even as Victor consoles himself with the thought, *It was just a nightmare and for now, it's over*, the thunder reminds him that for the men on the line, the nightmare continues.

Victor Franks was not a great student. At best he was average, mostly Cs and an occasional B. Neither was he a great athlete. He was too small for football, too short for basketball, and too slow for track. While he was always part of the team it was as "equipment manager" or "assistant coach" or whatever other titles were used for someone who did everything but play the game.

What Victor was good at were machines. He had an intuitive knack for them. There was nothing he could not fix or make better. When automobiles finally arrived in Victor's town, he took right to them, all of them.

There were the electrics, but their range was limited. There were the oil-steam and water-steam cars. The boilers needed for those were tricky, and after one or two spectacular explosions, Victor decided they were not for him.

What Victor loved was the internal combustion engine. He loved the sound, he loved the smell, he loved the gears and the belts and the cylinders that made it run. The cars that ran on gasoline, kerosene, or diesel were, however, out of the reach of most people in his town.

Until Mr. Ford's Model T.

Victor never got a chance to own one. He did, however, fix them for those who did.

When the circus came to town, the circus manager showed up at the garage where Victor worked parttime. His mechanic had quit in the last town they played and he had some mechanical rides that needed looking after. And some new trucks that did not yet run right. Victor went out to the fairgrounds and within a few days had the rides operating at the peak of perfection and the trucks running better than anyone had expected. To Victor, machines were all a matter of the right combination of gears, straps, belts, and pulleys along with something to make them go.

As the circus made ready to leave, its manager asked Victor if he wanted to leave with it. What young man has never dreamed of running away to join the circus? Victor certainly had, from the very first time he had gone with his parents. He was tempted. He would have trucks and cars to drive, rides and other machines to tend and make better. The food was good. The circus folk understood him better than his friends and family. And there were girls.

The women of the Burly-Q, who smiled at him and asked him to come into their tents to fix small things and who weren't shy about showing a young man their bodies. There were the female freaks: the mermaid, the tattooed and bearded ladies, and the strong woman who could lift Victor over her head with one hand. And there was the magician's daughter, who always seemed to hang around to watch Victor fix things. He loved her smile. He loved her laugh. He loved her eyes. He loved her… well, everything about her. And she seemed to love him. And best of all, her father liked him because Victor had found ways to make the magician's tricks look more like miracles.

Yes, Victor was tempted, but before he yielded to the temptation the letter came.

"Notice of Call and to Appear for Physical Examination," it read. "You are hereby notified that you are called for military service of the United States…"

There was a war in Europe. People called it the "World War." The United States was involved, and Victor had been summoned to take up arms.

"You don't have to go," the magician told him. "You can still leave with us. Half the people in this circus once had another life, another name. Leave Victor Franks behind and come with us. I know my Mary would be glad to have you."

Again, Victor was tempted. And he almost plucked the fruit. But before he bit down, he thought of the man chosen to fight and maybe die in his place. And so, after thanking the magician and after a sweet, tender goodbye with Mary, Victor Franks walked away from Paradise.

Soon Victor was on an eastbound train. He listened to the clack of the wheels, felt their rhythm, and smelled the diesel fumes. While on the train he relaxed and dreamt of Ferris wheels and carousels and of a brown-haired, green-eyed magician's daughter. When he woke, he felt himself a fool for having given all that up and prayed those who said the war would soon be over were right and that Mary would wait.

From the train they went to a ship, and if they had let him, he would have haunted the engine rooms, learning the secrets of the leviathan on which he sailed. It was not always a smooth passage. It was known that German submarines prowled the Atlantic and he volunteered to stand watch hoping and yet not hoping to see one. Twice he and his fellow soldiers were placed on alert and made ready to man the lifeboats. Victor tried not to think about how there were not enough boats for all the men and instead concentrated on the mechanics of submarines and how one might fire torpedoes from them.

From the ship to the shore, and from the shore to the trucks, and from the trucks to the front and the hell of the trenches.

No one in the military cared that Victor was a mechanical savant. They cared only that he followed orders and shot in a straight line. They did not even care how good a marksman he was or if he could hit a certain target. Where he was being sent there would be more than enough targets. Odds were that he would hit his share.

Hold the line, repel the enemy advance, and send them back. Go over the top, try to gain ground, fall back, and try not to give up what had been won. It was a deadly game, one that neither side seemed capable of winning.

Victor did not dream. He barely slept. When he did it was the exhausted sleep of the near-dead. Only fragments came to him — indistinct sounds, smells, and voices. The best were the times he dreamt that he was back at the circus. These were also the worst when he woke up and found that he wasn't.

Leave helped. Sometimes they were rotated to the rear for a rest before being sent up front again. Other times when they took a town back from the Germans, they had a brief respite before being sent forward to gain some more ground.

In one such town Victor encountered Henry Shelley. Victor wasn't on leave as such. His company had been assigned to guard a field hospital until the ambulance angels came to evacuate the patients. He had met Henry on the train. Henry was strong, a sportsman and a scholar, nothing at all like Victor. So, of course, they became friends. When they reached France, they were sent their separate ways and never thought to see each other again.

Henry was one of those awaiting transport back to the States. He and his company had helped take the town, but Henry had lost a leg doing so.

"At least you're out of the fighting," Victor said to his friend.

Henry shrugged. "Yeah, never expected to go back like this. Always thought I'd go home marching or in a box. Never thought it would as half a man. Yeah, I'll have my moment of glory, get to show off my medals, then I'll be forgotten and left to live off a pension that probably won't pay the bills. Ya know, Vic, if they tripled that pension, I'd trade it for a new leg. Not that either one is likely."

Victor's mind started working. He knew that he was born to fix things. He had fixed cars, trucks, and carnival rides. Why couldn't he fix his friend?

He excused himself and went out to do what most soldiers are good at. He scavenged. He came back with belts, straps, and other things and made Henry a workable leg, one with a knee joint and an ankle that moved. Henry had to use a cane to walk but he could walk.

"That's a pension you owe me," Victor said as a smiling Henry slowly walked over to hug him as two friends do.

"How about a dollar a week until it's paid up?"

"Done."

When the other wounded soldiers saw what Victor had done for Henry, they asked the obvious question, "Can you fix me?"

Of course, he could. He enlisted the able-bodied to help scavenge. He made rough legs and arms for as many as he could. They were not things of beauty, but they moved and some of the hands even gripped.

Then came that one soldier, the one whose bed was in the back of the tent.

"Vic," Henry said when he walked his friend over. "This is Adam."

In his despair, Henry had called himself "half a man." Adam truly was. His lower body was gone, his legs having been blown off, with not enough left to attach the kind of device Victor had made for Henry.

"I heard what you've been doing for others, giving up your free time to fix 'em. I know you can't fix me, but I just wanted to thank you for what you've been doing."

There was no way Victor could have foreseen what was going to happen. If he had, he might have thanked Adam and wished him well. Maybe Adam would have despaired, asked a friend for a gun or a knife, and found his way to a patch of ground in France. Or maybe he would have gone home to live a life of quiet depression. Maybe he'd have got a circus job as a freak. Or maybe he would have overcome his disability and lived a long and happy life.

Born to fix things, Victor saw Adam as needing fixing.

He told Henry what he wanted to do.

"You're crazy."

Victor thought back to before he got the letter. He thought of a life he once had and would probably never get back. A life he'd given away.

"Yeah, I know. You gonna help?"

"Wait here." Henry slowly walked back to Adam's bed. They talked for just a minute. Then he returned to Victor. "He said yes."

They did not have long. The wounded were scheduled to be evacuated at the end of the week. Then Victor and the other able-bodied would either move forward or fall back.

While others scavenged, Victor built the engine. It was worn like a backpack and powered the pistons that worked the gears and pullies that would give Adam a kind of life back.

The day before the ambulances came, they were ready.

Adam was raised and placed in his bulky harness. "You'll need someone to start the engine for you," Victor told him. "Here's the switch to shut off the gas. You'll need to do that if you want to stop. Otherwise, you'll keep walking and walking until the fuel runs out. To turn, pull this lever or the other one. And I've adjusted it so that you should be able to handle rough terrain. Ready?"

"Yeah, let's do this. Start me up, Vic."

Victor pulled the cord. The engine sputtered then started. There was noise and smoke, and the smell of diesel filled the air. Then Adam, the man with no legs, began to walk.

Or tried to. Adjustments had to be made—straps tightened, pulleys fixed. There was a problem with a belt. Adam had to get used to letting a machine walk for him. Twice he fell when trying to turn and had to be helped to his "feet."

"Anything we can do to keep that from happening?" he asked.

"Yeah," Henry offered, "learn to turn."

It took some effort but soon Adam was walking in a balanced motion, ten feet then another ten. He successfully turned in a wide arc and walked back to where Victor, Henry, and most of the company, wounded and able, stood watching.

"It's exhausting," a smiling Adam said, "but I can walk. Thank you, Victor, I feel like I'm alive again."

When the ambulances came, the nurses did not comment on how some of their charges had been "fixed." Adam and his walking harness went in two separate stretchers, the plans Victor had drawn up tucked safely on Adam's person.

The ambulances gone, Victor and his company went back to war. And that should have been the end of it.

Except that it wasn't. The wounded, those who guarded them, and the nurses who transported them talked about what they had seen and how some of the soldiers had been fixed. Adam was mentioned several times. Word spread.

A week went by. A week of no advances, just firing from the trenches at the charging enemy and driving them back. Sometimes, at the end of the day, they seemed to have gotten closer. At the end of other days, they seemed further away. But they did not overrun the Allied position and the soldiers settled for that.

On the line, Victor did as he always did, fired toward the enemy as a whole and not at any one particular soldier. That way he could tell himself that he had not killed a man. Had he caused deaths? Yes, probably several if not dozens. But they had not been deliberate, simply the luck of the bullet. Deep inside, he knew this for a lie, but it was one he chose to believe so that he could get what little sleep he managed.

A car pulled up, a Daimler from its lines. One did not see that type of car this close to the front very often. It spoke of command and importance. Rumors flew. One final winner-take-all charge. Retreat and surrender. Armistice.

A chauffeur got out. He wore a clean uniform and wore sergeant's stripes. He opened the back doors for a captain and a major. The captain asked questions. When he got the answers he needed he sent the sergeant into the trenches.

Victor Franks was pulled off the line. The sergeant led him to the rear and into the command tent.

Victor approached the two officers who were seated behind the campaign table from which the maps had been removed. He came to attention and saluted.

"Private Franks reporting, sirs."

"At ease, private," the captain told him. "Have a seat." When Victor did, the captain went on. "Sergeant, guard the door, from the outside if you please." Once the sergeant left, the captain turned to Victor.

"Private Franks, I am Captain Moritz. This is Major Clerval."

Moritz drew some papers from a briefcase that lay on the table and passed them on to Victor. "What can you tell me about these?"

Victor recognized them immediately, the plans for the motorized harness he had made for Adam. Forgetting whom he addressed, Victor blurted out, "Where did you get these?"

"We are asking the questions here, private," Moritz said gently but firmly. "I take it you recognize these plans. That you drew them and designed Private Lavenza's harness as well as the, what's the word, prostheses for the other wounded men." Seeing the surprise on Victor's face, Moritz explained, "It's a large war but really a small town. You are to be commended."

"What happened to Adam?" Victor demanded, worry overriding his sense of place and military protocol.

"Adam Lavenza is not your concern, private." The major's voice was harsh, its tone reprimanding Victor for his near insubordination. "What is your concern, our concern, is… can you make more?"

Of course, he could. He had made one, more would be easy. "How many more, sir?"

Moritz answered. "As many as you can, private, for as long as needed."

Although still worried about Adam, Victor got caught up in the problem of how best to accomplish the task. As much to himself as the officers he said, "With some men to help, and enough equipment and supplies, I think several a day to start. After that, if things go well, I think we'll be able to make more, sirs."

Major Clerval smiled and nodded to Moritz who said, "Based on these plans, Franks, we've begun to assemble what you'll need. If there's anything else, you'll let us know. We'll assign you working space and men to assist you. And since you'll be in charge of these men, you'd best get used to being called 'Sergeant.' Now if there's nothing else, Sergeant Waldman will show you to your new sleeping and working quarters."

It was a clear dismissal. Victor stood to attention and saluted. Then he dared to ask, "One thing, captain, major. All this is to help wounded men like Adam, isn't it? I think it's a wonderful thing you're doing. Thank you."

Again, Victor saluted, turned and left the tent, not seeing the look exchanged by the two officers.

Rumors run through an army like dysentery. The most current was that of a ghost company that fearlessly charged and routed the enemy. Every soldier on the line knew someone who knew someone who had been told by a friend that he had seen them. No one believed it any more than they believed that the Germans were using trained wolves.

Victor returned to the trenches, having been relieved of his detail after overseeing the making of roughly three dozen harnesses.

"It's not practical to make them here on the front," Captain Moritz told him. "You will, of course, be allowed to keep your rank and will be leading a platoon."

"Thank you, captain," Victor replied. "If I may ask, will this work be continued back in the States?"

"Sergeant, I can assure you that your work will be continued."

His platoon always seemed to be the one first over the top, taking the heaviest losses. "It's like they're trying to get us killed," one of his men said but that was just soldier talk. No one really believed that. What use would the army have for dead men?

The trucks pulled up just before dawn. That was not unusual. Many moves were made under cover of darkness.

It was the other noise that woke Victor, that of engines, the *whoosh, whoosh* of working pistons and the *clank, clank* of metal feet. The smell of diesel hung in the air.

These were the sounds and the smell he had first encountered when he fixed Adam. He had encountered them again while on his detail. Without even seeing what the trucks had delivered, Victor knew it as his work.

But why, he wondered, *why bring them back here? They should be home.*

Then he caught an odor every soldier knew, that of the freshly dead, maybe two, three days gone. He followed that scent and came upon the trucks just as soldiers finished unloading bodies and setting them into the harnesses he had designed and perfected.

"No!" Victor shouted and rushed toward the trucks. Guards stopped him and started to removed him.

"Let him stay, after all, this is his work."

Victor knew the voice. "Captain Moritz?"

"Yes, but it's major now, sergeant. Thanks to you. Come forward and see your creations."

Victor approached. It was now light enough for him to make out twenty harnesses. They were larger than he had designed, with extra fuel tanks. Strapped into each was a corpse.

"Why not use the dead and spare the living?" Moritz asked. "We made some changes of course, so we could use the whole body and not have to cut off the legs."

As horrified as Victor was, the mechanic in him had to ask, "Why use them at all? What good are they?"

"Good question, sergeant. We thought about just sending the mechanicals, but soldiers are men, and men are by nature superstitious. We thought the sight of walking corpses would frighten the enemy and it does. But yours is a good question. It implies that there might be room for improvement."

"But, major, sir, this is monstrous."

"Of course, it is, sergeant. Then again, war has been turning men into monsters for thousands of years. Anyway, Colonel Clerval thought you might want to see the results of your work, so this group was assigned here."

"This *group*? There are more?"

"Up and down the line. By the way, your squad will be assigned to follow behind our "ghosts," to mop up after they've done their work."

What work can they do? Victor asked himself. *They walk forward and scare the Germans.* Again, he asked, but silently, *What good are they?* And not even the mechanic and designer inside him could answer that question.

The harnessed dead marched out of the trenches just after dawn, clanking their way toward the enemy lines. Shots rang out and found their mark, but you can't kill what is already dead. The ghosts kept marching.

That's why the extra fuel tanks, to get them across no man's land. They have more than enough.

It suddenly occurred to Victor why they had more than enough fuel. The word "monstrous" came back to him when he figured it out.

"Spread the word," he told the men closest to him, "when we go over, keep as far back from those… things as possible."

"No worries there, Sarge. What sick mind thought of those things anyway?"

One who meant well, Victor thought as the order was given.

They advanced, all of them firing, some of them falling as the Germans shot back. But most of the enemy fire concentrated itself on the harnessed dead, which soon reached the German trenches into which they fell.

And exploded, sending fire through the trenches.

Timer, Victor thought, *or maybe a float switch.* Then he stopped thinking of how it was done. Shouting "Charge!" he led his men forward.

The attack was a success, but Victor's platoon had not been one of the lucky ones. The enemy fought fire with fire and a German soldier swept Victor and his men with a flame thrower before falling back. Munitions were nearby, and the flame and explosion took most of the men. Victor himself ended up as Adam had.

Victor lies in the hospital, dreading sleep, hoping that that night it will be his turn for the morphine that grants oblivion and chases the nightmares. He wonders when he and the others will be sent home. He asks himself if he will build his own harness when he returns, decides that he would rather be a circus freak, but not in Mary's circus. That would truly be hell.

Then he hears one of the nurses. "Sergeant Franks is right in here, major."

Moritz stands before Victor's bed. Without greeting, he says, "You asked me why use the dead? What good were they? And you were right. After all, the dead can't fire back. But soldiers like you, those who still have arms with which to hold and fire a rifle, can serve their country one last time. Thank you for the idea, Franks. See you on the front."

Not until then did Victor Franks realize that his dreams had been prophetic, that in them he is not the lone soldier but rather one of the risen dead. He thinks to scream but the practical part of him—the designer, the engineer, the mechanic—tells him that at least the nightmares will soon stop.

THE IMPOSSIBLE JOURNEY

DANIELLE ACKLEY-MCPHAIL

There are always those who will say it cannot be done.
— The British Interplanetary Society

ALOHA WANDERWELL GAVE ME THE WORLD. SHE TAUGHT ME TO DREAM. The first I ever saw her, I came to the realization that nothing was impossible. Nothing out of reach. Not even the Moon. Nor the stars. She taught me I could do anything, and polite society be damned.

The third of June 1924, Bombay, India

It wasn't all glamour like the broadsheets made out. There was nary a camera or reporter in sight. Not at first, anyway. My father was assigned to the British Raj, but we were housed at the Anglo-Indian Hotel. I was all of ten years old and quite motherless, and thus already inclined to be a bit wild.

I had crept from beneath the mosquito net tenting my bed and gone in search of some water. Even at four in the morning, the day already promised to be hot. But even so, I forgot my thirst at the sound of hearty swearing outside the kitchen window. I climbed onto the counter and peered out, not wishing to be seen, but I quickly jumped down and hurried out the door to the side yard where a veritable giantess bent over what I was later informed was a Ford Model-T, one of three embarking on the grandest adventure. At the sound of my footsteps, she glanced up and over her shoulder.

My eyes went wide, and my mouth likewise, to see her — Ms. Aloha Wanderwell, the first woman to drive around the world — standing there in men's breeches and an army tunic, with her hair pulled back in a tail. By the light of the electric lantern perched on the edge of the car, her hair shone like gold, and her eye sparkled like dark blue diamonds.

"Pardon my French," she said, with her mouth half-quirked in a smile, looking not the least apologetic.

I could not stop staring at the smudges of grease on her face. Twisting my arms behind me, I lowered my gaze and forced myself not to stare. "No pardon needed, mum."

Her laughter sparkled brighter than her eyes.

"Hey, doll, how about you lending me a hand?"

That was the first I ever held a spanner. It wasn't the last.

For hours we tinkered on that engine, as the sun slowly rose to outshine our lantern, with Aloha — excuse me, Idris, as she asked to be called — carefully explaining what each part was and what it should do. We both got frightfully greasy pulling that engine apart and putting it all back until the motor purred. Well, rumbled, more like. Model-Ts were not known for their melodious voices.

As we worked, and between the explaining, she told me of the wondrous places she had been, and those she would go to, waking in me a new thirst. One for adventure.

"Betina!"

At my ayah's outraged call, I all but dropped the spanner I held and dashed back inside, blushing at Idris's throaty chuckle as I called back my farewells over my shoulder.

The Wanderwell expedition left the next day.

I was not to see my new friend again, not in person, but I carried that spark she lit in me until I could fan it to flame, though it took nearly a decade to consume me.

The 13th of October 1933, Liverpool, England

My father despaired for me. His daughter who was more of a son. Wearing nothing but breeks and flat caps with my blouses, and sturdy boots on my feet, I never developed a taste for fashion plates or magazines, though I fancied boys well enough when I noticed them. They themselves scarcely noticed me. Between my short bob and functional attire, they more often mistook me for one of their own.

It made no matter to me, with my head, as they say, in the clouds. Clippings of Idris's continued adventures plastered my walls, and, ever since I'd read *An American Aviatrix Abroad*, Ruth Nichols and a slew of other pilots, both men and women alike, had joined her. I had it in mind to reach for the skies.

Instead of attending finishing school, I stalked the newsstands for the latest issues of all the engineering magazines, including my new favorite, *Practical Mechanics*, drawn to their bright-colored covers and fantastical artwork, projecting the future onto the page even as they revealed the secrets of modern machinery. I devoured their contents religiously late into the night. And during the daylight hours, I wandered down to the nearby airfield to gawk or perched atop the neighbor's wall to watch his driver maintain their Tantra 77. Automobiles had come a long way since Ford's Model-T, and I itched to take up tools beside him. I nearly fell off the wall trying to get a look at the rear-mounted, air-cooled v7 engine.

At my yip, the man yelled and shooed me away. Laughing, I rolled and dropped to the ground, running through the brush until I reached our street and ran beyond for the sheer joy of it. I kept going until I reached Dale Street, slowing at the sight of a slew of men entering No. 81, among them a vaguely familiar face. My brow furrowed as I probed the recesses of my mind for why. I wasn't known for noticing people, my thoughts more often turned inward, puzzling out science and mechanics I had mostly only read about. And then the spark connected. All the press was abuzz about Phillip E. Cleater's "The Possibilities of Interplanetary Travel." Even the Echo had run the piece. Whatever was taking place on Dale Street involved some of the most brilliant minds in Liverpool.

What I wouldn't give to follow them inside.

To think I'd witnessed the birth of the British Interplanetary Society, though I scarcely knew it at the time.

They moved away from Liverpool. The BIS. I despaired for my dream, now out of reach. A dream I had not admitted even to myself. As a child, I used to fall asleep to my father's voice as he told me of fanciful films by Georges Méliès, which he had seen as a boy, films since lost. My mind filled with the vibrant descriptions his words painted as he shared his memories, until I would swear, I could see the flickering images inviting me to dream. Papa's favorite had been *The Impossible Voyage*, but *A Trip to the Moon* had held me fascinated. It still did.

Men like Cleater and Clarke, Les Shepherd and Eric Burgess, Ralph Smith and Harry Ross, and others like them gave me hope the heavens were within reach. As my self-learning transitioned from aeronautics to astrophysics, those visionaries joined my wall of inspiration, and the flame in me fanned high as the stars, if not the sun.

The 4th of January 1945, London

My father stopped complaining about my manner of dress. He stopped complaining about anything, spending all his breath on trying to convince me to flee the city I had made my home, moving to where industry… and opportunity lived. In costly calls on the telephone, Papa wasted no time reminding me those were the very things the Germans sought to bomb out of existence. I couldn't tell him I would gladly wear my gas mask like a handbag the rest of my days for the chance to work in the factories, using the mechanical skills that a few short years ago had been nothing more than book learning. Today? Grease embedded my nailbeds and scarce a day went by when my knuckles didn't gain a well-earned scrape. The military didn't care about the anatomy under your clothes when it desperately needed hands that knew what they were doing. And if it so happened, I wandered by Vauxhall and South Lambeth Road of an evening, so be it.

See, I'd found the Society once more. The BIS, and lean as times had grown and worn my clothes, they never questioned my gender, to all appearances male. Oh, the things I learned, the theories I discussed. Rockets and landers and encapsulating suits. Tantalizing advancements all but begging to be put into practice.

I understood that yearning.

But the Explosives Act of 1875 kept all those plans on paper. Testing of rocket fuel by private individuals was against the law, and without all that, the rest remained nothing but enticing theory, right?

Who would have thought the scientific community housed rebels?

"I thought this was a group for serious scientists. Why wait? The world outstrips us while we are hobbled by rules not even made in this century," one young hothead muttered across the drawing room, exchanging sly glances with his compatriots. "How are they even to know what we're about? What are the laws of men when we seek to reorder the laws of physics?"

I stayed silent, out of the way, too cautious to bring attention to myself though I longed to talk sense into the barmy berk.

One or two others muttered agreement, but wiser heads stared them down.

Shortly thereafter, the young dissenters wandered off to what manner of mischief I couldn't say. With a sigh, I rose to follow, but not out of solidarity. Morning in the factories came before the sun even woke, let alone me.

I bid my farewells and exited the building, heading for my flat in Kennington Park. I'd gone just down the road when the sky briefly lit like day, and a rumbling roar rattled my noggin. I crouched and cried out as I nearly lost my feet, fumbling for my gas mask more by instinct than anything else. The rest of the night descended into chaos. Dust filled the air, coating the lenses over my eyes until I could not see more than the flicker of flame all too near as the muffled sound of running feet pounded all around me.

Someone gripped my shoulders and hurried me back inside BIS headquarters, where someone else pulled the mask from my head and pressed a scotch into my hand. We waited a very long time for things to settle. My nerves still jittered the next day, and all thoughts of work pled off against the overwhelming drive to hunker down and take cover.

The press blamed the explosion on the Blitz. A V-2 rocket strike purportedly leveled the Lambeth Baths, killing four dozen people. Or so they said. I hadn't heard any planes. But there was no disputing the damage. Any wonder the Houses held their ground on rocket fuel? I shuddered and hushed the little voice inside wondering where the hotheads had gone. None had resurfaced since that night.

I shuddered at the thought.

After that, I bowed to my father's wishes, though not as expected.

As we waited for the literal dust to settle, the senior, more level-headed members of the Society gathered around me, their looks considering.

"Well," someone grumbled. "They've nearly cocked that up royal."

Ross cleared his throat. "They were foolish. Reckless. But they weren't wrong. If we stifle progress, we will fall behind. Be *left* behind."

I frowned and turned to meet his gaze. "What they proposed was dangerous."

"But it needn't be," he countered, and the others nodded in agreement. "It isn't, done properly, with precautions and safeguards in place."

"You speak as if this is other than theoretical."

He half grimaced, and half grinned like a schoolboy caught out on a harmless prank.

"We may have gone a *bit* beyond the theoretical."

I looked from one to the other all around the circle, earnest expressions all, then to the diagrams and artwork gracing the walls of groundbreaking designs to shake off gravity's coil and gain the heavens.

"What are you proposing?"

"You are young and lean, with a sound head on your shoulders," Clarke said, leaning back, relaxed, as if what they discussed were not in the least radical or controversial. "Your thoughts are quick and cunning, and you do not speak without having thought your statement through. We have held back until now because we are past the age of exploration, our bones ill-suited to the rigors such flight proposes. Old men dream, young men make it happen."

I held back a scoff. These men were hardly geriatric. But still, their words enticed me.

"Why now? Why me?"

"Until now, none have held our confidence. All the others rushed forward with bravado. You carry yourself with thought and purpose, and your mechanical skills stand impressive."

Slowly, I shook my head, more in disbelief than rejection. Half of me scolded that I needed to be responsible. I barely heard it over the echoes of Idris and Ruth and Amelia and half a dozen other trailblazers in my head.

Their words fanned the flame inside me beyond my ability to constrain it.

We left that place. Together.

Sloughing off the dusting of war, I drew a deep, clean breath of air and marched toward progress, guided by these visionaries, eager for the adventure they led me to.

Driving deep into the country where strafing runs and air raid sirens were but a thing of buried memory, we came to a structure more barn than silo, and as the doors opened wide, my gaze danced with awe and delight. I pushed up my sleeves and strode with purpose toward my *own* grandest adventure.

I cannot yet say where I have been, but I can tell you, nothing is impossible.

STORMSPIKE

KEN SCHRADER

ROSAMUND THORPE STOOD ON THE FLIGHT DECK OF HIS MAJESTY, King George VI's flying fortress: the *Arc Royal*, scowling into the night over the North Sea. Wind tugged at her shoulder-length brown hair. Its chill fingers snatched each plume of breath as it passed her lips.

Stars glittered overhead, and a half-moon gave just enough light to see the fighter planes tethered to the flight deck around her. Two meters from the edge, strips of blue lights ran the perimeter of the deck. Not bright enough to make the ship a target, they were a safety precaution.

And they were out.

The blackouts started a few days ago. They hadn't lasted long, but on a ship like the *Royal*, they were as disruptive as a fishhook in the finger.

Worse, Rosamund and her crew hadn't been able to find the cause. Which made the whole mess officially her fault.

It made no sense. Not even a tripped breaker, but here she was, out on the deck, warding the edges because the bloody safety lights were out.

As if sensing her thoughts, the thin strips glowed to life.

"You could have had someone else ward the—what the hell?" A voice spoke from behind her.

Abigail Shaul, her second, stood hunched against the cold, her fists shoved deep into the pockets of her jacket. She stared at the safeties, head cocked, her brown hair whipping about her head.

"You look surprised," Rosamund said.

"I am surprised," Abigail said. "I came out here to give you a status update. We hadn't started on the safeties."

Rosamund frowned at the lights. "What did you find?"

"Not a bloody thing," Abigail said.

"That can't be right."

"It is," Abigail said. "Power has been restored, and we've been from one end of the outage to the other. Nothing."

Rosamund glared at the lights. Her breath exploded in a cloud of gray. "The deck safeties are on their own backup circuit. Why did they go down?"

"We hadn't made it there yet," Abigail said. "The crew'll look into it, but I have a feeling that they'll find the same amount of nothing."

"It can't be nothing," Rosamund said. "This is contested territory. If we run into the Germans during an outage…"

"We'll figure it out." Abigail turned up the collar of her jacket. "But we can only play what's in front of us, and everything appears to be working now."

A chill blast flowed across the deck, and Rosamund turned into it. The cold hitched her breath in her chest. She took it in and released it in a long plume. She hated not knowing. It got under her skin like a splinter.

A wall of clouds gathered at the horizon. A storm, probably — if the wind didn't change.

She turned to Abigail. "Is everyone accounted for?"

"Aye. At least the night shift." Abigail frowned. "What are you thinking?"

A sour feeling coiled in Rosamund's stomach. She didn't want to give voice to the thought. Tensions were already frayed among the crew.

A shiver rattled Abigail from head to foot. "Why are we still out here?"

"We've still got to brief the captain." A wry grin quirked Rosamund's lips. "Tell him we don't have any idea what's going on."

"Ah." Abigail's blue eyes glittered. "I suppose I'll get used to the cold eventually."

Her wristwatch chimed at an ear-splitting pitch, and it took every ounce of self-restraint to keep Rosamund from smashing it against the bulkhead.

She sat up, stretched, and her right shoulder popped. She'd gotten too little sleep over the past few days. So had the rest of her crew, and she wasn't going to ask them to do anything she wasn't willing to do herself.

As expected, Captain Ethan Bywater hadn't liked hearing that his chief engineer didn't know what was going on with the power aboard his ship. Of course, with the power back on, all Rosamund had was her assurances that she'd get to the bottom of it.

It wasn't his way to shout. Instead, he'd told her that he had every faith in her skill, while the look on his face was that of a disappointed parent.

She wished he'd shouted.

She stood, shivering as her bare feet hit metal. The chill of the deck meshed with a flash of frustration as she replayed their discussion in her head. She showered, dressed, and left her bunk wanting to dismantle some machinery — or the one responsible.

The first rays of dawn had yet to crest the edge of the world. Rosamund stepped onto the flight deck, her boots crunching a sheet of ice. The wind bit into her, coating the back of her throat with a pleasant arctic tang.

The weather soothed her, and she strode with quiet calm toward the forward weapon embankment the crew called the Fist of England.

The *Arc Royal* commanded a pair of Fists. One forward and one aft. Massive Tesla cannons, they were capable of throwing arcs of devastating electrical energy well over twenty-five kilometers.

Rosamund tested them every week, but recent events had convinced her to step up her schedule. There had been no outages for the last forty-eight hours, but that hadn't kept her crew from working overtime, testing and retesting.

She blew out a frosty breath and climbed the ladder to the gunnery station. At the door, she paused, turning to look out over the sea.

The storm drew closer. It would overtake them, probably by the end of the day, unless the captain decided to outrun it.

Rosamund stepped into the room and threw the switch. A pair of caged incandescents snapped to life, filling the space with a warm, yellow light. She removed a radio from its charging station on the wall, inserted the earpiece, and switched it on. A staticky pop sounded in her ear, then the hum of an empty channel.

"Abigail, are you there?" Rosamund asked.

"Bright and early, chief."

"Good." Rosamund stepped clear of the room, adjusting her volume and baffles against the wind. "I want this test to go as smooth as a sheet of ice, but don't hesitate to pull the plug if anything seems even slightly out of the ordinary."

"Understood," Abigail said. "Then it's a leisurely afternoon spent pouring over diagnostics." A trace of weariness entered her voice. "That should be fun. I'll make sure the coffee is in your quarters before we get there."

"Good woman," Rosamund said. Footsteps on the deck signaled the arrival of the first of her crew. She glanced over her shoulder into the smiling face of Engineer First-Class Sam Holmes.

"Morning, Sam," she said.

"Morning, chief," he said. "I thought I was early. Did you sleep out here?"

"You know I don't sleep."

Sam chuckled. "Must be a requirement for promotion." He pulled the edges of his jacket tighter. "Along with an immunity to the cold."

"I grew up in this," Rosamund said. "I'll let you know when it starts getting cold." Holmes snorted as he turned to the controls.

Rosamund repeated her instructions to Sam. She handed him her radio, clapped him on the shoulder, then climbed down to the deck.

The *Royal's* bridge sported a three-hundred-sixty-degree view. Plotting, helm, and communications formed the points of an equilateral triangle within the circle, with the captain's chair in the center.

Captain Bywater was already seated. He gave Rosamund a smile and a nod.

"Morning, chief."

"Good morning, sir."

"Rough weather coming," he said. "What do you think? Sundown?"

"A few hours sooner, I'd bet."

He raised an eyebrow. "Five pounds?"

Both of them had grown up on the northern coast of England. He from Whitley Bay and she from Seaham. Their weather sense was a source of good-natured competition.

Rosamund grinned. "Done." She stepped to the comm station, picked up a radio, and switched it on.

"Poppy," Rosamund said. "How do our levels look?"

Down in engineering, Poppy Harrison answered in her usual chipper tone. "We're green across the board and sitting steady as the horizon on a calm day."

"You know the drill." Rosamund turned to Bywater. "Ready to proceed, sir."

"Navigation," he said. "Radar contact?"

"No, sir."

"Action stations," Bywater said. "Condition Two."

The communications officer threw a switch, and a short, sharp alarm exploded from speakers all across the *Royal*. It repeated twice, then he called out the ready state via loudspeaker. This, too, was repeated twice.

Captain Bywater stood and walked to the starboard windows. "Go ahead, chief."

"Aye, sir." Rosamund signaled to the plotting station, who relayed firing coordinates to the Fists.

As one, the cannons turned, locking onto a point on the distant horizon. Beneath the grind of the weapons rotating, a deep thrum began. It overtook the turrets, rolling in an unstoppable wave of power.

The sound of the Fists priming to fire didn't simply reach the ears. It resonated in Rosamund's chest like a bass guitar strummed by God.

She keyed on her radio. "Poppy, how are we looking?"

"Still green across the board," Poppy said. "Not even a flicker."

Rosamund thumbed a preset switch on the radio. "Abigail?"

"Aft Fist is ready to fire and holding steady."

Rosamund gave a quick nod to the captain and switched channels. "Sam?"

"Green across the board, ma'am."

A pop of interference burst in Rosamund's ears.

"What was that?" Rosamund said. "Sam?" At her tone, Bywater turned from the window, striding toward her.

"A small spike," Sam said. "Probably no—"

A roar of static cut him off as a brilliant blue-white light filled the windows.

"Sam!"

A staccato growl ripped through the bridge as the Fist of England fired. Red-orange flashes bled into the discharge. Explosions roared outside.

"Emergency conditions!" Bywater said. "Clear that area. Fire and med crews to the flight deck."

"Poppy!" Rosamund said. "Cut the feed to the fore-capacitor."

As suddenly as it happened, the Fist stopped firing.

"Damage report," Bywater ordered. Rosamund raced to the window.

Oily black smoke rose from the flight deck. Three of the fighters lay in burning heaps. Others nearby bore nasty scorch marks and were in danger of going up themselves.

Fire and medical crews swarmed, battling the blaze and caring for the wounded.

"Chief." Bywater's voice snapped Rosamund from the scene outside. "Get down there. I want to know exactly what just happened."

"This place smells like ozone!" Abigail, head and shoulders in the Fist's left-rear quarter, shouted to be heard over the wind.

"It could be worse." Rosamund stood on the lip of the turret. A twelve-inch strip of steel and a safety harness kept her from a long fall into the frigid North Sea.

The blast from the Fist had shattered the gunnery room window and charred the walls. Sam had managed to find cover beneath the console. He was burned but alive, thank God.

As soon as the fire and med teams had cleared the room, Rosamund tore into the control console, determined to get to the bottom of the malfunction. If it had been a malfunction.

She'd found nothing.

The next place to look was the Fist itself. To get inside, she had to twist into an awkward position that had the muscles in her back aching within minutes.

She'd been in there so long, steel digging into her spine, that it had taken her a long minute to stand up straight once she'd gotten back to her feet.

On the deck, Rosamund's crew worked to remove the wreckage of the fighters. With a metallic scrape, they forced a chunk of wing over the side. She followed its fall with her eyes until it splashed into the sea.

"You were right," Abigail said. "Firing gap and range control have been tampered with. This was no accident."

"Damn it." Rosamund twisted at the hips and was rewarded with a crackle in her lower back. She blew out a breath.

The storm was nearly on top of them. Lightning flashed in its depths as rain fell in wispy streamers. They'd feel it soon—well ahead of sundown.

The thought brought her no joy. This had been a deliberate act of sabotage waiting for the next round of testing.

Which wouldn't have happened until Friday, she thought.

"That should do it." Abigail shifted with a groan. "It won't be pretty, but that was some miracle you pulled off. She'll fire again if she needs to."

Rosamund turned to offer Abigail a hand up when something in the clouds caught her eye.

Movement.

She hauled Abigail to her feet, aiming her gaze skyward.

"Tell me if you see anything in the clouds," she said.

"What?" Abigail bent forward, arching her back. "My back is killing me." She straightened. "What am I looking for? Lightning?"

"Not lightning." Rosamund stared at the churning gray wall. "I don't know. I thought I saw..."

She trailed off as the sleek, sinister silhouette of a German fighter emerged, followed by another. And another, and another...

"My God," Abigail said.

"Get back to the capacitor!" Rosamund shouted. "Reconnect the Fist."

Battle Stations sounded, but Abigail stayed transfixed. Rosamund gripped her arm and shook hard.

Abigail clutched at her, her eyes snapping to the thin strip of deck.

"Focus," Rosamund said.

Abigail nodded. She rushed back to the access ladder, disconnected her harness, and slid to the deck.

Rosamund replaced the access panel, making sure the seals were tight, then ran to the ladder. A new sound reached her ears, and she stopped.

Turbines.

She looked up as the bow of a massive flying fortress broke through the clouds.

She's larger than the Royal. Rosamund didn't need to see any more than she had to know that. *How did she get so close?* A mixture of dread and wonder filled her.

Cries from the deck snapped her back into the present. She reached the ladder, unclasped her harness, and slid down.

Scores of men and women—pilots, flight, and gunnery crews, sprinted to their posts.

"Get to your stations!" Rosamund shouted to her remaining crew. "I want to see how well that monster can swim! Move!"

Rosamund sprinted across the flight deck, the roar of the fighters taking off and the crack of the anti-aircraft guns hard on her heels.

Planes swarmed the sky between the two ships, a pair of hornet's nests kicked at the same time.

Gunfire filled the air. A Messerschmidt erupted in flames and tumbled so close to the deck that Rosamund braced for impact.

Her eyes fastened on the enemy airship. There was no way this was a chance meeting. Rosamund clenched her fists. The Germans had expected one of the *Royal's* main guns to be out of commission… She changed course, heading aft.

The world swayed beneath her feet as the *Royal* took evasive action. Ahead of her, a fighter, both wings aflame, engine screaming, smashed into the deck. The plane skipped and tumbled in a burning ruin, sliding off the other side. Rosamund cursed, dodging around pieces of flaming metal.

Ahead, the gunnery station was quiet. Panting, she slowed. The door to the firing room swung on its hinges. Someone should have been here by now.

A bone-deep thrum rose from the fore of the ship. A curse came from the gunnery room, and that was when Rosamund saw the blood staining the deck.

The Fist fired. Rosamund shielded her eyes as a thick cord of lightning streaked out from the cannon to the flying fortress above them.

The bolt struck home, drawing additional lightning from the storm. It skittered and jumped across the German hull. Strange bits of plating, too thin to be armor, sheared off her, falling like broken glass. The large ship shuddered, then returned fire from a set of twin turrets set in her belly.

The shots pounded the *Royal*'s flank, punching through armor.

Rosamund raced up the ladder as the gunnery door swung wide.

Ezekiel Hibbard, one of her crewmen, stepped out. Sinister stains blotched the top half of his working blues. He held a pistol in his right hand.

For a long moment, the two of them stared at each other. Zeke raised the gun.

"Shit!" Rosamund leapt out onto the lip of metal surrounding the turret. Clutching at hand holds, she swung herself around to put as much of the cannon between them as possible.

A bullet spanged off the walkway.

"Of course, it would be you," Zeke said.

The *Royal* took another hit. Rosamund held on for all she was worth, a foot slipping off the narrow lip.

"Who else would it be?" Rosamund filled her voice with anger, distracting from the plunge beneath her feet.

A bullet smashed off the deck. Too close. She skittered to the far side of the cannon, clutching at hand holds with chilled fingers.

"It was you all this time, wasn't it?" she demanded. "Randomly throwing breakers, making a mess of things on my ship?"

The darkening sky flashed a brilliant blue-white as the *Royal* gave as good as she got. Rosamund blinked the spots away, the taste of ozone coating her throat.

"You should have heard the grumbling behind your back," Zeke sneered. "Some of the crew would throw you over the side if they could get away with it."

"Started by you, I'm sure." The cold bit through Rosamund's jacket. The first spattering of rain struck her face. She peered back the way she'd come.

The deck was empty. She gasped, shuffling forward

Another bullet cracked off the turret behind her.

"You're my chief," Zeke said. "I stood up for you! Got a bloodied lip for it." He sounded proud, then the pitch of his voice changed. "Even after you passed me over for promotion a second time."

"That unstable and violent streak is hard to overlook," Rosamund said. "And honestly, I have seen better engineers—"

"Shut up!" Zeke fired but missed.

Rosamund tightened her grip as the rain poured down.

"You can't stay there forever," Zeke said. "I could just wait until your hands go numb and watch you fall on your own."

He was right. Rosamund's stiff fingers burned with the cold.

"I'll make it quick," he said. "I owe you that much."

"What about Sam? What did you owe him?" Rosamund asked. "Keep it! I can hold on until they come to see why the Fist isn't firing."

An orange-red flash lit the sky. Rosamund glanced away to see a Schmidt, missing a wing, tumble past. Farther away, one of their own fighters vanished in a ball of fire.

Rosamund hooked her wrist around a handhold, clasping her fingers together to warm them up.

"You're awfully quiet," she said. "Run out of nerve? Revert to the coward I always took you for?"

She expected an outburst and a shot or two, but only the sounds of the battle reached her.

Gritting her teeth, Rosamund edged around the Fist. The gunnery platform lay empty, as did the room beyond.

She whirled, certain that he'd gotten behind her, and nearly lost her footing. Frigid rain blew into her face. She scrambled off the walkway into the gunnery room, swinging the door shut.

Groaning, she hunched, shoving her fists in her pockets. The frozen edges burned her wrists, but the inner lining felt heavenly.

She looked around, torn between the need to undo whatever Ezekiel had done and running that traitorous bastard down.

A panel lay on the deck next to the console. Scowling, Rosamund grabbed a radio off the wall and snapped it on.

"Abigail? Are you there?"

"I'm here, chief. Where are you?"

The *Royal* shuddered under a hard hit. Alarms blared.

"I'm at the aft Fist." Rosamund shimmied under the console. "Ezekiel Hibbard did something to it," she said. "He's behind everything. If you see him, he's armed. Be careful."

Abigail cursed. "Understood."

Rosamund ripped open her jacket and fumbled a pen-light out of an inner pocket. Clicking it on, she stuck it between her teeth and pulled herself into the console.

Ezekiel hadn't had time to be subtle, but with the amount of power the Fists used, short-circuiting the line could have blown the entire thing off the ship.

She flexed her fingers to limber up, then repaired the damage as well as she could.

"None of the crew have seen him," Abigail said through the radio.

"He's got to have some way off the ship." Rosamund climbed to her feet. Outside, the anti-aircraft guns fired. Fighters roared past, their cannons ripping into the hulls of the struggling airships.

She leapt down the ladder as a gunnery crew arrived.

"Sidearm!" Rosamund stopped a man long enough to take his pistol, then raced from the deck.

A hollow boom echoed in the stairwell and the *Royal* shuddered. Rosamund stumbled down the last half of the stairs, hitting the bottom wall hard. She bounced off and hurtled down the next flight.

The *Royal* had a loading bay they used for restocking at ports where there wasn't room to land. That was Ezekiel's way off the ship.

A blast of wet, frigid air hit her as she charged into the bay. The ramp was down, letting the storm howl through.

Ezekiel straightened from a crouch next to an open crate and turned toward her. He held a long metallic plank with three turbines mounted to it. A hoverboard.

He dropped the board with a clang and drew his pistol. Rosamund ducked behind a crate as bullets chewed the wood behind her.

"I thought you hated those things." Rosamund checked her gun and peered around the corner. Ezekiel and the board were gone.

"No lie, chief." His voice seemed to be coming from everywhere. "Can't stand 'em, but it's better than a dip in the drink."

Rosamund slipped between the crates. Zeke was going to make for that open door, and she wanted to be in front of him when he did.

Bullets slammed into the cargo above her. Cursing, Rosamund crouched and ran forward. At a gap, she fired up toward the ceiling.

Ezekiel cried out in surprise, rocking the hoverboard back and away.

An explosion outside smothered the storm, and the *Royal* lurched. Crates tugged at their moorings as Rosamund hit a corner with bruising force and tumbled to the deck. Scrabbling forward, she swung out around the edge of her crate and fired into empty space.

"Nice try, chief." Ezekiel leered down from above her.

Rosamund leapt ahead, rolling even as her calf lit in agony. She fired, and the bullet spanged off the underside of the board. Ezekiel wobbled and fired back, bullets cracking into the deck ahead of her and to the side.

He gave her a cheeky wave before angling toward the open bay door.

Another shot rang out.

Ezekiel pitched forward. The board spun crazily, then dropped to the deck, sending his body tumbling through the door and down the ramp.

"Chief?" Abigail shouted above the wind. "Rosamund, are you alright?"

"I'm here," Rosamund said, the deck cold and wet beneath her.

"Hold on, chief," Abigail said. Rosamund hadn't seen her approach. "You'll be all right."

There was a ripping sound that Rosamund felt more than heard, then a fiery ball of pain erupted in her calf. She hissed in a breath, and the edges of the hold came into focus.

"Come on." Abigail's strong arms hauled her to her feet. "We need to get you to sick bay."

"Wait." Rosamund shrugged off Abigail's arm and limped toward the door.

At the edge of the ramp, Ezekiel hung by a single hand, the wind trying to shake him loose.

"Chief!" His eyes were wide and panicked. "I can't hold on. Help!"

The sky exploded in blue-white lightning as both Fists drove deep into the German airship.

The vessel shuddered, listing terribly. Pieces dropped off her hull like sleet.

"We were crew." Rosamund looked down at Ezekiel, unmoving. Her hair whipped in the wind as blood ran down her throbbing leg, soaking into her sock. Abigail stood next to her, hard-eyed and silent.

"Abigail!" Ezekiel said. "For God's sake, you can't leave me here. Please!"

Both women raised their guns and fired.

Ezekiel fell, joining his allies in a race to the bottom of the sea.

Rosamund swayed, but Abigail caught her and held her up. "All right, chief," she said. "Your work's done for a bit."

The setting sun hung lazy on the horizon, painting the sky a brilliant red-orange, shifting the scattered clouds a slate gray.

Wind swept across the flight deck. It had long since blown away the smell of char and gunfire, replacing it with a crisp cold that stung Rosamund's nose and tugged at her hair and jacket.

She braced herself with her cane, keeping weight off her leg. Flakes of burnt metal peeled off the deck where a Schmidt had come to a fiery end.

She'd hoped to find some of the plating from the airship that had baffled the *Royal*'s radar, but it was all at the bottom of the sea by now.

Footsteps sounded, and Abigail came to stand beside her. The two gazed out in silence, save for the wind and the rumbling whirr of the turbines.

The *Royal* sounded whole. She was hurt, tattered at the edges, but solid at her core again. She'd make Oslo with no worries, then Rosamund would leave her for a bit to heal.

Maybe.

"I didn't have the chance earlier," Rosamund said, "to thank you for saving my hide."

"Don't mention it," Abigail said.

"I am mentioning it. Zeke would have punched my ticket if you hadn't been there. Thank you."

"You're welcome, chief."

Rosamund held out her hand, and they clasped forearms, which turned into a full embrace.

Releasing each other, they returned to staring at the horizon.

"So does this mean I can call you Rosie?" A mischievous grin spread across Abigail's face.

"You only saved my life." Rosamund snorted. "How about I start calling you Abby?"

"Good Lord, no," Abigail said. "You've still got a bum leg, and we're not that far from the edge. I'd manage the extra work somehow."

"Is that what's keeping me going, then?" Rosamund asked. "You don't want the chief's workload?"

"I'm happy to be the power behind the throne." Abigail grinned at her. "For now."

My Mechanical Girl

Misty Massey

BILLIE GLIDED ONTO THE STAGE TO THE APPLAUSE OF THE AUDIENCE, positioned herself under the lights on her mark, and struck a pose. Her music swelled. "It's the loveliest of days when I'm near you," she sang, "Robins chase the clouds out of the sky…"

Billie's the headliner at La Fantaisie. Me, I'm her mechanic. I polish her steel face until she glows warm under the electric lights, lubricate her joints, and spend the dough to dress her in glam. I didn't create the valve system that lets her sing in a voice like warm molasses spilling down the back of a velvet chair nor the hydraulics that allow her to spin and dance, but I know how they work, and I can build off what the old inventor did. My grimy fingers carry permanent stains from years in a factory. My nails are bit back to the quick and I cut my own hair. At any time, there might be a streak of ash or oil on my face where I scratched an itch without bothering to wipe my hands first. The powerful gentlemen who frequent the Fant expect to see people like me fixing their cars, not standing in the club watching them drink brandy. It's okay, though. I stay out of sight, watching from the wings while my girl entertains the room. It's best that way, considering how I make the lion's share of my money.

La Fantaisie has always been popular with the higher-ups in the military, thanks to it being so close to the capitol building. Colonels and congressmen spend their evenings drinking expensive liquor and talking important talk while my Billie sings. I've installed nearly a dozen songs into her voice system, all the ones I like best. In between sets, she roams around the room on a magnetic track I built into the floor, stopping at every table to say something flirty. She knows eight different phrases, and I'm working on three new ones.

She's a toy. Metal arms and legs. A complicated hydraulic on the inside to keep her moving. A series of delicate valves connected to a circuit board that serve as her voice box. She's a mechanical girl. But I love her like she's real.

George Dupree, owner of the Fant, used to hire human women to sing in his nightclub, pretty ones with white-blonde curls who sang and danced and sometimes slid the necks of their dresses down to show off their bare shoulders. Between that Hitler guy and his Nazi thugs in the newsrags and women being found burnt to crisps in alleys, the military brass ordered their bigwigs to stay away from ordinary singers and dancers. Might have been for fear of them spilling secrets over pillow talk, or maybe the burnt-up women were the results of some experiment gone wrong and the generals wanted to put distance between their scientists and the victims. Who can guess? George was left without dames for his customers to ogle, and business dropped off. He was on the verge of closing down until he met my Billie.

Billie finished singing, took a bow, and the music for her next song began. "It's always summer when you smile at me..." she sang. Suddenly her chin jerked, and she stuttered, like a record player needle skipping. The music continued on, but instead of singing, her jaw fell open with a click, and words poured out, words I didn't understand. "Eian saprue prace sius ceva iot..."

The audience stared at my girl, as confused as I was. This gibberish was not one of the phrases she could say. After a few seconds, someone at a table said, "Is that German?" Silence fell again, until another said, "Sounds like a numbers station." Like a dam breaking, the whole room burst into chatter, and some of the officers rose to their feet.

I ran out onto the stage, grabbed Billie's arm, and drew her with me into the wings. "Sorry, folks," I called out. "Show's over for tonight." George met us backstage, his face redder than his cummerbund.

"Why the ever-loving hell did you teach her German?" he hissed. "You're going to get me shut down!"

It hadn't sounded like German to me. But George wasn't wrong. These days, the whole country seemed to be on a witch hunt, and Germany was the devil. It was time to hit the road before the bigwigs out front found their way backstage. "This ain't my doing. It's likely radio interference," I said, turning my girl toward the street door.

Her full-length coat hung on a hook next to it, so I slipped it over her shoulders and buttoned it at the neck, sliding the hood up to shadow her face. She'd stopped talking at last, thank goodness. The noise out on the main floor rose, and I heard snatches of unpleasant comments. Things like "spy network" and "treason" and "federal custody." "I'll recalibrate her vocal valves. Something's just gone out of whack."

"Send me a message tomorrow," he said, pushing his shoulders back and straightening his tuxedo jacket. "It's apology time, and I don't want her anywhere near here if she's spouting more of that kraut nonsense."

Thudding footsteps echoed from the direction of the stage. Time to make tracks. Billie has wheels set in the soles of her feet, so she rolls instead of walking. Tonight I was glad of it.

The streets were empty of everyone but tired working girls and drunks hunting for a bar they hadn't already been thrown out of, neither of whom had any interest in us. I felt a little bad for the women, defenseless as they were. Nobody seemed to know who was setting them on fire, or why. Some people said they were former spies who'd outlived their usefulness. I figured it was more likely a maniac on the loose. Thank goodness my girl wasn't the type to catch fire.

The old garage wasn't luxurious by any stretch, but it was perfect for us. Cheap rent, plenty of space for me to lay out diagrams and sort parts, and best of all, no one comes by. "Here we go, darlin'," I said, slipping the coat off her shoulders and hanging it on the tree by the door. "Time for your supper." She followed me, rolling across the floor to her charging station. I unzipped her dress to expose her back, lifted the smooth panel that hid the charging port in her neck, and pressed her gently against the plug. It clicked into place, and I did the same with the two in her back. She settled into the station, her eyes dropping closed. A machine like her ate a lot of battery power, but she was worth the cost.

Three years ago, I worked as a machinist finishing engine cylinders. Twelve-hour days for crap pay. I was lucky to have the job, but I stayed to watch the old man. He owned the place, and he built Billie. He'd been an inventor until his university closed and left him running a factory. Every day he tinkered on her. He thought he'd make his fortune selling her as a housewife's helper, but the patents never seemed to reach approval stage. One night, I stopped by his office on my way out. He sat slumped over in his chair. Dead as a doornail, face gray and skin cold. Billie stood in the corner, under a tarp. On a whim, I took her home with me. I showed up for work next day and played like I was as shocked as the rest. No one noticed the missing metal girl.

The old man's creditors took the factory and fired all of us. For a year, I took any job I could find, spending every dime I could spare on Billie. The old man made her say things like "May I help you?" or "The lady of the house is not at home." I learned how to adjust the tolerances in the delicate valves so she sang songs, and I mixed up a new lubricant that didn't stain her steel body. I didn't know what I wanted to do with her, but I knew we were both meant for better things than rusting away in an old factory.

When I heard about the Fant closing, I dressed Billie up fine and walked her over. At first, George didn't understand the opportunity I offered, until I pointed out that here was an entertainer who couldn't be tempted to sell important secrets she overheard, never fell ill or needed sleep. When I finally got through to him, he hired us on the spot.

It was only after the first week or two that my side job occurred to me. Billie can't be tempted, it's true. She only sings the songs I wire into her. But she listens. And records everything she hears. There's a recording machine in her belly, with a button on her side to activate it. Every night when we return to the garage, I play the recording and make notes. I know who's sleeping with who, which lawmakers are getting kickbacks from which businessmen, and where the cash for all sorts of hinky projects came from. Information sells for big money. I'm careful what I sell, of course. I stick with personal sins, nothing that might bring the government sniffing around. Forcing fifty dollars out of a fat cat's wallet to keep his love life quiet was less lucrative than asking the War Department for a thousand bucks not to tell the papers about the latest weapon they're testing, but it's a whole lot safer.

I slipped Billie's dress down from her shoulders, careful not to let it fall onto the dingy floor, and hung it in the wardrobe. I pressed her belly panel. It popped open, revealing the recording machine. The film whirred as it wound itself around the first spindle, rewinding to the beginning. She hadn't been on stage long, so there wouldn't be much to hear tonight, but it was worth listening anyway. When the film stopped, I flipped the switch to "play," took down my notebook and a pen, and settled myself at the table to make notes.

I heard a click. "Zener moc suovec?" I spun in my chair. Billie's eyes were open, as was her mouth, and the words were spilling out. "Sia remiajri. Eian saprue prace sius ceva iot."

I laid my pen on the table and walked over to my girl. She watched me, her face serene as it always was, and didn't speak again. I flipped the switch to rewind the film. I could listen later. Fixing this problem was more important. One of Billie's voice valve sets must have shifted out of place, tangled with another, or broken down entirely. An easy fix would please me no end, but my girl was anything but easy. Pushing my sleeves up above the elbow, I opened Billie up.

A little after sunrise, I admitted defeat. There was nothing wrong. Billie's valve sets were cradled securely, running exactly as they should. Her wiring was perfect, nothing loose or frayed. Her batteries were connected and optimal. Nothing bumped against anything else unless it was supposed to. While the sounds could have resulted from inappropriate levels of air moving through the valves, I couldn't make her repeat them. For a while I worried I'd accidentally created a receiver somewhere in her guts, something that maybe caught a faraway radio broadcast. There was no trace of such an anomaly. She remained in dormant mode, her eyes closed as if she slept. I stroked my thumb over her gleaming metal cheek. My poor girl. The best thing I ever did, so much better than mindless factory work, and safer than selling information. With a sigh, I pulled a chair over to sit down in front of her. "We've got a problem, Billie. I can't fix you if I can't find what's wrong, but I can't let you sing again until I fix you."

Her eyes snapped open. I started, nearly sliding out of my chair. I hadn't pressed the button to wake her up, so her eyes shouldn't open on their own. She looked straight at me. "Does your heart beat for me?" she said, enunciating each syllable.

I gripped the arms of my chair like it was a life preserver and I'd just jumped off the Titanic. Billie didn't know how to say that. Billie sang pretty songs, she didn't quote them.

Billie blinked. "Share together."

"Share?" My brain spun with the idea of her wanting anything. "Do you want to talk with me?"

She nodded. "Your fortune falling all over town." Billie's metal face wasn't designed to make expressions, but for a second I'd have sworn she frowned. "Warning voice in the night."

I stood up and paced in front of my gleaming girl. That's when it hit me. She was trying to tell me something by searching through the lyrics for phrases that might work. That implied awareness. I couldn't have created that even if I wanted to. Machines that could think existed in science fiction movies, not real life. So why was Billie talking? And how could I make her stop? George didn't need this kind of trouble in his place, and unless I returned her to proper function, our show business days were over.

A sudden pounding on my door made me jump. "Open up, Frankie Harvey! Federal agents!"

My blood ran cold. Who called those guys? Other than my landlord and the kid who delivered groceries, no one knew I lived here. I looked at Billie, but she said nothing, her face impassive. The last thing I needed was for her to start spouting gobbledygook. I unlatched the door locks. It swung open. Two men in matching black suits stood on the sidewalk. The shorter one wore glasses and stood with his arms at his sides. The other held both hands behind his back and scowled at me. "You Harvey?" the taller one asked. I nodded. He swung his right hand up, pointing his black revolver inches from my face. "Back up and let us in. Right now."

I raised both hands and stepped slowly backward. My heart beat like a bongo against my breastbone, and I kept swallowing against the tightness in my throat. "No need for guns," I said, my voice sounding weak and scared in my ears.

The shorter one stepped close to me and pushed a finger against my forehead. He stunk of old cigarettes. "We'll tell you if we need guns, Nazi."

Damn. Someone from the club reported what happened. "I'm no Nazi," I said.

"You are if we say you are. Your machine over there talked Kraut the other night, and a whole lot of people heard it. People who know what they're listening to. You're lucky if you only go to jail."

I couldn't take my eyes off the gun. At this distance, he'd splatter my brains onto the next block. "She wasn't broadcasting. I never built her with the capacity to pick up signals. It was her valve system malfunctioning, I swear."

Agent Gun-Guy drew the pistol back and uncocked the hammer. I relaxed so hard I almost fell on the floor. Agent Glasses turned toward Billie. "Never said it was broadcasting anything. We have plenty of smart people who've been looking for something just like your mannequin here. They'll take it apart, see how it works, and build more to choke Hitler right out of Europe."

"Please." My head was spinning. "She's just an entertainer." They wanted to take my girl away. A tiny voice in my head tried to remind me she was only a toy. But I didn't care—Billie was mine and I didn't want to let her go. Especially not to jerks like these.

"We can do anything we like. Frankie... is that short for Frankenstein?" He snorted at his joke, but I didn't smile. "We're the government."

Agent Gun-Guy holstered the weapon and ran his hands over Billie's curves. I hadn't dressed her since last night, so she wore a tea rose pink brassiere and matching tap pants. I didn't need to give her underclothes, of course, but the glam dresses she wore to work hung better with such garments underneath. The agent positioned himself behind Billie and cupped her breast. "Sexy. Too bad it's metal."

"Leave her alone," I said, letting my hands fall.

Agent Gun-Guy swung his gun back up in my face. "What are you going to do about it, Frankenstein?"

A crowbar lay on a table a few feet away, but Agent Gun-Guy and Billie were between me and it. He stepped forward and pressed the muzzle against my forehead. My breath came fast and shallow, my pulse thundering in my ears. I'd worried more than once about being beaten up by someone I blackmailed. I never once thought I'd die. I closed my eyes.

A dull crack, a groan, and a thud were not sounds I expected. I raised one eyelid. Agent Gun-Guy lay on the floor, unconscious, his gun a few inches from his hand. Billie held the crowbar in one hand, and Agent Glasses was grabbing for it. Before I could move, though, his face fell blank, and his arms dropped. He turned to me. "Tie him up and take his gun."

I looked from him to Billie and back again. "Oh no," I said, putting some distance between us. "Not happening. You'll say I was resisting and shoot me."

Agent Glasses shook his head. "I can't stay in here long." He coughed, a phlegmy sound that turned my stomach. "Damned smokers. Listen, do what I tell you, and maybe you'll survive."

"Oh, I get it. You're the advance team? Your backup's on the way, and you want to steal Billie before they get here?"

Agent Glasses was sweating buckets, beads of perspiration rolling down his face. When did that start? "Please. I can help you, but you have to hurry." His face went suddenly slack again, and his knees buckled under him. He fell to the floor, breathing hard. "Tie him..." and he passed out.

A machine starts throwing sparks, I can diagnose the problem easy. People, though, have always been a mystery. And these guys were currently topping the list of weird behavior.

"Don't you know, little fool, you never can win." Billie still held the crowbar in her hand. Was she going to clock me next? I backed up a step, but she let it drop with a clang on the concrete floor. Billie rolled over to my worktable, picked up a pencil between her thumb and palm, and started writing on a scrap of paper. Messy, tilted words, like a child would make. *Tie men up.*

The same thing Agent Glasses said before he passed out. "Both of them?" I asked. She nodded. I kept a reel of manila rope on a shelf nearby. I grabbed it up while Billie arranged two chairs back to back and lifted each unconscious man into one. I wrapped them round and round, tying a knot under the chairs every few feet so as to make escape more complicated. At least, I hoped so. I'd never bound a person before. Once I ran out of rope, I noticed Billie writing again. She pushed the paper toward me. *Pack bag.*

Agent Gun-Guy groaned softly. He'd be coming around any second. I kicked his gun under the shelves at the back wall and dug my carpetbag from under my bed. I shoved Billie's fancy clothes in — I could always sell them if I needed cash. My battered strongbox, full of money and old recordings, went in next, followed by my toothbrush. Billie's charging station was too massive to carry. I'd have to hope we found somewhere to hide that I could steal electricity to keep her juiced. Otherwise, she'd be nothing but a pretty statue in a day or two.

By the time I was ready to roll. Agent Gun-Guy was awake. "You've made a mistake now, Frankenstein. I work for people who'd scare the hair right off your head." I didn't know how to answer, so I steered

Billie toward the door. I opened it and peered outside at the quiet street. This early, the only people around were milkmen.

Before I could walk out, Agent Gun-Guy's eyes rolled backward, and his body trembled, rattling the chair legs under him. I ran to the chair, thinking to catch him before he fell over, but by the time I reached him, he'd stopped shaking. "This one's better." He struggled against the rope. "Good knots. Should hold them a while. Now listen."

For the life of me, I had no idea what to do.

"I didn't mean to hurt those women. I didn't know how fragile humans are."

"You killed them?" My head spun. "You're a federal agent."

"No, no, you're not getting it." He took a breath and blew it out. "I'm *inside* a federal agent. Gotta tell you some things Billie doesn't have the vocabulary for. Human bodies overheat when I slip inside, burn up trying to contain me. I've been hiding in Billie, hoping to find a way to talk to you." Sweat glistened on his skin, and I remembered how Agent Glasses started sweating when he insisted I should tie up his partner. "Unhealthy bodies wear out faster. I was minutes away from burning the other man before."

"Are you a ghost?" I said. My heart pounded, and my throat tightened with fear. "What do you want?"

"Let me live inside your singing girl. Until I can figure out how to go home."

"And where's that?"

He shrugged. "This guy doesn't know the words to describe it."

"Okay, then how'd you get here?"

"A swirling black hole spitting lightning opened in the sky above me. It pulled me out of myself. I woke up trapped in a transparent container, screaming at the humans to let me out. They acted like they couldn't hear me. Eventually, someone opened the container. I slid into the first body I saw and ran for the outside." He dropped his head, looking ashamed. "He only lasted until night, when he caught fire. Once he was destroyed, I noticed I couldn't move without a body around me. I floated above him for hours until a woman came along, and I hitched a ride. But my rides kept burning up. Until one day you and your girl walked by, and I took the chance."

"Didn't you think the people who captured you could have answered your questions? You could have threatened to burn them up if they didn't send you home."

"All I could think about was jumping back through that spinning hole. But it's gone, I'm here, and I don't know what to do."

"I don't even know if you're telling the truth. You might slip into my head, drive me for a while until I catch fire, too."

"Not worth it to me. If you let me stay in her, at least I'm safe. And I can watch for the spinning hole to open again." He blinked. "For now, though, we need to leave here. I'll slide back into Billie and leave the decision to you." He shivered and threw his head back, bumping into his companion.

"Untie me right the fuck now!" he bellowed. Agent Gun-Guy was back.

Billie touched my arm, so I put her coat around her and steered her toward the door. There was only one place I could think to go.

The front doors of the Fant were closed, and a sign pasted there read *Closed by federal order*. I slipped down the alley to the stage door, which was, blessedly, unlocked. Shadows filled the place, and the only light came from over the bar where George stood, his sleeves rolled up, packing hooch into cardboard boxes. He stopped dead, a bottle of rum in each hand, when he caught sight of us. "I'm closed," he said, his face tightening into a scowl. "I spent most of the night being questioned by two unpleasant G-men. They ransacked my office and slapped the sign on the door. I'm surprised they didn't smash all the bottles, just to be nasty."

"You told them where to find me?"

"No, stupid. They found your address in my files. I had to have it for taxes, remember?" He closed up the box and tied it with a length of twine. "Should've paid you under the table."

I felt terrible about George's problems, but there wasn't anything I could do to fix them. "I need a place to lay low, long enough to arrange for a train ticket in whatever direction looks best."

George tilted his head. "Frankie, you saved me from ruin when you brought your metal girl around, and I'm grateful, but the world's caught up to us both. Hide in the basement if you want. I'm headed to my brother's in Savannah." He smiled at me, the saddest smile I'd ever seen. "Maybe I'll start another club there. Stop in sometime, if you can avoid prison."

The doors behind us burst open. Agent Gun-Guy walked in. He'd found another gun and he was waving it in my direction. "Well, well, Frankenstein, thought you were supposed to be smart? You couldn't think of a better place to run?" He swung to George. "Have a seat, Fancy Pants. I'm still inclined to leave you alone."

"Where's your pal?" I asked.

The agent snorted. "Hospital. He was having palpitations after what you did."

Behind the agent, another man in a suit stepped inside and cleared his throat. "Please, Agent Simmons, put your weapon away. Even under the circumstances, we can behave like civilized people."

So Agent Gun-Guy had a name. He scowled and slid his gun into the holster under his jacket. The suit looked at me. "I apologize for the heavy-handed tactics."

"Who might you be?" I asked, surprising myself.

The suit smiled, an unpleasant expression that sent a chill down my spine. He waved at a table, so I sat. Billie stood behind me, silent and still. "My name is classified. You can call me Mr. Brown. I am the director of a top-secret research agency working to keep this country safe. You love your country, do you not? And you don't want America's soldiers to sail across the ocean and die for a war we don't want, do you?" He waited as if expecting me to agree, but I kept quiet. "We've found an energy source we can use to destroy the enemy, but we need your assistance to make it feasible."

"That's out of my depth," I said. "I'm just a mechanic."

"True. It's not really your help we require. We want your automaton." He smiled again. "For the good of the country, of course."

"Build your own."

"We could, but since yours is already functional, it would be simpler for us to copy it. You'd be well-compensated."

"That's funny," I said. "Your muscle over there called me a Nazi and said I was headed for prison."

Brown glanced at Simmons, who didn't meet his gaze. Turning back to me, he said, "They weren't authorized to make any such threat."

I stood up slowly and faced my girl. I put my hands on her waist, and moved her toward the bar, pushing the recording button as I did. I've made a living off other people's information, and it was almost habit. "You don't want to use Billie as a template," I said. "You're hoping to capture the ghost living inside her. The one that's been burning women." I glanced over my shoulder at the scientist. His face gave away nothing, but I'd hit a nerve. He glanced at the agent and jerked his head. Simmons moved toward me, grinning. "You're going to kill me?"

"You know too much. It's a matter of national security. You've been in contact with the being, and you are clearly compromised. We can't allow you to share your story with the public. If it got out that we opened a passage to another dimension and brought an otherworldly being into Washington... remember the panic over the War of the Worlds radio show last year? And that wasn't even real."

Simmons pressed his revolver to my forehead and drew the hammer back. "Any last words?"

"I don't want to die," I said. Before I could say anything else, the agent's eyes rolled back, his lids fluttering, and his gun hand dropped. He recovered himself, and smiled again, but this time, it wasn't creepy. Because it wasn't Simmons.

"He's not dying today." Not-Simmons walked over to the scientist, pushing the gun into his chest. "You're going to leave him alone from now on. Him and me."

"Simmons, what are you—" Brown began, and stopped. "Oh my God. You're the experiment. How did you transfer from the automaton?"

"You stole me from my home. You made me kill people."

"No one important. And we don't hold you responsible. Come back to the lab with me. You can help us. You could slide inside Hitler himself, burn him to ashes. The United States would be the savior of the world, all thanks to you." Brown talked quickly, almost babbling. "Don't you want to be a hero?"

"I want to go home," he said. "Open the spinning hole, right now."

The scientist looked at me, his eyes pleading. "Call him off, Frankie."

I crossed my arms and said, "Why don't you open the hole, like he says?"

"Because I can't!" His voice was shrill. "We don't know how we managed it the first time. It was an accident." He opened his arms, and stared, wide-eyed, at the agent. "We can keep trying. If you return to the lab, you can live in the container and help us figure out how to open the way."

"Would you want to live in a jar?" I said.

Brown looked from the agent to me and back again, now speechless.

"If you can't send me home, I see no reason to keep you," Not-Simmons said, his finger tightening on the trigger.

"Wait," I stepped forward and laid a hand on his arm. "If they promise to keep working on the problem, and leave you safe inside Billie, will you let him walk out of here?"

Not-Simmons' face gleamed with perspiration. He drew the gun back. "What guarantee do we have that he won't burn this place down with us in it?"

I looked at Brown. "I've recorded our conversation. Just to be safe, I'll make copies, hide them all over the place, and notify trusted people what to do if anything hinky happens. In exchange for me not releasing the recording to the papers, Mr. Brown will continue to try and open your way home. He will not bring any others through. He'll report to us regularly on his progress." I leaned over the table. "And the order on my friend's nightclub is lifted. Today. Deal?"

The scientist stared at his hands for an eternity. "Agreed," he said.

These days the Fant's clientele runs more high society than military brass. George hired some cocktail waitresses, and even gave me a salary boost. The mysterious, unsolved burning deaths have stopped, and the papers moved on to other stories. Brown sends reports to me once a week, by courier, care of the nightclub, and I read them to the ghost. I don't know when they'll figure out how to send it home, but for now, it's content to live inside my mechanical girl.

It likes the music.

On the Fly

Heather E. Hutsell

Sweat dripped from Sofia's forehead as she angled the end of her flat-head screwdriver to reach the barely visible screw nestled inside the glitchy motor on the workbench before her. She gave an impatient huff as another drop landed on her hand. Flicking it off, she rubbed her hand dry against the grease-stained smock that protected her dress from her work. The friction and moisture stirred the pungent odor of machine oil and grease wiped onto the cotton fibers many times before. The smell kindled a mix of anticipation and satisfaction. Working her screwdriver into place, she gave the stubborn screw a hard turn. Sofia sucked in a sharp breath as the screwdriver slipped, gouging her other hand. She clenched her jaw to keep from letting out more than a groan while tightening her grip on the screwdriver. It had left an angry, red crease in her skin, but the initial sting passed with a quick, dismissive rub.

From a few feet behind Sofia, the runners of her grandmother's rocking chair ground out a steady rhythm against the boards of the porch. The sound had been lost to Sofia's concentration moments before, except when the woman paused to shuffle a deck of worn, once-colorful tarot cards in hands gnarled with age and equally worn from years of a hard life as a washer woman. She *tsk*ed at Sofia's little mishap and cut the cards before forcing the two stacks back into one. She did this several more times, slapping a card that tried to fall loose from the others into place, and then muttered a foreign rebuke at the shuffle-softened card as though it could understand her.

Sofia sighed and turned back to her project, wishing her grandmother would get back to her rocking, the shuffling a distraction that

Sofia couldn't quite block out, as the cards were enough of an annoyance all on their own. It wasn't that Sofia really believed in her grandmother's predictions or any of that sort of mumbo jumbo, but the woman spent more time communing with spirits than taking an interest in anything else going on around her. Worse was that she'd been *mostly* right enough times that no one could convince her she didn't have the "Gift." Like the time she'd drawn the Wheel of Fortune and told Sofia's mother that she would never have a son.

Gloria Clay *did* have a son, but he died shortly after his birth, as did Gloria. Sofia had been ten years old at the time. Her grandmother swore the cards had told her this was going to happen. Sofia had taken a slap across her face for calling her senile, but how could old, faded images printed on cardstock reveal such events? To her, for something to be real, it had to also be solid, visible—something she could experience with her senses, and it most definitely had to be tangible. She supposed that was why she craved taking things apart to see what made them work.

Sofia picked up the motor, its weight making it awkward to hold in one hand, despite how it wasn't more than six inches long. Much of the heft was in the legs of the base that had once been attached to a larger machine. She turned the cylinder to inspect the screw that had been giving her trouble in more direct sunlight.

"*Great,*" she grumbled, seeing that her fiddling had stripped the head. She sighed and tapped the screwdriver's handle against the motor, contemplating her next move, when the screen door opened, and her father stepped outside.

"Thanks for getting the carburetor off the kitchen table, Pip." He noticed the black object in her hand and went to stand beside her. "What've you got there?" he asked.

"It's the motor from the Singer," Sofia said, absently gesturing to the rest of the machine that sat a few feet away, her eyes still on her dilemma.

"What—the sewing machine?"

"Yeah," Sofia sighed, wondering if they had a gum band in the house that she could use to help compensate for the screw's stripped drive.

"You don't sew," her father pointed out, curiosity edging his tone.

"No one here sews anymore," Sofia muttered, then paused at the insensitivity of her comment. "Sorry, Dad."

"So, what are you doing with it?"

"I'm trying to get this casing open so that I can clean the motor. I want to attach it to the clothesline—"

Taking a sudden interest in the conversation at the mention of the familiar, Sofia's grandmother pointedly stated, "You need some clean clothes."

Sofia ignored the comment.

"I think I've figured out a way to attach it to the pulley, and if we route the clothesline directly to the porch, then Gram can just have the line bring the laundry to her without having to go out into the yard to get it. This motor should be strong enough, right? Or I could take a bigger one out of something else—"

Frank considered this while shaking his head at Sofia's eagerness over her backup plan.

"I think that one could work," he concurred. Then, remembering why he was out there, said, "I need you to pack it up for now—I've got another job, and I need your help with it." Frank patted Sofia on the shoulder. "You're gonna want to put on some trousers."

Everything he had said roused enough of Sofia's curiosity to make her forget about the trifle with the screw and look up at him just as he checked his watch.

"Why? What is it?"

"Because we're going to be in the fields, and the ticks are high this year. And pants would just be better. C'mon—"

He headed into the house, leaving Sofia to scramble to put her things back into their greasy cardboard box before hurrying to follow him inside.

"What are we working on? A thresher? A baler? A combine—I wouldn't mind working on one of those again."

"None of those."

"Another tractor?" she said with slightly diminished enthusiasm.

"No, Pip. We've got about a half hour's drive, though, and need to get a move on, so can you—?" He gestured to Sofia's clothing. "The sooner, the better. I need to get your grandmother ready."

Sofia's excitement waned further, and while she knew the sound of their Model T's motor would drown out the old woman's shuffling, it still irked her. "Does she have to come?"

Frank paused on his way toward his mother's bedroom to retrieve her sweater. "We can't leave her here. Remember what happened last time?"

"So, she almost burned down the house once." Sofia shrugged, not bothering to add that she was guilty of other near disasters back when she had first started tinkering with their few small kitchen appliances. At least her episodes hadn't involved something as trivial as filling the entire living room with lit candles to summon a dead *someone or other*.

"*Sofia.*"

"Okay, of course—Gram's coming, too. But *what is it*? What's the job?"

"You'll see. And Sofia—*pants*."

With the possibilities stacking up in her head, Sofia hurried off to her room to change from her smock and dress into a pair of corduroy trousers and a blouse just nice enough that she wouldn't embarrass her father by wearing something filthy, should they be in polite company, but one she wouldn't get in trouble for spilling grease on it either.

Her thoughts jumped and jumbled, trying to figure out what they might be working on—farm equipment was an obvious guess and their usual source of income, but could it be a generator? A motorcycle? Or maybe an automobile! She had seen a fancy Duesenberg once, and her excitement swelled at the notion that they might be getting under the hood of one of those or even a Ford newer than what they owned. As far as automobiles go, Sofia's experience only went as far as their own, which she'd learned to drive and service when her father returned from the war. Sofia had been only eight at the time and couldn't reach the pedals without wooden blocks attached to her shoes or by sitting on her father's lap, but he needed her to learn, stating that she couldn't properly know how to fix the thing if she didn't even know how to use it. And this was only made necessary because of the one other time Sofia's grandmother had half foretold the future, stating Frank would die in an explosion.

Shortly before Sofia's father had returned from the war, he'd been caught in a bombing raid while loading a shipment of military radios into the transport truck, throwing him in the blast. He had landed, unconscious, next to the small building where he'd been working, the truck in pieces all over the yard.

"But I didn't *die*," he'd insisted, which had been part of Sofia's grandmother's prophecy.

"You should have blown up, too," the woman had insisted, almost petulant.

"*Nice, Mama,*" her son had said. "I didn't, though."

He hadn't come away from the event unscathed, however, having lost all but his thumb and index finger on his right hand. It had been both a nightmare and blessing for him to discover upon his return home that Sofia had found some of his tools and taken to disassembling items around the house — the bread warmer, the phonograph, and a few other modern conveniences, leaving the household without them until he could put them back together. Once, before she had died, Sofia's mother had only just stopped her from dismantling their telephone. That was when Frank had the idea to include Sofia in the repair work. All it took was putting a few old issues of *Popular Mechanics* into her hands to broaden her interests beyond electronics, to tinkering with things that left her hands sore and dirty, but her appetite for learning was always stronger than when she'd started on them. Frank had no regrets about any of that, and the decision had proven to be the right one more than once.

Sofia met them outside and at the car, where her father was helping his mother into the back seat. Sofia took the wheel, waiting for her father to climb in on the passenger side before she started the engine. She waited for further instructions as he unfolded a map, adjusting her side mirror when all she really wanted to do was ask again where they were going. Their destination couldn't be too far, seeing as how they hadn't packed to stay overnight, and as far as Sofia knew, the picnic hamper still sat empty inside the house. That left the surrounding area, and, as she had suspected, this job would likely involve another piece of farming equipment.

"Head out toward the state route," her father instructed. "We're gonna take that for a bit."

"Yes, sir."

They rode in silence for a few minutes, the air flowing through their open windows still hot but refreshing, and the road they were on straight and empty, allowing Sofia's thoughts to drift.

It was on the tip of her tongue to press her father for answers about where they were going, how long — exactly — it would take to get there, and what the job was. But she had learned that *"you'll see"* was his gentle way of telling her to be patient. By then, she had talked herself into being content with this just being another tractor job — she had helped work on so many of them now that at least she could count on it being easy, which would get her back home to her project. But then, why the secrecy? She was always glad to work on anything mechanical but hoped for something new and interesting enough to lessen the threatening twinge of boredom.

The sudden rustling of the map as Sofia's father refolded it drew her attention. She waited for him to speak, to offer a hint about their destination, but he only replaced the map into the leather pouch on the door before resting one arm on the edge of his window.

Sofia's patience finally cracked. "So, whose farm are we going to?"

"We're not going to a farm."

"But you said we'll be in a field."

"Yes, I did."

When he didn't elaborate, Sofia wondered out loud, "Why else would we be in a field?"

A quick glance at her father prompted no answer, but he smiled softly with his gaze focused straight through the windshield. Sofia could keep asking questions, and she could keep coaxing him for information, but she knew better and was just going to have to wait. The remedy for this was to gently press on the gas pedal and subtly increase the car's speed from the steady thirty-five miles per hour they'd been going to its maximum of forty-two. Sofia managed to get a short way down the road before her father gave a soft warning.

"It's hot, Pip. Let's not overheat her before we get where we're going."

Sofia reluctantly slowed down, but another glance caught her father grinning.

"Don't worry," he said before she could needle him further. "You'll like this."

It wasn't too much longer before Sofia's grandmother interrupted the silence. Her cards escaped her hands, and a few landed in the front of the vehicle, startling Sofia enough to make her jerk the steering wheel.

"*Birds — birds —*" came from the back seat.

Sofia ignored the outburst, brushing away the cards that had landed around her. But her grandmother persisted, leaning forward to point past Sofia's head toward something in the distance before sticking a single card in front of her face.

"Gram!" Annoyed, Sofia grabbed the card, giving it a glance before she dropped it to clutch the wheel. *The Hanged Man.*

"*Birds — birds —*"

Already queasy from the ominous card, Sofia's shoulders tensed with each repetition, but it melted away when something caught her eye through the windshield.

Not birds, but several dark objects flew and darted through the air. From their location, she couldn't make out what they were, but her heart gave a sudden hard thump.

"Planes? *Planes*, Dad?"

Frank beamed. "They're Jennies."

Sofia gave the engine some extra gas, now squinting and craning her head to get a better look out her window. "What are they doing?"

"Just pay attention to your driving, Pip. We're almost there."

But Sofia couldn't focus with her thoughts bouncing every which way and her surprise quickly yielding to a mix of apprehension and rivaling anticipation. "The job is a *plane*?"

"You're going to make a left up here at that red barn—slow down, or you're going to miss it—"

Sofia cut the turn, sending the three of them pitching a little harder sideways than intended before slowing down and regaining control of the vehicle. She had turned into a lot where other vehicles were parked, and a few people were heading in and out of the barn. She pulled up beside another car and pushed open her door to get out almost before she shut off the engine. She didn't wait for her father and grandmother before hurrying around the back of the car to read the white lettering painted along the side of the barn: *Nike's Flying Circus*. There was no time to comprehend what that meant as a small plane came in for a landing, buzzing low overhead.

Sofia knew a little about airplanes from magazines and broadcasts about the Wright Brothers on the radio, but having one flying so close above her that she could practically make out the seams in its fuselage exhilarated her.

"Was that one?" she asked as her father and grandmother caught up. "Was that a Jenny?"

"That was a Fleet model 2. You'll probably work on one of those at some point, too."

In that moment, just off in the distance, two planes of similar size flew straight toward each other before splitting off at the last second to return in the directions from which they'd come.

"*Wow*," Sofia breathed.

"*Those* were Jennies. Come on—"

Sofia followed but couldn't keep her eyes off the planes in the sky. Some did loops and barrel rolls; others left long, thick clouds spiraling behind them. They all appeared—from where she stood—too close to each other to be safe.

"They're plenty far enough apart—"

Sofia jumped, not realizing someone had stepped up beside her. She afforded the young man a quick look, but the mesmeric spectacle drew her gaze back to the sky.

"They look like they're going to crash into each other."

"They won't. They know what they're doing." After letting Sofia take in another few seconds of the aerials, he said, "I'm Abie."

Sofia looked at his extended hand, immediately noticing that it was splotched with a brown sheen despite the grimy rag he held in the other. Undeterred and sensing she was in the presence of a kindred spirit, she smiled and shook his hand.

"Sofia Clay."

Abie's eyes grew wide in pleasant surprise. "Your Frank Clay's girl?"

"Yeah—that's my dad—" Sofia looked in the direction her father had gone, seeing that he had stopped to speak with another man. "I should probably catch up with him."

"I'll come with you. I believe we're heading the same way. You're here to help me with the barnstormer planes," he said as they began to walk.

"Barnstormers—?"

"The Jennies—they're the ones that fly through the barns without ripping their wings off. They do other stuff, too, but that's their specialty."

"Oh—yeah, I think so. That is, my dad is working on one—*of them.* I'm here to help him."

Abie grinned. "No, doll—you're helping *me.*"

As if the chance to get a look at the inner workings of one of these planes wasn't thrilling enough, the prospect of going completely hands-on just about took Sofia's breath away. She had so many questions.

They reached her father's side, their presence interrupting the conversation in progress.

"Charlie, this is my daughter—Sofia," he said, introducing her to the man he'd been speaking with.

"Sofia. I see you've met my nephew."

"Sofia, Charlie is one of the pilots," her father explained. "You'll be going with him and Abie to learn about his plane and a few of the others."

It was then that Sofia noticed how her father had his arm looped through that of her grandmother's, guiding her toward some nearby bleachers.

"You're not coming—" she concluded.

He smiled warmly at her. "No. This one is all yours. You'll be in good hands, though. I'll let you all get to it," he said, giving Charlie's hand a departing shake and a nod to his daughter. "Have fun, Pip."

"Shall we?" Charlie asked, clearly ready to get down to business.

Sofia followed him and Abie, hurrying to keep in step with their long strides as her head reeled. She was going to *help*? What, exactly, did that mean? This wasn't a tractor or car, and definitely, not a little sewing machine motor they were talking about!

"I've never worked on a plane before," she blurted, a tiny hint of doubt creeping in. "But I want to!" she added.

Charlie looked at her as he led them into the mowed field. His smile was soft and pensive, while Abie continued to grin knowingly.

"Your father has told me what sorts of things you've worked on and how long you've been into this kind of thing. You afraid of heights?"

"N-no, sir. Well, I don't really know."

"He said you get pretty absorbed while you're working on stuff."

"Sure. Usually."

Charlie patted Sofia on the shoulder. "You'll be fine."

"Yes, sir."

Sofia's pace slowed a bit, allowing Charlie to get a few steps ahead of her. Abie paused to step in time with Sofia.

"I've only read about plane engines in magazines," she confessed in a hushed voice. "And I've only worked on farm stuff and our car and—" Sofia stopped, but at Abie's interested nod for her to continue, she added, "And I'm modifying a sewing machine motor. I do a lot of different things, but not any one thing."

"That sounds neat."

"But it's not—" She gestured to another plane that was landing.

"Look, the thing you need to know about planes versus automobiles is that their engines are a bit more—*precise*. They're lighter, and since they're up in the air and don't have the stability of the ground beneath them, they can't have the same level of vibration. You get me?"

Sofia began to relax, understanding what he meant.

"Things gotta be tight, and these engines have a fair share of problems. You've gotta stay on top of their maintenance. But you've got a decent foundation of experience with fixing stuff, Sofia. The details—the bits and bobs—are gonna be different, and there'll be lots to learn, but I'm sure you'll get it."

They walked the rest of the way in silence, heading toward a yellow JN-4D. Sofia's thoughts still swirled with a mish-mash of questions and anticipation. *Could she do this?* She trusted her father—he was her greatest teacher for these things, after all, and if he hadn't thought she could do it, he never would have talked her up to Charlie and his nephew.

Sofia stopped next to the plane and took a deep breath, all doubts having passed as a wave of clarity washed over her. Charlie went climbing up onto one wing and, without so much as a pause, stepped into the front seat.

"First things first—" Abie interlaced his fingers and held his hands down for Sofia to step onto.

"First—what?"

"You gotta know how she feels to fly before you can know how to work on her."

The familiar advice was enough to cause a bubbling up in Sofia's chest, leaving her breathless again. She didn't need any further prompting. Placing her foot in Abie's grip, she let him boost her up, climbing into the seat behind Charlie.

"Don't let the altitude scare you," Abie offered, pulling himself up to sit on the edge of the plane. "Charlie's one of the best pilots there is."

"Put this on—" he instructed, picking up a radio headset.

Before Abie had even jumped down to the ground, Charlie had the engine going and the propeller spinning.

"This is going to be a short flight," Charlie said. The new experience of having his voice sound right in her ears made Sofia smile while her heart raced. "Take a few minutes to acclimate once we've lifted off. This plane was just maintenanced, so I want you to get familiar with what a well-working Jenny feels like."

"Roger, that—" Sofia replied, immediately wondering if it had been appropriate, but Charlie's soft chuckle put her at ease.

In moments, they were speeding across the field, the Jenny giving an occasional light bounce before it lifted, and Sofia's stomach sank into her seat. Despite the terrifying notion that they were no longer on the ground and climbing farther from it, she peeked over the edge of the plane. Everything below was shrinking into something surreal. From their new altitude, she could better see the other planes in midflight, noting that, while they passed quite close to one another, there was still a good amount of space between them, and they were nowhere near enough to collide. From this vantage point, she could also see wing walkers practicing their stunts. It was exhilarating.

Charlie flew them away from the others until the only engine buzzing was theirs. "All right, Sofia—what do you notice?"

For a moment, she focused on the feel of the plane, her attention running from nose to tail. "Everything is smooth—I don't really feel anything. Just the constant vibration, but it's even."

"Exactly. What about the plane? What do you feel?"

Not knowing exactly what Charlie was asking, Sofia pressed her hands to the outer edges of where she sat and closed her eyes. The metal was cool and otherwise not much different than when she'd put her hand on the car door while it was in motion. After a minute, she stated, "Nothing, really. No variations, no shaking."

"Good."

Charlie kept them in the air for a little longer to let Sofia get a feel for a good flight, then turned them back toward the landing field. Before they reached it, the engine stalled out of nowhere, leaving them in startling silence as the plane lost altitude. Sofia's heart began to race, and she felt like she was lifting from her seat.

"Can you tell me what's happened?" Charlie asked, calm and cool as the plane gently swayed back and forth. There was no indication— no beeping, no peculiar odors of leaking fluids, or anything beyond the silence that Sofia could detect, and even as a seasoned pilot, she thought Charlie too calm to suspect disaster.

"You cut the engine."

"The throttle, yes."

The plane continued to rock back and forth, reminding Sofia of a cradle, and she realized Charlie was performing a trick.

"What's this called?" she asked.

"This is a *falling leaf*," he said, sounding impressed. "I'll show you some others soon, but we have things to get done."

Then, as though he'd done it a thousand times, Charlie got the engine going again, righted the plane back into steady flight, and brought them in for a safe landing. Abie was there to help Sofía climb out of the plane.

"How was your first flight?"

"It might take some getting used to," she offered as they hurried along in Charlie's wake to another plane.

"This one has some minor problems," Charlie stated as they reached it and climbed into it. "Nothing too dangerous yet, but it's not up to standards. Let me know if you can tell the differences between it and the first plane."

As soon as the engine started, Sofia noticed something shaking. Their takeoff was only slightly bumpier, but the flight itself wasn't nearly as smooth, and she detected a strong chemical smell that wasn't present with the other plane. She was grateful when Charlie began his descent much sooner than the previous flight, imagining all that could go wrong.

"What stood out to you?" Charlie asked as the flight concluded.

"The shaking right away—there was too much of it. And there was definitely leakage."

Charlie nodded. "Good. These planes are notorious for mechanical problems—we have to constantly check to make sure all the housings are tight. This particular model has to be lubricated before every flight. It also leaks coolant, so that is something that must be kept under control. Engine failure can happen often, so it's crucial that they undergo frequent maintenance checks."

"Is this one that I'll be working on?"

"One of many."

"Yes, sir!" Sofia replied, excited to know that this would be an ongoing job.

On the ground, Abie took over. As they walked toward the hangar, he pointed out the other types of planes, pausing here and there to introduce Sofia to more pilots and stunt men and women along the way.

"So, what's your specialty?" he asked as they paused just outside the hangar.

"Mostly farm machines."

"Yeah?" He dug further with a notable look of mischief on his face. "You like it?"

"I like it okay," Sofía said, then admitted, "But it's a lot of the same thing, and farmers are pretty boring—they don't trust modifications. *'If it ain't broke, don't fix it.'*"

"Well, we all gotta eat, so we should thank them for being a little on the drab side. Here though—" He nodded at the array of planes still overhead and then toward the hangar.

"We have a little more freedom to get creative—so long as the general safety stuff is intact."

This piqued Sofia's curiosity more than anything else had so far, and that was saying something. "What do you mean?"

"Have you ever fixed something—not just to make it work again, but to make it *better*? More interesting?"

"Yeah, of course. I love doing that!"

"You'll fit right in. Come over here—"

They went inside, and he took her to a Jenny that was already opened up and being worked on. The engine was somewhat familiar from her magazines, but as Abie named each part and explained what they did, the diagrams slowly started making more sense. Sofia itched to pick up a wrench and get started. Abie even pointed out a clever little toolbox tucked under the pilot's seat for emergencies, though Sofia couldn't imagine trying to fix anything in flight!

As their tour continued, Sofia found herself torn between paying attention to what Abie said and taking in what she saw. Moment by moment, she recognized the differences between one model versus the next, but the performance modifications intrigued her the most. One plane was equipped with copper compound mechanisms that allowed it to shoot green flame for the night shows. Another had mini jets that boosted the plane's speed so it could execute a longer series of loops. Fascinating as it all was, Sofia preferred to be getting her hands dirty with everyone else. Fighting those urges, she started picking up any nut, bolt, or other piece of hardware she saw on the ground and dropping them into her pockets.

"Those are everywhere," Abie warned, having noticed. "If you pick up every one you see, you'll never get anything else done. Here—" He steered her toward one of the planes that was opened up to be worked on but sat unattended. "We're going to do some basic stuff on this one—making sure everything is properly greased and moving smoothly, and then we'll check all the connections," he said, pulling a couple of wrenches from his toolbelt.

The simple lesson commenced. A calm settled over Sofia with the weight of the tools in her hands and getting in there and connecting with the plane.

"What do you work on when you're not fixing stuff for other people?" Abie asked as he guided her.

"Oh, all kinds of things. My most recent—I was just working on it this morning—is a motorized pulley—" Sofia's cheeks grew warm. "For our clothesline," she added, hoping Abie didn't think it too ridiculous.

"Sounds neat."

Sofia gave a bolt several hard twists, pushing her weight into the act before it came loose enough to turn with less effort. Her head swam with images of all she'd seen outside, still processing who was doing what as she tried to catalog her new world. She paused in her work.

"Say, do you think something like that—a motorized pulley, I mean—could be used for the wing walkers? Make it easier to pull themselves up if they fall?"

Abie looked up from what he'd been doing with a grin. "Funny you should ask—we've been working on something just like that."

Sofia perked up. "Can I help with it?"

Abie shrugged. "I don't see why not." After a pause, he set his wrench on the plane. "You know what? Keep working on those bolts, and I'll go get what we've got so far so you can take a look at it."

Sofia was nearly done by the time Abie returned.

"Here it is." He handed her a motor several times larger than the one she'd pulled from the Singer. "We've tested it some—it'll definitely hold the weight of a wing-walker. We've got a plane to install it on— probably tomorrow."

Sofia looked the mechanism over and gave it back to Abie. "I think it looks good." She sighed and looked around at all that was going on around them and how many things were being done. "I wish I had this kind of space for all of my projects at home. My dad doesn't like it when I use the kitchen table—not that it allows much room for more than one or two at a time, and the same with the porch. I think I can have three going there."

Abie smiled in wonder. "How can you focus on so many at once and keep them straight?"

"I don't know. I'm just used to it."

Just then, Charlie approached and, having overheard this last part of their conversation, said sternly, "You're going to need to focus on one thing at a time in this work. The safety of everyone depends on it."

Sofia bit her lip as her cheeks reddened, already well aware of the vast difference between her hobby and something like this without needing it pointed out to her. She nodded, taking up her wrench to finish loosening the bolts. "Yes, sir. Of course."

"How's it coming?" Charlie asked, nodding toward the plane.

"We're almost ready to grease her up," Abie said.

"When you've finished on this one, you two can work on *The Buzzard* and *Madam Flutterby*."

"You got it."

Sofia waited until Charlie moved out of earshot to explain, giving her wrench a hard shove. "I don't work on them all at the *exact same moment*. That's impossible. Just maybe a few of them on the same day."

"I knew what you meant," Abie assured her in good humor. "Charlie's just really serious about safety. We've had a few accidents, and they're…" He stopped, having gone solemn.

"I get it," Sofia assured him. "I'll do my part, so it doesn't happen."

Sofia, her father, and grandmother stayed on to watch the evening show, enraptured not only by the performances but the fascinating effects coming from the planes and how they filled the sky with patterned flashes and streams of colored light. Sofia found herself only half watching, more caught up in wanting to explore how it all worked. She needed to get a closer look at the aircraft, to study and piece together the familiar parts with the devices and inner workings that were new to her. As much as she tried just to watch and enjoy the show, she couldn't help reflecting on what modifications she had seen and what improvements she might make to them.

On the ride home, Sofia regaled her father and grandmother with frenetic, chatty ramblings and hardly a moment of silence, during which the rumble of the Model T's engine only reminded her of all she had seen, prompting her to start talking again.

"So much of it was new, but it was so—comfortable. Inviting, I guess. It felt right—natural—"

Catching a pause, Frank interjected. "So, are you saying you enjoyed yourself today?" he teased.

Enjoyed? A dozen responses tripped on her tongue, resulting in her blurting out a simple and emphatic "*Yes!*"

"Glad to hear it. The job is yours for as long as you want it."

The unexpected proposal stumped her with welling surprise. "Do you mean it?"

"There are a lot of different things to work on, and with your taste for variety, I had a feeling you'd enjoy it."

"And how," Sofía agreed, finally settling into silence for the rest of the drive.

But her thoughts replayed the entire day and all she'd seen, as well as scenarios and conversations that involved what more she could do and help with back at the airfield. Sleeping was next to impossible, and as tempted as she was to get out of bed to resume working on one of her projects, she finally quieted her mind with thoughts of being up in one of the planes, focusing on the gentler, even the sound of a perfectly working engine.

The next day, Sofia was up with the sun and dressed in dungarees and a blouse that had already seen some grease and could stand to bear some more. *In fact,* she thought, as she threw together a quick breakfast of eggs, toast, and coffee for the three of them, she hoped the new day would send her home downright filthy after a full and satisfying day of tune-ups, repairs, modifications, and whatever else she could take part in.

They ate their breakfast, with Sofia dominating the conversation.

"I hope we can test the pulley today. Oh, and I want to see the installation of jets on one of the planes — Abie said they have a new set all ready to go. One of the others is supposed to get a new engine — do you think I could bring one home at some point? We'd need a trailer — I would probably need to just work on it at the hanger, though — don't you think?"

Frank just smiled and appreciated the joy in Sofia's rambling.

When it came time to leave, Sofia headed toward the car, stopping with the door open, when she realized her father still stood on the porch with his hands in his pockets.

"Aren't you coming?"

"You remember how to get there?"

"Sure," she said with confusion setting in. "But aren't you — ?"

"Nah, Pip. I told you — this is all yours. Besides, I've got a few quick, easy things coming by the house, and I want to keep your grandmother out of the heat. You'll be fine," he said with a wave when Sofia hesitated. "Tell me all about it when you get home tonight."

Sofia shrugged with nonchalance. "Okay." But once she was in the vehicle and heading down the road, she could hardly contain her elation.

Abie was waiting for Sofia in the parking lot when she arrived. There were less cars and people around at that hour, and instead of the buzzing of airplane engines, the air was filled with the sound of cicadas.

"Lots to do today," Abie said as they approached the hangar. "Oh, hey—" He pulled something from his pocket and held his hand out to Sofia. She put hers beneath it, and he dropped a small heavy object into her palm. "I have a few hobbies, too," he revealed as Sofia held up a bolt suspended from a ball chain by a soldered loop. There were three nuts screwed onto it. "One is for adventure, one for luck, and a third for whatever you want. I know it's clunky and heavy—you don't have to wear it."

Touched, Sofia grinned and immediately put the chain on over her head. Abie smiled at the gesture and continued smiling for the entire rest of the day.

They got to work, spending the day side-by-side, not just seeing to the basic routine maintenance of the planes but observing some of the more intricate workings of modified aircraft. For the first few instances, Sofia held back a bit, just watching and not wanting to get in the way, but it took no more than Abie giving her an encouraging nod for Sofia to start posing questions, including asking if she could try whatever was at hand.

"I hope I didn't annoy anyone or step on any toes," she said afterward as she headed toward the parking lot at the end of the day. Abie shook his head, looking pleased. ?"Not one bit." He shut her door after Sofia was in her vehicle. "See you in the morning."

It was just dusk as she left, and Sofia was pleasantly exhausted by the time she reached home, giving a recap of her day over supper, but once finished, she was off to bed.

Tired as she had been the night before, Sofia bounded out of bed and hurried to get ready for work, grabbing her trousers from the day before. Among the many things they had talked about, Abie had revealed to her that the motorized tether was ready to be secured to a plane for use. She was thinking about this as she told her father goodbye and was just stepping outside when her grandmother rose from her rocking chair with a spryness she hadn't exhibited in some time.

"I'm off to work, Gram. See you later."

But before Sofia could take a step past the woman, she thrust a card at Sofia's chest.

"Not now, okay?" Sofia pushed it away, only to have it pushed back.

"It's for *you*," her grandmother insisted.

Knowing she wouldn't get out of it any other way, Sofia looked at the card: the Hanged Man again. She made another, this time successful, attempt to return the card, saying quickly, "Thank you, Gram. Thanks! Gotta go!"

This time, the woman snatched it out of Sofia's hand and went back to her chair, leaving Sofia to be on her way. The entire drive, Sofia tried to think of anything else, the image having left her with a lingering uneasiness, but by the time the barn at the airfield came into view, the entire incident had evaporated.

Once again, Abie was there to greet her, but this time he looked ready to burst. "I got here early, and we got the new tether attached to one of the planes—are you ready to test it?"

Sofia paused to look up, seeing one of the wing walkers transferring between two planes. The sight made her stomach twirl. "I don't want to watch—but I can't help it."

"It *is* mesmerizing—but I meant from *on* the plane. You can't really get a good handle on how it's working from down here."

"True—"

"Come on. The wind is perfect right now, and Charlie's ready."

Sofia was ready to jump right in, but at the slower, more concentrated tasks. Still, she had been looking forward to this, too, and there was something about Charlie being the one who would pilot the plane for this new apparatus that intrigued Sofia.

He was already at the plane when Abie and Sofia arrived, looking eager to get going. One of the wing walkers, whom Charlie introduced as Jane, was there as well.

"Good luck," Abie said once Jane was secured into a frame on the top wing and just as they were pulling away to take off.

Not having had a chance to work on her clothesline, Sofia was even more eager to test out this new contraption. Abie had assured her that it was in perfect working order, and even if the motor failed, as long as Jane was attached, it would still hold. There was next to nothing that could go wrong.

As the plane left the ground, almost at once, Sofia felt a mild, almost lopsided shaking. It wasn't anything like the second plane she had been on, and no one else reacted, so she dismissed it as Charlie started talking about what Jane would do on this flight. But as they climbed higher, the irregularity grew, and with it came a sort of noise that wasn't quite a clank or rattle, and the sick feeling and rush of adrenaline it gave Sofia prompted her to speak.

"Charlie—" she interjected. "There's something wrong with the plane."

Charlie went silent.

"Do you feel it?" Sofia asked. "I think it's beneath us—do you hear it?"

Again, there was only silence as Charlie pushed his headset off one ear and listened.

"I do," he finally said. "Definitely sounds like it's below. Something with our landing gear. I'll have to climb down there and look—I'll use the tether—"

"*You can't*," Sofia interjected as a wave of dread washed over her. "It's not built to hold you—it's not strong enough."

"If it's what I think it is, we can't land safely unless it's fixed—"

Sofia's head filled with fog, her body went numb, and the words blurted from her mouth before she could stop them: "I'll do it."

"Sofia—"

Clarity struck her like a punch in the chest. "Well, I can't fly the plane," she argued, "but I can probably fix what's wrong."

"*Probably?*"

"*Can,*" she whispered before saying aloud and with determination, "I *can* fix it."

After too long of a moment, Charlie finally conceded. "There's a safety harness under my seat, along with a small toolbox. Put the harness on and hook the tools to the rings."

Sofia nodded. Abie had pointed that out when he'd shown her around. She stood and did as instructed.

Realizing that the plane was making a slight descent, Jane unfastened from the frame and lowered herself onto the bottom wing. Charlie made an urgent gesture to the rig to the new tether and then back at Sofia. Jane hurried to attach one of the static tethers to herself before removing the motorized one and passing it back to Charlie. By then, Sofia was in the harness, ladened with half a dozen tools clipped to it. She took the tether from Charlie and hooked it on. Thinking there was only one way to do it, Sofia slowly climbed out of the plane, gripping so tightly to whatever she could that her hands ached, and her knees grew sore from pressing hard against the plane. She paused when Charlie reached back to take hold of her arm, grateful for the few moments he afforded her his stabilizing hold.

"I'm going to take us lower," he explained. "About five hundred feet, but we're still going to be a long way from the ground. I'll lower you down the side, stay as close to it as you can, and grab hold of the gear once you're down there. We're going to take this one moment at a time."

"Okay," Sofia said, as though they were speaking of something as simple as parking a car and not a mission that might kill her and would most assuredly kill them all if she failed.

"The gear is your *only* concern," Charlie added. "Here we go—"

There wasn't another moment to contemplate what was happening, and certainly, no chance to change her mind as the tether began to slacken and Sofia slipped down the outside of the plane. The wind current was fierce. She clung to the edge of the plane and tried with every ounce of her strength to stay against it, even as the current fought to strip her off. The tether continued to slacken.

"Let go, Sofia. Get down there—"

Knowing there was no other option, she flattened against the fuselage, one hand holding onto the meager stability of the tether while the other, slippery from sweat, struggled to guide her down to the underside of the plane. There wasn't far to go, but even a mere couple of feet seemed to take forever to cover.

The source of the noise was immediately clear: one of the wheels had come loose, and while the other spun nice and evenly with the threading of wind through the spokes, this one wobbled hard enough to reverberate through the rest of the gear. On the ground and properly raised, it would be an easy fix, but of course, it was the wheel on the opposite side from where she'd come down, leaving Sofia no choice but to climb onto the axle.

"I need more slack—"

The tether suddenly loosened too much at once. Sofia lost contact with the plane, still secure but hanging upside down with one foot caught in it. The image from her grandmother's card of the Hanged Man flashed across her mind. Shuddering, Sofia shielded her face from the tools dangling from the harness. They clanged against each other like a horrible wind chime. Sofia reached toward the axle. With the wind threatening to make her spin, it took a few swings before she caught hold.

Charlie's voice came through Sofia's headset, tinged with panic. "Sofia—you still with me, kid?"

"Just taking in the view," she said breathlessly once she regained her voice.

There was a pause before Charlie spoke again, his tone now calmer. "Take a breath. Focus. You got this, kiddo."

Sofia hooked one leg and then the other onto the axle, then quickly pulled herself toward the outer wheel. Bracing her feet against the underside of the plane, she grabbed the tire to steady it. The shaking immediately lessened but did not stop altogether.

"What is it?" Charlie asked.

"The right wheel—it's loose," she responded, her voice hitching as she realized a much bigger problem from feeling the bare end of the axle jutting out the other side. "The parts that hold it on—they're gone."

"The cap?"

"The cap, the bolt, the nut—all of it."

Her mind raced, wondering just how she was supposed to fix this. She glanced around at the rest of the landing gear, wondering if any of the connecting parts could sacrifice at least a bolt, but even as a novice, she knew that every bit was precise and vital for the rig to work properly.

Charlie muttered an expletive before asking, "Will any of the parts on the tether fit?"

Sofia closed her eyes, the axle pinching the backs of her knees. This was not at all where she wanted to be. But this was part of the job. She cataloged the elements of the pulley in her mind, and her assessment resulted in a groan.

"*No*—they're welded on, and anything we can remove is too big."

In the next pause, Sofia began patting her pockets—*hadn't she stashed a few nuts and bolts somewhere?* For an instant, she feared these were in her other trousers, but elation and relief struck when she felt the hard lumps.

"I might have something—"

She let go of the wheel so she could shove her hand into her pocket, but just as she pulled it back out, the wheel gave a terrible wobble, forcing her to reach for it so it wouldn't come off. The hardware she'd been retrieving all fell toward the ground.

"Well?" Charlie prompted. "We can stay up here for a while, but not forever," he warned.

"I know," Sofia replied, hoping that her utter disappointment in herself didn't translate in her voice, and more than that, she hoped Charlie hadn't lost confidence in her. "I just need a minute."

"Roger that."

Something about the phrase and Charlie having used it caught Sofia off guard and renewed her strength and determination. There just *had* to be something. She examined the various connections of the landing gear and the plane itself and gritted her teeth. There was nothing she could remove.

Still holding the wheel in place, she shifted, hooking her other arm around the axle to take some pressure off her legs. It was enough to move the forgotten weight on the chain around her neck, and the bulk of it — Abie's pendant! — rolled from where it had been sitting on her chest, zipping along the chain to hang down under her. She quickly pulled it back up and sighed in relief. It should do the trick! As she contorted herself, wrapping one arm around the wheel to free up her hand while still keeping the wheel in place, she made a mental note to tell Abie what a genius he was.

It took a few moments to get the nuts free from the bolt. Sofia put them between her tightly pressed lips so she wouldn't drop these like the others, not daring to entertain the notion of swallowing them, and after removing the chain and wrapping it around her hand, she sought out the hole to thread the bolt through. The wind pushed against her hand and the wheel, trying to force it out of alignment.

"Any luck?" Charlie asked.

Unable to respond, Sofia found one hole and got the bolt through it, shifting herself again to straighten it and feed it through the other side of the axle. *"This is the easy part,"* she thought, feeling the resistance give as the bolt slipped into place.

Easiest or not, she shook with adrenaline. No sooner had she gotten the first nut onto the bolt and began to turn did she just as quickly knock it off. She took the second try at a slower pace, able to screw it on partway and enough that she could let go of the wheel to search for the right sized wrench to tighten it. None of them was a perfect match, but one was close enough. Sofia's muscles quivered with fatigue at hanging there, and her head swam with vertigo as she caught sight of the ground, causing her to fumble the wrench. She closed her eyes, locked the tool back onto the nut by feel, and resumed tightening it as quickly as she could, finally able to use both hands to hang onto it and give it full torque. The rapid-fire tapping of the loose wheel ceased.

"I'm liking the quiet," Charlie stated.

Sofia removed the last nut from her mouth and added it to the bolt for good measure. "Me, too. I think I'm about ready to come up."

"Glad to hear it."

Sofia shimmied across the axle and braced an arm against the side of the plane.

"Okay, bring me up."

She was back in her seat in moments, still shaking but full of relief.

Charlie was the first to speak. "What did you end up using?"

Sofia laughed softly at the irony. "*Adventure* and *luck*, I imagine."

THE MAPS OF OUR SCARS

JAMES CHAMBERS

"HERE'S A BAD OMEN. THE BIG MAN HIMSELF HAS COME TO GREET US IN place of Dorrie," Morris said.

"I thought he never left his workshop," Madame Marceline said.

Morris tipped a luggage handler a few coins as the man finished piling his and Marceline's bags onto Morris's steam dolly. He plugged a guidewire into the dolly—the other end terminating at a battery-powered controller mounted atop his walking stick—then toed the dolly's ignition switch. Its miniature steam engine huffed to life. The dolly trailed the slender Morris Garvey, dressed in a tailored suit and fitted long coat, like a hungry puppy as he and Madame Marceline Rene, a brunette in the latest Paris dress, waded through the crowds bustling outside the gargantuan, brick structure of Cadillac City Central Station. The throngs parted in curious surprise at the oddity of Morris's mechanical porter trailing a thin tail of steam. A red-white-and-blue banner strung thirty feet between flagpoles above the Station entry read:

CADILLAC CITY AERIAL CRAFT COMPETITION
WELCOMES THE WORLD.

"Only rumors. He hasn't entirely turned his back on his globe-trotting past. We both know how easy it is to fall down a rabbit hole in the shop." Morris raised a hand, waved, and called out: "Hank!"

A broad-shouldered man, nearly six-and-a-half-feet tall, lit up at the sound of his name. He wore a gray jumpsuit, mottled with an uncatalogable variety of stains, its legs tucked into well-worn, calf-high leather boots. The zipper, open to the waist, revealed a pie-slice of immaculate shirt, tie, and vest under the coverall. The man himself sported a gray-streaked mane of black hair, spectacles, a day's worth of stubble, and a wide smile at the arrival of his guests.

"Morris," Hank Van Buren called across the buzz of roving travelers.

He stepped away from a gray-and-silver, ramshackle truck, seemingly assembled from junkyard parts scavenged with no regard for form, only function. Morris thumbed the dolly control, bringing it to a smooth halt with a soft, mechanical exhalation, then extended his free hand, which Hank grasped with both of his and shook warmly.

"It's a miracle to see you in Cadillac City, Morris. I thought we'd never pry New Alexandria's favorite son away to the heart of motor country," he said. He released Morris's hand and turned to Marceline. "Madame Rene, has it really been five years since Le Mans?"

"Six, I believe, Hank, but you look as if you haven't aged a day."

"The same goes for you." Hank took Marceline's hand and pressed it to his lips. "As always, you're a restorative sight for tired eyes." Hank gestured to his monstrous, patchwork truck. "My friends, your chariot awaits. Let's stow your luggage and take a ride."

Morris steered his dolly around the back of the truck, where he and Hank stacked the luggage in its open bed. Morris deactivated the dolly engine then disconnected it from his cane, folded it closed, then shoved it between the cases.

"Handy gadget, that," Hank said. "I could use it around the shop."

"I'm sure you could with all the sliding under things you do," Morris said.

"I've never been afraid to get my hands dirty."

Marceline grinned. "Or your coverall."

Hank laughed then further unzipped his jumpsuit and slid his arms free. The upper portion hung at the backs of his legs, revealing his immaculate, perfect-fitting suit, minus its jacket. "Better? Lost track of the hour. I ran right from my hangar without time for a proper change."

"We appreciate it," Morris said, "but I'd expected Dorrie to fetch us."

A pall fell over Hank's face. It flattened his smile and shadowed his eyes.

"I've got bad news. There was a crash. Dorrie has been in the hospital for three days. She woke up only this morning. The docs say it was touch and go for a while."

"Oh, Hank, how awful, I'm terribly sorry," Marceline said.

Reading into Hank's expression, Morris scowled. "What else, Hank? Don't hold back."

Hank's jaw tightened. His cheeks reddened. Anger flared in his eyes.

"The crash," he said, "was no accident."

Despite its cumbersome appearance, Hank's truck drove as smooth as a sailing ship as it departed the seventeen-floor edifice of Central Station. Morris occupied the passenger seat. Marceline sat between him and Hank, feigning a lack of concern about the two men crushing her delicate dress. Overcast gloom and a thin drizzle darkened the brick-and-asphalt landscape of Cadillac City, an oil-and-electric metropolis younger and more modern than New Alexandria, where cobblestone streets and gas lamps still ruled. Cadillac City, thanks largely to Hank's ingenuity, willpower, and persistence, had modernized by filling its municipal fleet with diesel-fuel vehicles, wiring electricity to its neighborhoods one by one, and drawing international investment in the emerging motor-vehicle industry—founded almost single-handedly by Hank. The booming local industries gave inventors and manufacturers in the Northeast, such as Morris, a run for their steam-damp money, making the future of mechanics and technology more uncertain and exciting than ever. Morris admired the steady glow of electric lights along the roads and in building windows. He knew in his bones change would come for his dear, gaslit city one day, where his steam-powered chimney sweeps had won him his own fortune. In fact, he'd already developed plans to manage the evolution, secured in the vault at his Machinations Sundry headquarters, ready for the day the city councilors needed them.

"We were testing a lighter weight version of my autogyro," Hank said. "Weight is a factor in the Aerial Competition, and we'd shaved a second off our time from last year's challenge course when we brainstormed substitute materials to drop another three pounds. Dorrie insisted on flying the new configuration first. The damn thing took her up to 1,500 feet, no trouble at all, ran through maneuvers, then stalled and dropped like a stone."

"What do you mean dropped?" said Morris.

"I mean that thing that happens when gravity clutches you, Morris. The motor sputtered into silence then the rotors stopped spinning. Thank heaven, Dorrie had managed most of her descent. She plummeted only about fifty feet and landed in our reservoir. That's all that saved her life. If she'd flown higher or longer, the outcome would've been tragic. Still, she broke two ribs and took an awful blow to her head."

"Did the equipment fail?" Marceline said.

Hank shook his head. "Not how you mean. After we saw Dorrie safely to the hospital, I dived the reservoir and recovered every last scrap of the gyro, horrified I'd made a mistake that caused the crash. I examined every single piece until I found the culprit."

The truck rolled deeper into the city, made a series of confounding turns, then settled on a long, straight highway that appeared to terminate at a complex of brick buildings that sprawled like a bruise beside the heart of the smoky metropolis. Hank overtook a slow-moving milk truck, honked twice, then sped past it, his anger over Dorrie's plight given voice by the truck's growling motor.

"Don't keep us in suspense, Hank. What caused it?" Morris said.

"Someone drilled tiny holes into the cylinders of the prototype motor we cast from the new materials. If you didn't know what to look for, it would've seemed like a materials flaw. The bird ran long enough to gain altitude before the holes caused a full stall."

"Suggesting the saboteur aimed to kill the pilot, ruin the craft, and discredit your innovation." Morris scowled. "Who'd want to do that?"

"That's a question I hope you can help me answer. I inspected every piece of that craft pre-flight, fabricated half of them with my own two hands. Eight hours before take-off, that machine was flawless and built exactly to specification."

"That narrows the window of opportunity," Morris said. "Who had access during the time?"

"Me and Dorrie, of course, and, officially, half a dozen of my top technicians."

"Was the main target the autogyro or Dorrie, do you think?" said Marceline.

"Neither." Hank slammed one hand against the wheel. "They were after *me*. I was scheduled for that morning's test flight. The change in materials was Dorrie's idea. She was so damned excited that I gave in when she asked to take my place last minute. She took a fall meant for me. After all she suffered during the Czar's Gas Wars—losing her family, her home, damn near losing her mind—she winds up with the one blockhead too stupid to keep his promise to protect her from any more horror."

"Oh, Hank, don't blame yourself. You couldn't have known," Marceline said.

"Couldn't I have?" Hank said.

"You have an idea who'd want to hurt you?" said Morris.

"Not hurt, *kill*. Someone meant to kill me," Hank said.

"All right, but who?"

"It's a short list. Only all my competitors and half of Europe."

"Why half of Europe?" Marceline said.

"To answer that, I'll have to show you my latest project. You won't like it much, but it'll explain quite a bit."

The truck carried them through the entrance checkpoint into the Van Buren Motorworks complex, barely slowing as Hank honked his truck horn, hollered, and waved to his frantic security guards. He cut a sharp right then two more turns, tires spewing gravel, and aimed them toward the largest building on the campus, a brick-and-stone hangar larger than any other single building Morris had ever seen. In New Alexandria, it would've occupied a dozen city blocks, maybe even a quarter of the city below 14th Street. Observing the truck speeding toward the main doors, a crew rushed from stations outside the structure to operate mechanisms that opened the passage. Hank sped in then slammed the brakes, screeching tires and burning rubber, before he parked beside two similarly asymmetrical trucks.

"You absolute madman," Morris said after Hank killed the motor. Marceline held his hand in a panicked steely grip that mottled it bright red and white. "You can let go now, dear."

Marceline's face flushed. "I shall never grow accustomed to the chaos of your wild driving, Hank, nor your internal combustion motors."

"Wave of the future, my dear," said Hank. "Don't stand in the way of progress. You'll only get steamrolled."

Thinking of Dorrie, Marceline cringed at Hank's poor choice of words, unsurprised he missed their irony. They exited the truck, and Hank led them into the vastness of his workshop. A third of it seemed dedicated to the autogyros upon which Hank had built his fortune. Other sections housed more ragtag trucks, each in a different stage of repair. Two- and three-wheeled vehicles, standalone motors, fixed-wing aircraft, and gadgets far too numerous for Morris to decipher all their individual purposes occupied still other spaces. Mechanics and technicians roved around, filling the air with a concert of clinks, clanks, and conversation that produced a cloud of industrious noise. As the trio progressed, Hank greeted some of the busy men and women, but most ignored his presence, heads down, focused on their work. Despite the sense of weight created by the impressive display of steel and iron parts, not to mention the caustic aroma of diesel fuel and motor oil, Morris felt at ease here. Regardless of the different materials and technologies, he understood the dedication, ingenuity, and labor on display. It reminded him of his own steam-based workshop pulsing with activity back home. His shop occupied a quarter of the area filled by Hank's, but the upper Midwest offered a great deal more open space than the densely-packed island of New Alexandria.

"What about our bags, Hank?" Marceline said.

Hank waved away the question. "Don't worry. Someone will take them to your quarters."

"Not much security with all these people around," Morris said.

"I stored the autogyro in my personal shop. Most of these people don't have access." Hank swung open a heavy steel door and ushered Morris and Marceline into a twelve-foot-square room. The door latched shut behind them, and they seemed trapped.

"Should we understand the significance of this empty room?" Morris said.

Hank smiled. "If you're worried about security, check this out." He put his right pinky to the corner of his lips then whistled four distinct notes. Invisible machines grumbled in reply. "It's not a room."

As if to prove his point, the floor trembled then commenced a slow descent. Marceline gave out a surprised gasp and grabbed Morris's arm to steady herself. Patient, curious, Morris nodded at Hank. A dozen questions spun through his head, about the technology of the elevator, Dorrie's condition, Hank's business, his competitors, and more, but he held his silence, content to wait for Hank to reveal the answers in his own time. The floor eased to a stop at the conclusion of its journey, presenting its passengers with another door, which Hank opened. They exited into a small vestibule. Odors like those upstairs flavored the air, but mingled with another scent, one Morris intensely disliked: gunpowder.

"It only responds to my whistle. I bring the team down here every morning."

Hank closed the elevator door then led them around a corner into a workshop entirely filled with a single type of machine: guns. From pistols to rifles to artillery cannons stout enough to hurl a projectile miles over the horizon, weapons of all sizes and types filled the cavernous space, and dozens of workers tended to them. A terrifying, multi-chambered reimagining of Gatling's famous gun mounted on iron wheels caught Morris's eye, a mechanical Cerberus that looked capable of chewing everything in its path to nothing in seconds.

Morris's heart pounded in rage over the incredible array of death machines. He read Marceline's silence as an expression of her own anger, too cold for words.

"My god, Hank. What is this arsenal?" Morris said.

"This is why half of Europe wants me dead," Hank said. "There have been seven assassination attempts against me, eight now, I suppose, at least that I know of. No one's ever used the Competition for cover before. It has always been neutral ground for nations and industrialists. A chance to show off for the world and show each other up. That only works if we call a truce. No industrial espionage, no poaching each other's top engineers, no hostilities. This year my enemies feel much closer. I'm afraid I won't survive the next attempt. That's why I took the liberty of building you a present, my old friend."

Still angry, Morris and Marceline followed Hank past a barrier that separated a corner of the workshop from the armory.

"I followed your design, but I'm sure you'll want to refine it," Hank said.

"What is it?" Marceline said.

Morris raised his walking cane and tapped one shining brass panel of the construction with the tip. The machine resembled a gold scarab with its thorax and legs wrapped over a large, elliptical void. The upper carapace housed a cockpit for two, and along either side of it spread panels, like the layers of a beetle's wings, which contained different size fans, steam-jets, ailerons, and flaps. Mounted on a scaffold, it resembled a giant insect pinned to an entomologist's table.

"It's my Steam Bug. The space beneath houses a helium bladder. When fully inflated, it lofts the entire mechanism into the air. The steam-driven gear in the wings enables navigation. Hank helped me refine it. I built a single-pilot prototype for the New Alexandria Police

Department. Imagine the benefits of aerial pursuit and surveillance. Alas, they never found an officer brave enough to fly it." Morris lowered his walking stick and leaned on it. "Hank, why on earth have you built this?"

"If you're going to enter the Aerial Competition, Morris, you're going to need something to fly."

"Let's visit Hank Van Buren, you said. Let's have a change of scenery, you said. Let's watch Hank win yet another aerial competition and relax for a few days, you said." Marceline's hands drew invisible symbols of her frustration in the air. "Instead, right now, we could be sipping wine by the Seine. Every time, Morris. Every. Time."

"What about Cuba?"

"Cuba, *oui*, we spent two days finding the Persian ambassador's missing teenage daughter, who turned out not lost but only hiding in a salsa club to escape strict parenting."

Morris raised his glass of merlot from the table between him and Marceline and took a long sip while considering his next words. Except for a small group of technicians on the far side of the employee club, they were alone. "You didn't have to come, Marcy. You had such a good time with Hank when he won the Le Mans race, I figured you'd appreciate another victory celebration."

"My enjoyment of Le Mans had far more to do with access to my native wine and cuisine than with cheering on Hank in his motor car. And even there two people turned up murdered. *Et puis quoi encore*?" Calming herself, she reached across the table and took one of Morris's hands in hers. "Please don't misunderstand, Morris. I enjoy all of it. I only marvel at these adventures, these risks that seem to gravitate to you like the Moon hangs to the Earth. They're part of who you are in a strange fundamental way, but it would be nice to have a quiet day now and then."

"Hank caught me off-guard as much as he did you. I had no idea he'd turned to making weapons. It's... well, it's disturbing is the kindest thing I can say. Hank, it seems, is no longer the same man I knew who pledged himself to technological progress to elevate humanity and ease our sufferings. I'd say it's a reaction to seeing Dorrie hurt in his place. After what they suffered together in the Gas Wars, she's like a daughter to him. But he didn't build that arsenal in days. That took years, as if he started the day he returned from Eastern Europe."

"I did," Hank said. Neither Morris nor Marceline had noticed him enter the clubroom. He waited by their table, which occupied a window space overlooking the Van Buren complex. Brilliant sunset hues streaking the horizon rendered the buildings dead black. "I'll leave if this is a private conversation. But I thought I might explain."

"Yes, do that, sit down and explain," Morris snapped. "Explain why you're building death machines you once swore never to make. You called me here, built my steam Bug, and roped me into a competition I never planned to enter. Fine. I'll compete because my dear friend and confidant, Hank Van Buren, who never acts without purpose asked me to, but I need to know why. We've never kept secrets before."

Hank lowered his eyes. After a moment's hesitation, he seated himself, then waved at a waiter who brought him a wine glass and placed a second decanter of red on the table.

"You don't know half the things I saw during the Gas Wars." He poured wine into his glass, lifted it, and inhaled the aroma. "Those horrors are well, if incompletely, documented, but not the madness of them. I fear that madness is contagious, and it has taken root in that region of the world. I won't speak of the details here, not in comfort with wine and good friends. All I'll say is there's a condition like shellshock that afflicts folks who never set foot on the battlefield, a shock that grows on you from witnessing how utterly savage humans can be to each other, how some people see no value in human life. Living under the shadow of menace hits you even if your life never feels its touch firsthand. It creeps into the back of your thoughts, takes root, and becomes—well, almost liberating, you see, this idea that others matter less than you thus you owe them nothing. It frees you from your conscience if one ever shackled you."

Morris shook off a chill. He had read every in-depth report of the Gas Wars he could find and knew most of the details Hank alluded to, but he still didn't understand. "What are you saying?"

"The Gas Wars ended but their savagery is only hibernating," Hank said.

"You mean the Czar plans to restart the war?" said Marceline.

"No, the Czar is done with war. For him, the war ended the day he lost all his sons at the Battle of Krakow. But the conflict ground nearly all humanity out of the region. Another war is inevitable, and the Czar's top advisor stokes it. He's an unpleasant man who carries himself like an ascetic, but who in fact possesses not a spark of the divine. He's a rabid dog cleverer than his hunters. After the war's end he fled to Austria, welcomed by a secretive group who believed the Czar's efforts to refashion society didn't go far enough. Imagine that? A million dead, more lives ruined, and how many cities destroyed, but it didn't go far enough? Among them, there's a man who peers into corners of science and technology the three of us have only speculated about, beyond aether and magic, into cosmic energies untapped since the birth of the universe. He's a genius and utterly amoral. He's partnered with the lunatic who midwifed the Czar's mad aggression, a pair of sharks swimming in a stew of dehumanization, hatred, rage, and numbness. Trust me, one day it will erupt into terrors unlike any in history."

Morris sat back in his chair. "You're building weapons against them."

Hank nodded. "I've kept it as secret as I can, but spies are everywhere. These men hold seats of power in the nations closest to the conflict. They have resources far beyond mine. They understand the risk I pose to their ambitions if I should arm their enemies."

"Horrors suffered and witnessed should move people to rise above such conflicts, to seek better ways to live, to cherish life," Marceline said.

"Dear Marceline, the world simply doesn't work that way," Hank said. "Instead of learning from our history, we follow the maps of our scars."

"So our work here isn't only to protect you and win the competition, but to root out the spies in your midst," Morris said. "Fine, here's what we'll do..."

A thunderous rumble drowned out Morris's voice. The building shook. Windows rattled. Wine quivered in their glasses. The sunset had ended, leaving an indigo canvas for a brush of glaring fire and smoke that rose from one of the buildings in the complex. As the tremors faded, Morris, Marceline, and Hank rose from the table in stunned silence to peer out the window. The technicians at the other table did the same while uttering gasps of shock. All of them stared in awe at the conflagration that whipped itself into a whirlwind frenzy.

"No, oh, no, no, that was my personal shop. The new parts for the autogyro were there." Hank restrained a scream of anguish as he glanced at his watch. "And I *should've* been. I work there at this time every evening. If not for you two, I'd be dead right now."

The morning of the competition brought clear, still weather. Marceline dubbed it a blessing for their flight. Morris considered it a deceptive start to a day he knew would not go easy, but he tried to take Marceline's view. Without her technical acumen and inventiveness, his Steam Bug would still be sitting in Hank's workshop. Hank had overbuilt everything, applying truck sensibility to a machine that held more in common with a bicycle. Marceline swiftly grasped the concept of Morris's design, and their many hours laboring together in the Machinations Sundry shop had trained them to work as though they shared a mind. The refitted Steam Bug, the only craft of its kind among the diesel motor autogyros, garnered stares from dozens of people. At the neighboring staging station, Hank adjusted his own vessel to compensate for the destruction of the new parts. A steady mutter of curses telegraphed his mood.

Morris tested the pressure of the Bug's primary helium bladder. Satisfied, he packed away the last of his borrowed tools.

"She's magnificent, Morris," Marceline said. "Why didn't you ever show her to me?"

Morris shrugged. "After the NAPD rejected my prototype, Hank took the world by storm with his autogyros, and she seemed obsolete before she got off the ground."

"You may surprise yourself today."

"Our purpose is to keep Hank—and everyone else here—alive, and see if we can't out his would-be assassins." Morris looked along the length of his Steam Bug, seeking any imperfections, then, finding none, turned his attention to Hank's autogyro. "I have the most troublesome sense we already have part of the answer, but we haven't yet recognized it."

Marceline tilted her head, thoughtful, but before she could reply, the crowd along the roped-off perimeter produced a loud murmur. People parted for a chauffeur, trundling a wheelchair under the rope toward Hank's site. The young woman passenger managed a frail smile through obvious fatigue, her eyes dark in contrast to her pale face, sunken as if they had retreated from the world for having seen too many atrocities. She wore a mechanics jumpsuit, embroidered with the bright Van Buren Motorworks logo. A flannel blanket covered her legs.

"That's Dorrie," Morris said.

"Is it? I've never met her before," said Marceline.

The chauffeur brought her to Hank, who hadn't yet observed her. When Dorrie spoke his name, he dropped his wrench and spun around, his face beaming with joy. As gently as he could, he embraced her. Afterward, he beckoned Morris and Marceline and introduced them.

"You're Hank's idol, Mr. Garvey," Dorrie said.

"The regard is mutual," Morris said. "I don't expect you to remember after so many years, but we met when Hank first brought you to Cadillac City. You were much younger then and distracted by your new environment. It fills my heart with joy to see you're recovering."

"I feel fine except for my ribs. Those damn doctors insist I use this chair," Dorrie said. "I had to sneak out."

"They don't know you've gone?" Marceline said.

Dorrie laughed. "They never do. Hank, you weren't going to fly this thing without my seal of approval, were you? Or without this?"

From beneath her blanket, Dorrie produced a mechanical part that Morris didn't recognize but which lit excitement in Hank's eyes. A kind of valve, the size of a grapefruit, it produced a diffuse gleam in the morning light. Taking it from Dorrie's hands, Hank hefted it and grinned.

"You knocked out another… three ounces?" he said.

"That's a whole *five* ounces lighter," said Dorrie.

"Someone sneak a machine shop into your hospital room?"

"I fabricated it before the crash but used the heavier version for our test. This ought to give you the edge you need to win."

His spirits lifted, Hank rolled Dorrie alongside the autogyro. "Let's swap it out for the old one."

Morris and Marceline retreated to the Bug, while Hank and Dorrie worked rapidly to install the new part. Dorrie winced whenever she reached into the machine to help. Before long, a horn blew, announcing the final countdown to the first challenge. Morris gestured for Marceline to board the bug and prepare for take-off. On the neighboring lot, Hank hugged Dorrie farewell, then one of his technicians wheeled her back to the perimeter, where her chauffeur met her and steered uphill toward a line of parked cars.

Another horn blew. Two dozen motors growled to life. Rotors whirled, accelerated, spinning into blurs of motion, and raised an astonishing array of autogyros into the air, casting shadows on Marceline and Morris, who threw off the restraining lines, allowing the Steam Bug to float into the sky. He yanked a cord, flipped switches, and seized the controls, operating jointly with Marceline, who worked pedals and levers at her station. They guided the chugging Bug along with the purring aircraft swarming toward the starting line. Ahead flew Hank, at ease and as confident as Morris had ever seen him.

Cool air whipped Morris's face as the Bug surged ahead of many of the heavier autogyros. He could've occupied a lead place, but he held back to keep a watchful eye on Hank's bird, flying ahead of the pack. The first challenge combined altitude and navigation checkpoints over a seven-mile course above wilderness sculpted by rocky hills and bristling with trees. With Marceline's aid, Morris guided the Bug into fourth, keeping two aircraft between them and Hank.

"Can't we go faster, Morris? We can win this!" Marceline cried.

"We can, but we're not here to win. Hold us steady, will you?"

Morris reached into a compartment and withdrew a set of binoculars. He held them against his goggles. Magnified trees, grass, rock, and soil sped by at a nauseating pace.

"What is it? What do you see?" Marceline said.

"Nothing yet, but it's best to watch...." Morris trailed off as steel glinted within a stretch of wild brush. He dropped the glasses and floored the Bug's accelerator. "Now, Marcy! Open her up!"

The Bug hopped straight up as Morris lessened the vertical dampeners and its helium bladder shot them skyward. It maneuvered like a dragonfly, hovering then darting as it passed the second-place autogyro. Morris poured all of its power into overtaking Hank and swung the Bug across his path, forcing him to drop altitude and swerve. He glimpsed Hank's furious face, which faded as metal slugs grouped in three tight columns slashed the space Hank's bird had occupied. Failing to see the danger, the second-place pilot seized the opening and accelerated into the deadly stream. It ripped his craft apart, ignited its fuel, and birthed an explosion of flame, steel, blood, and bone. The concussion rocked the Bug.

On the ground, a smaller version of the Cerberus Gatling gun in Hank's shop spit lead into the air until its chamber ran empty and only wisps of smoke emerged from the barrels. A man in black clothing fled from the emptied gun, too fast for Morris to catch him in detail.

The aircraft sped onward and out of range.

Morris and Hank traded glances, unspoken acknowledgment to seek survival over victory but stay the course in hopes of revealing the assassin. The explosion turned back many of their competitors, but the two aircraft flew side-by-side ahead of those still in the air. Regaining competition altitude, Morris and Hank aimed their craft at the next navigation checkpoint, the shallow canyon of the St. Joseph River. Their course required them to pass the river by one mile then circle back for the final stretch. Rushing water sped by beneath them, a rippling quilt of blue and white. Then earth returned. They flew to the checkpoint, marked by a bright, blue flag before turning.

Morris spied the oily gray trail of Hank's bird before Hank realized his jeopardy.

Hank's motor sputtered. His craft dipped. He worked the controls, tyring to return to altitude, but the motor refused to cooperate. The autogyro lurched and bounced in the air, tipping toward a spin. Morris flew nearby, hoping the Bug could hold Hank's weight if he bailed out. Hank pounded his fists on the console, a useless outburst Morris cursed until the panel broke loose, revealing Hank's true goal. He tugged wires loose from underneath it, and, struggling to keep control of his bird, stripped them with his teeth. He tapped them together in search of a spark, which refused to come.

Morris grabbed his cane, stowed by his feet, and unscrewed its top. "Hank!" he screamed.

He threw the object into Hank's cockpit.

Startled, Hank recovered his composure as he recognized the lifeline Morris had thrown him. He unreeled the guide wire it contained, entwined it with the console wires, then switched on the battery. Steady electrical power flowed into the autogyro's works. Its motor sputtered, coughed, then stilled for a breath, during which the craft hung poised at the apex of a doomed arc — then reignited. The rotors spun, and Hank regained control. The dark cloud he'd trailed dissipated. Only half a dozen other aircraft remained in the challenge, all of them gaining on Hank and the Bug. With a roguish grin, Hank pushed his wounded bird to its maximum and pulled way in front.

"Damn him," Morris said. "Does he have a death wish?"

"You're doing too good a job of saving him," Marceline said, her voice fighting the wind. "You've made him feel invincible."

Scanning the terrain for new threats, Morris allowed himself to hope that no more awaited, but his hope vanished when a new autogyro rose from the forest directly in their path. Its design resembled Hank's but it bore no markings. It hovered as the competitors approached, then dipped forward on a collision course with Hank's craft. As it neared, Morris recognized the pilot, a flannel blanket still spread across her legs. His heart sank; a leaden sensation filled his entire body.

"Dear god," he said. "It's Dorrie!"

Marceline compensated for his shock and accelerated the Bug, bringing it close enough to Hank for Morris to read the confusion and horror on his friend's face.

Hank veered off course to avoid a crash. Dorrie, seemingly determined to force one, flew after him. Or did she intend to send Hank to the ground, Morris wondered, as she maneuvered Hank lower toward the treetops. Hank would fly himself into the earth before harming Dorrie. She had found the perfect weapon against him, herself, only Morris couldn't fathom what compelled her to use it.

"She means to crash him," Marceline said. "What do we do?"

In the heartbeat available to decide, Morris's brain couldn't consciously catalog all the factors that formed his choice. The answer tasted bitter on his lips. "Save Hank."

He and Marceline flew the Bug between Dorrie and Hank, close enough for all of them to see each other's faces for a shard of a second. The Bug forced Dorrie to turn. Morris spun his flyer in a maneuver impossible for an autogyro and rammed Dorrie's craft. Two of the Bug's wings sheared off as Dorrie's bird tipped into a fatal spiral and plunged to the ground. It cratered with an eruption of earth, metal, and smoke. The damaged Bug, off-balance, remained in the air, buoyed by its helium bladder as it limped toward the crash site in a rocky clearing. Doubling back, Hank beat them there and landed.

By the time the Bug touched down, Hank had recovered Dorrie's body from the wreck and cradled her in his arms.

"We're leaving for New Alexandria this morning," Morris said.

Slouched on a work stool in his secret armory, devoid of its workers, Hank nodded. He refused to look Morris in the eye.

"Please know how terribly sorry we are, Hank. However we can help, we will," Marceline said.

"You've done enough." Hank's low voice quavered with grief, fury, and uncertainty. "You've done plenty."

Morris eyed a letter on a workbench behind Hank, who had carried the missive with him like a totem since he found it in Dorrie's pocket. Written in case of her death, it explained why she'd tried to sabotage and kill him. Hank had shared it with Morris and Marceline. It rambled about the horrors and tragedies of Dorrie's life, and how she idolized Hank—so much, in fact, she refused to let him become like the men who'd destroyed her world. She wrote of all the times she tried to persuade him to give up his death machines, of staging her crash to scare him from proceeding, of arranging the Gatling gun attack with a spy from the Eastern Europe cabal he feared, of tampering with his electrical system while helping him install the new part—and, if all else failed, her plan to throw herself at him. *Whatever it costs the world*, she wrote, *you must never become like them. You must keep all your goodness intact even if we both must die.*

"You have our support whatever you decide to do, Hank," Morris said.

"Shut up, Morris." Hank stood with fists clenched. "You've no idea what the future holds for this world. No idea at all. Whatever I decide? Ha! That decision has already been made for all of us. Now, go on, shut up, and get out of here."

Waiting for the elevator, Morris studied his old friend, who resembled a humbled giant, resting, regathering his strength and his fire.

THE HARLEM HELLFIGHTERS

DEREK TYLER ATTICO

May 15, 1918

LIKE WORLD WAR ONE, THE HOLES STARTED SMALL. DITCHES DUG WITH muscles, sweat, blood, and haste by boys that wanted to live long enough to become men. Then the ditches grew, expanded by men that wanted to return to their girlfriends, wives, and mothers.

Men that wanted to go home.

The ditches became trenches. Long, narrow interconnecting hallways dug twelve feet down and six feet across. Six feet to help you stay alive, with another six in case you weren't so lucky. Two hundred and fifty miles of trenches stretched through France and Belgium. Some housed hundreds of men, while others could only hold a dozen. They constituted subterranean worlds where men could sleep and piss and shit and dream of love and life.

All while they waged war.

There were trenches on both the German and French sides. Deeprooted scars in the earth that divided war from peace, liberation from subjugation, victory from defeat. Just above the trenches, at ground level, miles of barbed wire lay stretched out across the terrain, a last line of warning and defense. Bodies of animals and men could be found all along the length of the barbed wire, like pieces of rotting meat stuck between the teeth of some angry beast.

And on the board of this senseless game, in the vast space between where both sides kept their chess pieces, lay No Man's Land. A barren desert of dirt and death, where very little moved for very long. No Man's Land was ruled by the dead and those that presided over them.

Vultures and flies gorged themselves on the flesh of fools that dared to venture to the other side with the ambition of killing the neighbor that was their enemy. Craters the size of automobiles pockmarked the empty space, telling the tales of shelling that had failed with blackened holes and succeeded with crushed bone.

In a small observation post of sandbags and barbed wire inside No Man's Land, near a French trench, three men lay unmoving in the mud, bathed in the shadows.

Henry Johnson looked to his right at the two men he'd been on lookout duty with for the last three days, Truffaut and Roberts. Louis Truffaut was as pale as he was French, but he was also one of the most easygoing people Johnson had ever met, with piercing blue eyes and a boyish face that balanced out his inquisitive nature.

"Another quiet night," Johnson whispered. "Anything you want to talk about, Louis?"

Roberts kept his eyes peeled on No Man's Land, but his smile belied what he was thinking. "See. Now, you know you're gonna get Louis started," he said.

Louis Truffaut looked over at Johnson. Before a few days ago, he'd never met a Black American man. They were different from other Americans he'd met. They possessed a confidence and an ease that he didn't expect. Johnson had bronze skin with a medium build. The young man had a smile that was easy to greet and eyes that were easier to trust. At twenty-six, the American soldier seemed calmer and more in tune with himself and life than Truffaut did at thirty-two. But what he really didn't understand was the patriotism exuding from the man. "But this makes no sense to me," he whispered. "You both join your military, cross the Atlantic, and come all the way to France to fight for America, no?" he asked.

Johnson realized that while this was his first time across the Atlantic, he hadn't considered until now that his ancestor's first and only trip across the same ocean wasn't by choice. And even with that being said, America was still his home. "Yes," he replied to his new friend.

Truffaut now turned to Roberts. It was clear this younger Black man and Johnson were so close that the two men might as well have been brothers. Roberts was less rugged than Johnson, with a smaller frame and smoother features that made the young man look like he should be a young Hollywood movie star instead of a soldier. At only seventeen years old, it was clear Needham Roberts looked up to the older Johnson, sticking beside him even when he didn't have to. The more Louis thought about it, he realized Roberts did indeed act like Johnson's younger brother, idolizing Henry at every opportunity, but still, this teenager showed signs of becoming a fine man in his own right.

Truffaut wasn't surprised when Roberts admitted he'd lied about his age so he could fight in the war. Many young French boys had done the exact same thing, but unlike America, France was grateful when boys that looked like Roberts enlisted. "But your country won't let you fight with other Americans, so the only way your 369th infantry can fight is by being loaned to support the French, no?"

Roberts smiled. He knew that Louis was being polite. The 369th infantry was made up of all Black volunteers but, despite their training, they weren't allowed to fight on behalf of America. At least not alongside their white American counterparts. Thankfully the French agreed to take in the 369th temporarily and have the American unit fight with them. Roberts was thankful and wholeheartedly believed that the American military and people back home just needed to give them all a chance. "Yes," Roberts said, then added, "but that will all change once America sees us fighting for her!"

Truffaut looked back to Johnson, reminding himself to keep his voice down as he spoke. "So you fight for world freedom and for respect for your people, yes?" the Frenchman asked.

Henry Johnson looked over at his eager new friend and his young, old one. Roberts was too naïve, and Truffaut too hopeful. But he had to admit he'd heard similar questions many times before. He had a good-paying job as a mechanic for the Ford Motor Company, which wasn't very easy to come by in America. So when he gave it up to enlist, his friends thought he was crazy. They wanted to know why he was leaving his job to fight in a war that had nothing to do with him.

Johnson thought about what he told his friends as he answered Truffaut. "No, it's not that simple. We do it because —"

A low, metal-snapping sound pierced the darkness ending their conversation.

In unison, the three men turned toward the direction of the sound. No Man's Land, just beyond their observation post and much closer than expected. After a few seconds, they heard it again and again. Finally, Johnson identified the noise.

Someone cut the barbed wire ahead of them.

Johnson placed two fingers in front of his eyes and then pointed those fingers toward the sound. Understanding the silent message, Truffaut and Roberts began to crawl out of the makeshift sandbag outpost. From somewhere deep in No Man's Land, Johnson heard a cough that sounded more mechanical than biological.

A half second later, Louis's head exploded.

Blood sprayed in all directions, covering the faces of the two remaining men lying along either side of their friend. Roberts was about to say something when two men jumped him out of the shadows, both taller and bigger than Roberts. A trio of arms and legs went down into the mud. Johnson saw a glint of moonlight off of metal in one of the assailant's hands.

Why were the attackers using knives instead of guns?

Henry Johnson jumped up, grabbed his M1903 Springfield rifle, and stepped forward. He brought the rifle up to his face for a precision shot among the tangled flesh as his friend fought for his life, two-on-one, and Roberts didn't have much time. As Johnson lined up his shot, his peripheral vision caught the edge of a shadow to his left. Without hesitation, the Army soldier turned and fired, shooting a young German man squarely in the chest. As the soldier fell, two more behind him rushed forward. Johnson squeezed the trigger and let off two more shots in quick succession. Both approaching men fell to the muddy ground limp, like marionettes with their strings abruptly cut. In one quick motion, Johnson reached for the pistol on his left side with his right hand. He pointed the pistol into the air and fired the flare, illuminating the night sky and warning the French trench.

As Johnson dropped the pistol and turned back toward Roberts, something slammed into his right shoulder and nearly spun him around. Henry Johnson knew he'd been shot, more from the blood he could feel soaking the inside of his uniform than from any pain. He looked back to where he thought it came from, somewhere out in No Man's Land. Now, with a dwindling sunset afterglow across the killing fields, his eyes caught a glimpse of something unnatural approaching from several hundred yards away. Two shadows walking quickly toward his location, much larger than a man but still shaped like one, moving almost as fast as a tank.

Whatever they were, they would be visible soon.

Somewhere in an ocean of pain, shock, adrenaline, and confusion, a name floated to the surface.

Roberts!

Henry Johnson snapped his head back around to where his friend fought, realizing the bullet lodged in his shoulder slowed him down in more ways than one. But where three men had been struggling a few seconds ago, only one remained. A knife jutted from his neck. Johnson's gut clenched, and he fought the urge to cry out. In a few more seconds, the man's beating heart finished the knife's job, pumping the last few remaining pints of blood out of the severed artery. Johnson rushed over to the fallen figure then sighed with relief.

It wasn't Roberts.

Johnson looked out into the diminishing light. The black shroud of No Man's Land was about to reclaim the Germans and his friend. A few yards away, he saw the shadow of a man with another slung over his shoulder. The Germans hadn't killed Roberts. They were attempting to take him prisoner. Racing the dying light, Henry closed one eye and fought the pain in his shoulder. Bringing his M1903 bolt-action rifle back up to his face, he lined up his sight with the legs of the man hauling away his friend, took a breath, and slowly squeezed the trigger.

Nothing happened.

Johnson repeated the action, but again nothing happened. His firearm had found the most inopportune time to jam. Without thinking, Johnson set off into a sprint after his friend. Ignoring the one sacrosanct rule when you manned the observation post.

Never go into No Man's Land unless so ordered.

The space between the warring armies formed a chasm of death. Often during the day, sorties were attempted to take one side or the other. At night, as both sides tried to retrieve their wounded, sharpshooters picked off the uninjured soldiers, creating more wounded in a vicious cycle. By now, Johnson knew the French trench had seen and heard what was happening, but unless it was an assault on their line, the officers wouldn't fall into the trap of sending anyone else out to rescue one or two men, and rightly so. For the Germans, this was a win-win. If the French acted abruptly out of emotion and attempted rescue, they would be literally walking into the dark unprepared. If they did nothing, a lone soldier like Roberts could be captured and tortured for information.

One way or another, Johnson knew he had to get his friend back.

As he approached the German soldier carrying Roberts, Johnson flipped his rifle in mid-air, grabbed hold of the barrel with his left hand,

and used the butt of the weapon as a bludgeon against the enemy's head. The three of them tumbled to the ground. The German struggled to push through his rifle-induced stupor as he rolled and reached for his sidearm. Without hesitation, Johnson took out his bolo knife and plunged it through the man's eye. Pulling out his knife, Johnson noticed that the soldier wore black fatigues, not the traditional grey-green or brown fatigues worn by German troops. He also wore no rank markings or other identifiers, just a black-and-silver patch on his right shoulder. A monstrous wolf with the word FENRIR underneath.

A bullet zipped by Johnson going toward No Man's Land. He tracked back to where the shot had come from. Roberts had gained his feet but remained unsteady. The young man pointed a German gun with one hand and held his head with the other. Blood coated his face, whether his own or Truffaut's, Johnson couldn't say. He flinched as Roberts let off two more shots, screaming, "Behind you!"

Johnson turned to see about ten men in those same black fatigues coming toward them. Behind those men strode the two creatures he'd seen before. No longer in the distance, and out of the shadows and in the moonlight, he could see these weren't creatures at all, but mechanical constructs. Each stood about eight or nine feet tall, with triangular-shaped feet and tank-like treads for soles. Their legs were thick plates of metal that reached up and connected to a similar metal torso. The Wolf emblem from the soldier's patch etched each chest. The plate-armored arms, like the legs, had dividing joints, and there were no hands. Instead, where the right hand would be was a dual machine gun with an ammunition belt running up the outside of the shoulder. For the left hand, there was a large box-like attachment with four holes and what looked like the tips of rockets inside. The head of the creature confirmed what he feared. Metal grating protected the face of what was clearly a man inside this metal suit of death and destruction.

Roberts gave a quick, low whistle, getting Johnson's attention. The young man reached into his uniform and pulled out a Mills grenade. He pulled the pin and let go of the spoon on the side of the explosive device, activating its four-second fuse. Roberts threw the grenade over Johnson's head toward the advancing group and dove into a nearby crater. Johnson retrieved his own grenade from his kit, but instead of lobbing it, after pulling the pin, he tossed the deadly device like a bowling ball toward the approaching onslaught and dove for a crater of his own.

Screams immediately followed the explosions. Johnson crawled up to the edge of his crater and watched as several men staggered out of the blast radius on fire, only to be caught on barbed wire. About fifty yards away, Roberts had found another rifle and was picking off German soldiers as they stepped out of the smoke from the blast. "Thattaboy," Johnson said to himself, smiling.

Johnson was scanning for the machine-man monstrosities when one stepped out of the haze of smoke and flame. From this perspective, he noticed some kind of chassis on the back of the behemoth. His experience as a mechanic told him it was probably a good bet there was some kind of engine under that chassis. The machine-man was only about twenty yards away from Roberts. It pointed at him with its right arm and unleashed machine-gun fire in the soldier's direction. Roberts dove back into his crater for cover but had nowhere else to go. With him no longer firing, more men in black streamed from behind the metal-man monstrosity. The armored man himself lowered his right arm and raised his left, pointing it not toward Roberts' crater but at the French trench. Johnson watched in horror as the missiles illuminated the night. Two of the missiles set a section of the French trench aflame, dousing it in something that turned the night into day. The other two missiles were far more deadly. As they hit, they didn't explode but emitted a green gas among the French forces. Inhuman screams erupted from the trench. Johnson reached into his uniform pocket, took out his last grenade, and pulled the pin.

"Turn around slowly, American, or I will kill you where you stand," a German-accented voice said from behind Johnson.

Grenade in hand, Johnson turned around in the crater. Just a few feet away stood the nine-foot-tall mechanical creature. At this distance, it was clear that the behemoth was a brilliant work of engineering, with a man inside of it. More accurately, somehow, the Germans had put the best parts of a tank onto something that a soldier could wear. From behind the Man-Tank, Johnson heard the low hum of what sounded like an idling car engine and recognized the pungent aroma of diesel fuel in the air. It was clear to Johnson now that the chassis he saw on the back of the other mechanized soldier was indeed the protective casing covering the engine that powered the Man-Tank suit. The low hum told the mechanic everything he really needed to know. It sounded eerily similar to the engine on the Büssing A5P German armored car. A six-cylinder engine known for its reliability and power.

The artillery crater Johnson was in was four or five feet into the ground. As Henry looked up from this vantage point, the German machine seemed even more frightening. Henry smiled, doing his best not to show his fear, "I've already pulled the pin." Johnson raised his hand with the grenade so the German soldier could see he wasn't lying.

The Man-Tank pointed his machine gun at Johnson. "I know. It is the only reason you are not dead yet, American." The German soldier stepped backward, "Slowly, put the pin back in the grenade."

Johnson took the pin he'd been holding in his other hand and very, very slowly started to reinsert it.

The Man-Tank took another step back while keeping his gun trained on Johnson. A chuckle came from behind the metal face grating protecting the man inside. "Tell me, Hellfighter, after everything America has done to your people, you fight in their name. Why? You should be fighting with us!"

Johnson smiled. Since the 369th had joined the combat forces, the Germans themselves had named them the Höllenkämpfer — the Hellfighters. The Black American unit had turned the name given to them by their enemy into a badge of honor and made it their own, calling themselves the Harlem Hellfighters. The unit wanted the Germans to know exactly who was kicking their asses. Johnson realized now it wasn't by chance that these new Man-Tanks had attacked his unit. With the pin now halfway back into the grenade, Henry stopped and looked at the German. "We built America with our blood, sweat, and tears. America is our home."

Gritting against the pain in his shoulder, Johnson tossed the grenade over the Man-Tank's shoulder.

Stunned, the German soldier jerked backward, turning as he tried to follow the grenade's trajectory. The mechanized suit reacted to his involuntary motion, stumbling back and overbalancing. Johnson dove for cover at the base of the crater closest to the Man-Tank, and tried to make himself as small as possible, hoping any shrapnel would overshoot him.

As the soldier inside the Man-Tank landed on his side in the mud, the grenade detonated just ten feet away from him. Shrapnel tore into and through him. Johnson could feel biting white-hot shards dig into his leg. He screamed into the mud and fought to stay conscious as the edges of his vision blurred and darkened.

Johnson came to standing over the German Man-Tank. He didn't remember crawling out of the ditch and making it over to the death machine. The front of the armor had taken most of the damage from the grenade. The concussive blast and shrapnel had torn through the German's protective face grating, leaving a puddle of flesh and blood where the man's head should've been.

The popping of gunfire pulled Johnson's focus away from the dead man-machine at his feet and a hundred yards away across No Man's Land. Remarkably, Roberts was still alive and in the fight. The young man crouched behind metal-and-wood barricades taking shots at the Germans with a rifle. In between taking shots, the young man looked at Johnson and shouted something, but he couldn't make out what his friend was screaming. Henry looked back at the Germans surrounding the second Man-Tank that Roberts was firing at.

Then he understood.

That Man-Tank had exhausted its munitions and missiles. They were reloading him, and there wasn't much time.

Johnson knelt next to the Man-Tank he'd killed. Hot searing streams of pain tore up and down his leg. The American blinked hard, pushing away the shell shock and his body's impulse to pass out again. Amazingly, Johnson noticed that the engine for the Man-Tank still ran and appeared to be relatively undamaged. This was good because Johnson guessed that the engine powered the suit's mobility and weapons. The pungent odor of diesel now forced him wide awake as he examined the mech. Tubes ran from what had to be the primary and backup fuel tanks into the engine. Johnson realized the stench of diesel was so strong because the primary fuel tank was busted, probably when the Man-Tank fell. If what he had in mind was going to work, he had to keep the engine running, if only for a few more minutes.

This may have been a man wearing a tank, but now that he could see it all up close, Johnson realized the technology wasn't anything he hadn't seen as a mechanic. He knew he needed to switch the fuel line from the primary to the backup tank. Replacing a fuel line is something he'd done a thousand times before, but he had to do this one with the engine running and not blow himself up in the process.

No problem.

Johnson reached out for the fuel line, but his hands shook so badly that he had to stop. Taking a breath, Johnson realized what he needed to do right now.

Stop thinking.

In a series of swift actions, the mechanic tied off the main fuel line, isolating the busted tank. Then he took the backup line and fed it into the primary housing. After securing the line, Johnson stopped and waited a moment to see if the engine would sputter and stall, but it didn't. With one hurdle overcome, the mechanic moved on to the next.

Then Johnson noticed what he was looking for.

On the armor, where the man's ribcage would be, there was a small red lever on the right side. Johnson pulled the lever toward him, and the armor splayed open, revealing seams he hadn't noticed before. The dead officer inside was strapped into some kind of harness within the body of the machine. As quickly as he could, Johnson unbuckled the brown leather straps, took hold of the corpse, and began to pull him out of the metal contraption. Oddly, the pain from his shoulder was bearable, but what worried him was that he could barely feel his left arm. With one final heave, Johnson pulled the carcass out of the machine. A few seconds later, gunfire erupted around him, spraying dirt and mud everywhere. The Germans were nearly finished reloading the Man-Tank. He knew this because it ignored Roberts and turned in his direction.

"Shit," Johnson mumbled under his breath and slipped into the machine.

Johnson tried not to think about why the Man-Tank was warm and wet as he strapped himself in. His hands and feet disappeared into areas he could tell had controls in them, but they were designed to be operated by touch and not by sight.

Great.

Johnson thought about all the times he lay under a car with a wrench in his hand, fixing something not by sight but by how it felt, and knew this was no different. Both hand controls felt basically the same. There was a trigger the hand naturally wrapped around and a switch that toggled left and right. In the right hand, there seemed to be something added, a small lever. Henry used his thumb to pull the lever down, and the suit closed around him.

Gunfire from the German rifles bounced off the metal behemoth's side. "Damn," Johnson said, smiling.

The foot controls had pedals in both feet, and then it dawned on Johnson. Even with his experience as a mechanic, he had no idea how to get this thing up. He thought this Man-Tank would be his salvation, but now he realized it would probably be his coffin.

The other Man-Tank faced him squarely now. It opened up with its machine guns. Johnson instinctively raised his hands over his face. He could hear the suit's metal gears and pulleys responding instantly to his body's actions. The gunfire hitting his metal forearms sounded like rain falling on his tin roof back home in North Carolina. When the gunfire stopped, Johnson knew he'd have one last chance.

The rockets.

The missiles were his last and only chance of survival, but he didn't know which side of the switch was for bombs and which was for gas. If he chose the wrong one, he'd not only be signing his death warrant, but Roberts's also.

As the gunfire stopped, while still on his back, Johnson pointed his mechanized left hand toward the other Man-Tank and surrounding Germans. "Fuck it," he whispered as he toggled the switch to the left and fired twice. The rockets raced out of their small silos on command, the first hitting the other Man-Tank directly in the chest, the second hitting the German soldiers next to him.

Both exploded on impact.

Johnson could see Roberts running over to him. The young man limped badly, and his right arm hung lifeless, but his smile told Johnson everything he needed to know. Johnson lay back and breathed a sigh of relief. This time as unconsciousness rose to claim him, he didn't resist it.

Footnote: Henry Johnson, Needham Roberts, and the exploits of the Harlem Hellfighters are real individuals and situations that inspired this story. For more information on these American heroes, we encourage you to visit: https://en.wikipedia.org/wiki/Henry_Johnson_(World_War_I_soldier)

Under Amber Skies

Maria V. Snyder

I haven't seen my father in months. Not since I overheard the rumblings of war in town. According to my mother, he has retreated to his basement workshop, not to be disturbed. Every night, I fall asleep listening to the comforting sounds of metal clanking, machinery humming, and a hammer banging.

Every morning my mother makes me breakfast using my father's Chef's Helper device—a gleaming sleek cooker. Even with the kitchen gadgets, deep craters of exhaustion hang under her brown eyes. Her pale face is lined with strain and she moves like an automaton. I offer to take a turn assisting father at night.

"No, Zosia. Your father is working to keep Poland safe from the Nazis. You will only distract him and it is too vital. We all must make sacrifices during these uncertain times."

The Chef's Helper beeps then trundles to my plate. Halfway across the table, it stops with a screech of metal. It strains and shakes. I pounce on it, dragging it closer as I yank my screwdriver from my pocket. Popping open the control panel, I quickly adjust the tension on the mechanical limbs. After rummaging in a basket filled with an assortment of parts, I find a replacement gear for the broken one. Fixed, I set Chef's Helper back on the table. It quivers for a moment then resumes its journey. When it reaches my plate, it squats and deposits a steaming heap of slightly singed scrambled eggs.

I point to the Chef's Helper. "See? I can help him. I won't be a distraction." I try.

She ignores me. No surprise, as she's a firm believer in the children-should-be-seen-and-not-heard adage.

I gnaw on my bottom lip, debating if I should ask her about Inek. He too has disappeared, but for very different reasons. "Mother has Inek—"

"Zosia Jadwiga Nowak, you are not to mention his name to me again! Do you understand?"

"Yes, ma'am." My lip throbs. I taste blood from clamping down on what I really want to say to her.

"Good." Handing me a list of supplies, she says, "I need you to go into Leba today."

"But Father needs more amber—"

"And it will still be on the beach for you to collect for tomorrow." She snaps. "I don't know why Casimir insisted on decorating his inventions with that useless amber. It's impractical. I'm so glad he's now concentrating on *vital* machines. Poland will become a force to be reckoned with. Then the Nazis and the rest of Europe will be terrified of us!" Glowing with national pride, my mother hustles me out the door.

I could have told her why Father uses amber, but she never asks me for my opinion or wishes to have a conversation with me. Instead, she orders me about as if I'm a Polish soldier, sending me to fetch supplies. Mother has swallowed the propaganda about being ready for the war. I shouldn't be surprised. She's been a staunch patriot since forever. There were only two Queens of Poland throughout history, and my middle name, Jadwiga was one of them. Anna was the other. If it wasn't for my father's protests, I would have been named for both of them.

Perhaps if my name was Anna Jadwiga, I'd stand up to her. I'd refuse to be ordered about. I'd demand to see my father. But I'm just Zosia, named for my father's sister who died in the first World War.

Outside my home, I clutch the paper and a purse full of zlotys. Dark gray smoke pours from the chimney and stains the bright blue sky. Our wooden two-story house appears deceptively small as it huddles in the middle of our farm.

Although calling it a farm is being kind. Weeds choke the fields, the pasture fence is broken and rotted with decay. Our single cow has long since wandered away.

I fetch my wagon from the barn. The roof droops at a dangerous angle, but it's quite safe. My father allowed the outer walls to fade into dilapidation while he strengthened the inner ones, keeping his workshop hidden inside. The windows even trick the eye, allowing light to enter. But if you try and peer through them, all you'd see is black.

When the barn was deemed too small, he moved his workshop underground. Then my nights were filled with the scrapes of shovels, the chugging of augers, and the smell of damp earth while the barn was filled with mounds of dirt and rocks. I always wondered why he hid the piles.

A slight sound grates against the normal morning noises. I pause to listen and catch a flutter of squeaky wings. Scanning our farm, I search for the source. The Nazis have developed winged creatures to use for spying on their enemies. My pulse beats out a quick march, but all I see are real birds.

Unease crawls along my skin as I settle in the seat at the front of my wagon. I press the ignition button. Its small engine puffs out two tiny black clouds before settling into the quiet purr I'm used to. Since the day is so bright, I toggle on my umbrella. Sized just for me, the wagon resembles a miniature truck and has been one of my favorite projects I worked on with my father.

Steering the wagon, I recall his deep laugh and his grease-stained beard as the tires buzz over the dirt path. Every half mile or so, a bright flash of sunlight grabs my attention and I spot one of my father's machines working in the fields of our neighbors' farms. His Mole Plow digs deep grooves in the soil and a Beaver Saw's sharp whine cuts through the air as its blades cut through wood. Because of his equipment, our hamlet near Leba is prosperous. I'm sure my father would have been content to create farm apparatuses for years.

Except the threat of war creeps toward us. And a few of our neighbors claimed to have seen the gleam of the Nazi's spy owls in the trees and have smelled the diesel fumes from them.

We live on the very northern tip of Poland at the edge of the Baltic Sea. The supposedly Free City of Danzig is east of us—supposedly because the city's population is seventy percent German. And looming behind Danzig is East Prussia, also full of Germans. Across the narrow Polish Corridor to our west is Germany. We're almost boxed in by Nazis.

Jula's strident voice calls, jolting me from my train of thought. She waves me down. I brake. Her long ponytails bounce as she jumps in my wagon. She talks nonstop during the rest of the trip to town. Rattling on about boys, fashions, and the war. I let her words flow around me like the hot August air.

Instead, I focus on Father's Octopus Pluckers working in Teos's apple orchard. An odd clunk interrupts the cadence of the metallic pincers. If Teos fails to oil that joint soon, he'll be bringing one of the Pluckers back to us for repairs. Perhaps I should —

"Zosia, are you listening to me?"

"Of course."

"I'm glad you're not helping him with his metal beasts anymore. Aren't you glad not to have grease under your fingernails all the time?"

"Jula, why do you think I'm not helping my father?" I ask.

"Because of the war."

"Why would the war matter?"

"You haven't seen his new machines?"

"What new machines?"

"War machines, of course," she says. "It's all hush-hush. The Polish government's involved, and they say once he's done the Nazis will be too scared to cross the border."

If it's all hush-hush, then why does everyone know about it? Instead of pointing out the obvious to Jula, I concentrate on navigating over a set of deep ruts.

Eventually, the wagon clatters over cobblestones, announcing our arrival in the heart of Leda. The buildings are all huddled tight together as if they can't stay upright without the help of their neighbors. Townspeople fill the narrow streets with their loud voices, drowning out my wagon. Horses clop and carriage wheels thump and clunk. The rare automobile chugs by, followed by an occasional lumbering truck. To me, the sounds are raw and unrefined. Noise.

Jula and I part company as she heads to the pharmacist to purchase a tonic for her mother. The hardware supply store is a refuge of calm. Inside the scent of sawdust, metal, and grease mix into a familiar aroma. The shopkeeper hustles to take my order as the other customers drift closer to see what parts are carried out to my wagon. I must admit to my own curiosity as each item is placed inside, wondering why my father needed that particular device or gadget, imagining what I'd build from the various bits of machinery.

"…could be for a big trench builder for our boys," one man says about a stack of metal scoops.

"He's not going to dig trenches," his friend chides. "They're for a weapon. Maybe one that can run right through the Nazis."

"Those springs could launch bombs," another says.

"Or could help with suspension for a huge walking machine," says the first man.

Their guesses get wilder, and a couple are physically impossible, but I don't bother to teach them the laws of physics. My hard-earned knowledge came from working with my father over the years, building gadgets like the Poodle Pooper Scooper. It resembled a Poodle with copper wires for hair and four metal legs. It even barked. It ran around outside, but instead of leaving droppings, it cleaned them up with its wide tail. During those late-night sessions, we had such fun until…

I shy away from thoughts of war. Instead, I notice one customer staring at me with a keen interest. I ignore him. But when I pass by him to pay for my purchases, I smell the faint tang of machine oil. The hair on my arms stands up in warning.

After I receive my change, I bolt from the shop. Thankfully, the strange customer doesn't follow me. I wait for Jula at the place we parted. An odd creepy sensation slides between my shoulder blades like I'm being watched. I search the streets, but no one is staring at me.

My father said my imagination would get me into trouble someday. I wonder if today is that day. Or is today the day I need to be smart? I run my finger over the clear crystal of my wristwatch. The numbers and hands are crafted from pieces of amber. Below the face, tiny gears spin, keeping time. It looks so delicate, yet the watch is thick and heavy on my wrist. My father gave it to me on May 22, 1939, the day I turned eighteen.

I remembered when he hooked his finger under my chin to pull my gaze away from his marvelous gift to meet his, and said, "Zosia, this will tell you when it's time."

"Time for what?" I asked.

"Time to be smart. Time to stand up for yourself." He refused to explain anymore, and the next day he disappeared. Well, not completely as my mother claims he comes in late at night to check on me. And I have a collection of the little presents he occasionally leaves for me on my bedside table. Smiling, I recall the miniature amber statue of a girl with springs for her hair. I still haven't figured out how to turn her on.

Jula is slow to return. The other shoppers ignore me as I scan the various storefronts. My attention snags on Inek and his three younger brothers—all blonds—sitting on the steps of the butcher's shop at the opposite end of the street. Probably waiting for their father to finish haggling over the price of beef.

Inek's family's cattle farm is about two kilometers away from our house. Inek used to work at our farm, helping me with the chores. That was before my father caught us kissing behind the house a month before my birthday. Father, wearing an oversized pair of crystal and amber spectacles, waved his large wrench and chased Inek, yelling at him to stay away. Inek didn't come back, to my mother's delight. She never liked him.

Inek catches me staring and frowns. I jerk my gaze away, but the damage is done. Even though I'm hurt that he hasn't tried to contact me this summer, my insides still twist tight. My mouth goes dry in an instant. I can't help remembering the impish spark in his sky-blue eyes, his sense of humor, his wide smile, or the way his long fingers tangled in my hair.

I tuck a few curls behind my ear but know it's hopeless. Most of the long strands have sprung from my braid by now. My mother once claimed in exasperation that my curls were a force of nature. My father agreed, saying the color of my hair matched the color of the Baltic Sea's amber. He then proceeded to use a few strands of my hair to build a very accurate rain detector.

I'm jolted from my memories by two men who block my view. One look at their black suits, fedoras, and dour faces and I know they're from the government. Problem is, which one? Germany's or Poland's?

The thin-faced man on the left says in German, "Miss Nowak, we'd like a word with you." The language isn't a clue as most people around here speak both German and Polish.

The suit on the right touches my elbow. He gestures to a side street, and I catch a glimpse of a Luger holstered on his belt. "In private," he says. His hand remains on my arm.

My heart rate spikes, but there's nothing I can do as the men guide me to a quieter place. I catch a whiff of machine oil and fear rolls through me.

Thin-face asks, "Where is your father, Miss Nowak?"

Surprised by the question, I reply in German, "At home."

They exchange a glance.

The man holding my elbow says, "No one is at your house. Where are the Poles hiding him?"

Cold sweat drips down my back. "My mother—"

"Gone, too."

Unable to comprehend, I stare at Thin-face. "They were there this morning."

His expression softens a tiny bit. "Did you see your father today?"

"No, but—"

"When's the last time you saw your father, Miss Nowak?"

He sees the answer in my face, but asks, "How long ago?"

"Two, maybe three months," I say.

Elbow-man swears. His fingers tighten around my arm, digging into my skin. "Now what?" he asks his partner.

Thin-face studies me. His gaze lingers on my wristwatch. "We have his daughter. Perhaps we can use her to lure her father from his hiding place." He grabs my watch, ripping it from the leather strap.

"Hey!" I yell. "That's mine."

Elbow-man slaps me, ordering me to be quiet. Pain spreads from my cheek as tears well.

Holding my birthday present in his palm, Thin-face says, "This will provide the necessary proof."

It's almost as if my watch knows it's the center of attention. A strident clicking emanates from it and then an extraordinary thing happens. Metal legs unfold from the sides of the watch. The gears inside spin faster and faster. In mere seconds it transforms into a metallic crab, complete with two sets of nasty-looking pincers. Thin-face is fascinated until the crab grabs his finger.

Its claw cuts through the skin, exposing metal. A blue spark arcs through Thin-face's hand. He yelps and knocks the crab off with his other hand. It immediately scrambles sideways toward Elbow-man and clamps onto his ankle. Again, the electric hiss and blue bolt.

Elbow-man releases my arm to swipe at the crab. Thin-face is yanking at his unresponsive arm.

Inek appears in the midst of the chaos, urging me to run. I race after him. We weave through the streets and alleys until we're certain the… men haven't followed us. Then we collapse to the ground, gasping for breath.

Inek recovers faster than me. "Were they Nazi agents?"

I connect the clues—machine oil, metallic limbs, and the comment about Poles. "Yes," I puff.

"Enhanced?"

"Oh yes."

Inek curses. "Did they capture your father?"

"No. They were looking for him."

"Good." Inek relaxes. "Someone in the village must have warned him."

Over two months ago. As my fear ebbs, my irritation increases. My mother has been lying to me. Then I remember what Thin-face said.

"Mother!" I jump to my feet and run in the direction of home.

Inek catches up. "What about your mother?"

"The Nazis said she's gone."

"She's probably escaped with your father."

"No. My father's been gone for months."

Inek grabs my shoulders and stops me. "Wait a minute."

I'm struck by how tall he has grown since I saw him last. Inek's suspenders strain over his muscular chest. His white shirt is untucked and stuck to his sweaty skin. The early August heat has been hotter than normal. I'm sweating as well, but I resist the temptation to wipe my brow.

"I need to find her." I try to push his arms away, but they're solid muscle.

"I understand but think about it. The Nazis know where you live."

His matter-of-fact statement sends icy daggers into my heart. They know where I live. Two separate pieces of information click together in my mind. The Nazis have been watching us, and my mother's been putting on quite the show for them. It explains all those nights of mechanical noises, the smoke puffing from our chimney, and her exhaustion.

Pride that she has been fooling them into thinking my father was still at home wars with my anger over being kept in the dark.

"If you return home now, the Nazis will find you again," Inek says. "You need to hide until we can locate your mother."

He's right, but my desire to return to my house overrules logic. "What if she left me a message?"

He bites his lip as he considers.

"And I'll need a change of clothes and money." I left my wagon and supplies behind. "I'll go after dark."

"We'll go," Inek says. "You can't go alone."

"Why not?" I snap. "I'm quite capable of taking care of myself. It's not safe for your family. Or you. The Nazis are scarier than my father."

Inek squeezes my shoulders and anger flashes across his face. But he drops his arms. "You're not going alone. We'll cut through the fields while it's light and then wait until dark."

I open my mouth to protest, but a familiar clicking sounds behind me. Spinning around, I see the metallic crab, but not the Nazis — a minor relief until I realize it's heading straight toward me. Fast. I step back automatically as Inek hunts for a weapon.

Afraid of its dangerous pincers and electric shock, I hug my arms to my chest. My fingers brush the leather strap still wrapped around my wrist and I finally remember the crab was a gift from my father. Feeling a bit foolish about my panic, I crouch down.

"Get back," Inek yells.

"It's okay." I press my hand flat on the ground.

The crab climbs to the strap. Humming and clicking, it retracts its legs and pincers and reverts back into my watch. I tug on it, but it is secured to the leather.

Inek stares at my watch. "And you wonder why your father scares me."

After we make sure the Nazis didn't follow my watch-crab, Inek and I hike through the fields. I hold up my skirt as I'm careful not to crush the plants with my work boots. We keep out of sight. There is no breeze and the heat presses on my skin. My tunic is soon soaked with sweat. Insects buzz around my head and our footsteps seem overly loud.

Something's wrong. I stop, gazing at the rolling countryside.

"Did you see someone?" Inek asks.

"No. It's just… Too quiet." Another sweep of the neighboring farms confirms my suspicions. "My father's machines are gone."

"Nazis probably stole them," Inek says. "You can't be too surprised. His machines are efficient, compact, and don't require a heavy combustion engine or diesel fuel. They probably want to tear them apart and see how they work."

He pauses and I wait for the inevitable question.

"Do you know what fuels them?" he asks.

"No." I lie to him because my father swore me to secrecy after I figured it out on my own. He worried the Nazis would learn the secret. My father refused to tell my mother or anyone else. When asked, he deadpans that it is the sea air—the Baltic's very own electrons that power his equipment.

"Can the Nazis figure it out?"

"I've no idea." Which is true. My father rigged the power block on his machines to incinerate the fuel when it was tampered with, but I don't know if it works or not.

Inek and I walk for a while in silence. My stomach growls and I long for water. When we reach the woods that border my home, we stop and wait for dark. It's hard for me to sit there doing nothing. Worry over my mother's disappearance churns inside me. And where is my father? Does he know the danger he's put us in? Does he care?

I search my memories for any clues to his whereabouts. My parents arguing bubble to the surface. My mother insisting he help the war effort, his quiet response, and Mother using my name as a weapon. I also recall my mother flinging his Catfish Rug Sweeper—a vacuum cleaner— into the kitchen wall. Unable... or rather unwilling to explore those events further, I ask Inek about his family.

Inek chats aimlessly about his brothers and how their antics have gotten them in trouble. I realize I've been so preoccupied with my own problems that I forgot Inek left his brothers to help me.

"Will your family be worried about you?" I ask.

He shrugs. "Probably not."

"I guess they're used to you running off without saying a word."

Inek's expression flattens. He gives me a cold stare before he stalks away.

Alone with my thoughts isn't fun. I try to think of happier days. Like when I mastered the installation of the reticulating gears needed to move a four-legged device. Or when my father beamed with pride after I designed my first gadget—a page-turning music stand. Or when I spent hours and hours on the beach with both my parents. As I played in the sand, my father would collect amber while my mother dug for clams. My heart lurches as I remember the day when I was eight years old, and a green crab bit my toe. I yowled and begged my father to build a metallic fish to eat all the crabs in the sea.

Instead, he drew me into his lap. Beads of salt water clung to the ends of his short curls and grains of sand peppered his beard. "Zosia, the crab didn't bite you out of meanness or anger," he said. "You were probably going to step on her, and she was defending herself."

"Or her babies," my mother chimed in.

"Yes, that's it," he said. "Mothers are very protective, and she didn't want you hurting her family. You see they're planning a very long journey to Finland to attend the king of the crabs' wedding." Then he proceeded to tell the most outrageous story about the mother crab's trip across the Baltic, and how, in the end, she protected the future crab queen from a giant herring.

I touch my watch, trying to imagine the protective mother crab's shape in the gears, but am unable to focus due to the tears in my eyes.

Inek returns a few hours after he stormed off. He brings sugar beets and a jug of water from a neighbor's house. The beets taste delicious.

"Mr. Sobczak said the Nazis have been posing as Polish officials and going house to house asking questions about your family, and confiscating your father's machines," Inek says. "No one has seen your mother. And he thinks the Nazis have left the area, but it makes sense that they would leave someone, or a few of their spy owls behind to wait for you. You're going to walk into a trap. Come to my house. My mother will—"

"No. I need to see for myself. I know it's dangerous and I appreciate your help and the beets. You've done more than enough. Go home, Inek."

"No." Inek sits down. He leans back on a tree trunk and crosses his arms.

It takes a long time for the sun to set this far north. A long time of sitting in uncomfortable silence. Complete darkness finally descends after midnight. The chirp and trill of the nighttime insects help fill the emptiness, but as we approach my house from the back field, the silence is eerie.

No lights shine. The doors are closed. No smoke from the chimney. The place already has an abandoned feel.

Inek remains outside to watch for the Nazis as I sneak toward the house. The moon is three-quarters full and gives off enough light to illuminate the steps to the back door, which is unlocked.

I slip into our kitchen and stifle a gasp. The floor is littered with broken plates and glasses. Drawers hang open or have been flung to the ground. Careful not to step on any debris, I look for a note or some clue as to where my mother has gone. Our table has been broken in two and most of the chairs smashed into splinters. The rest of the house is in the same state as the kitchen. Outrage and fear churn in my stomach as I realize the Nazis have taken all of Father's machines.

In my room, I grab my tools and gather a few things from where they had been carelessly flung and shove them into a knapsack. Except for the statue, the Nazis have taken my father's gifts. I find another one of Father's gadgets in one of the pockets of my bag. It's a bug light and it's the same flat round shape as my watch, except it's bigger than my palm and amber covers the entire face. When I twist the bottom, the amber glows with a soft orange light.

Throwing the knapsack over my left shoulder, I clutch the bug light in my right hand as I go down to the cellar. My father's workshop is a mess. What couldn't be taken has been destroyed. A quick look around confirms that all his tools are gone. The amber I collected for him has been strewn about. More amber than I'd expected, but when I consider my mother has been down here making nothing but noise and smoke, it made sense.

I spot a stack of papers half hidden under an overturned workbench. Odd. I yank it free. The papers are tied with copper wire. My name is written on the top in an unfamiliar hand. I take them with me as I return to the kitchen.

The drawer where my mother keeps her purse has been upended, but underneath I find her purse still bulging. Strange that the Nazis would leave the money behind.

"Zosia," Inek whispers from the doorway. "I heard voices. Let's go!"

I turn off the light, shove the papers and purse into my knapsack, and join him. We press against the back wall, listening.

"I saw a light," a man's rough voice says in German. "Check the house, I'll go around the back."

Boots crunch on the gravel. My heart slams in my chest, beating a frantic rhythm. Inek points and we slip around the side. More voices call out, growing louder. Lights fill my house. If we stay here, we'll be caught. I gesture to the barn. Inek nods.

The desire to run pulses through my legs, but we keep an even and quiet pace. Every inch of my skin burns as I strain to listen for the shout of discovery. We reach the barn and I thank my father for keeping all our hinges well-oiled. Or should that be my mother?

Inek and I climb up the side of one of the dirt piles and crouch behind it. My hope that they give up searching when they find the house empty shatters with the shuffle of footsteps.

"Gimme that light," a man orders.

A yellow glow fills the barn and casts a shadow on the wall.

"She has to be here," another voice says. "Footprints."

My whole body is shaking, but I don't want Inek to get caught. "Stay here," I whisper to him. Then I rip off my watch, drop it, and, before I can chicken out, I step into view. Holding my hands wide, I flinch when they shine the light on me.

"Don't shoot. I surrender," I say.

"Come down nice and slow," one of the men says.

"Told you she'd come home," his companion says.

I slide down the pile. The noise of my passage masks the sound of my clicking watch. Except the clicking grows louder and is joined by others. Dozens of metallic crabs erupt from the dirt pile. They swarm toward the two Nazis, who yell and shoot at the skittering mass.

Inek grabs my arm and pulls me from the barn. Soon we're running full out. Shouts and shots follow us, but we don't stop. We're a kilometer away before we slow to a walk. I'm amazed I'm still clutching my knapsack.

"That was… incredible," Inek says. "I'm glad you knew they were there."

I don't bother to tell him they surprised me. I hoped my crab would attack like before, but I'd no idea there were more. Another reminder that my parents have been keeping secrets from me. What else have they hidden?

Inek leads me to his home. I'm too exhausted to protest, but I plan to leave in the morning. Light glows from the living room and Inek's father and mother are at the door before we reach it. Mrs. Adamczuk hugs her son while his father demands an explanation.

"Nazis," Inek says.

I let him explain. His mother doesn't hesitate. She takes me upstairs, lends me one of her nightgowns, and tucks me into Inek's bed. I haven't been tucked in since I was six and my mother chided my father for babying me.

"You're welcome to stay as long as you like," she says, sweeping a stray curl from my eyes. "Inek can sleep in Marcin's room."

After she leaves, I breathe in Inek's musky scent as the day's horrid events swirl in my mind. I don't think I'll be able to sleep, but I do.

When I wake in the morning, I notice my watch has returned during the night. It's creepy and comforting at the same time. The watch is covered with dust, and even after traveling two kilometers to find me, it still keeps the correct time. I wonder what my father meant by knowing when it was time to be smart. My mother fooled me for months, and the Nazis almost captured me. Not very smart.

Getting out of bed is difficult, I'm stiff and sore from running. Mrs. Adamczuk's nightgown reaches the floor. She's tall and thin like her husband and sons—all blue-eyed. Unlike my family. We all have brown hair, but I inherited my father's gray-green eye color and his cursed hair.

I sit on the floor of Inek's room and sort my meager possessions. Money, a clean blouse, my favorite green skirt, the amber statue— which I now realize my mother built, the bug light, and the stack of papers. I untwist the copper wire and realize the papers are letters. Perhaps my mother or father has explained everything to me, but instead I learn about something unrelated to the Nazis or the war effort.

When I finish reading the last one, tears flow down my cheeks. The letters started out so sweet, then confused, and finally angry. Not that I blame the letter writer. I'd get upset if my letters went unanswered.

Conflicting emotions overwhelm me. I want my mother to comfort me, and I want to yell at her for concealing these letters. After a few minutes, the tightness in my throat eases. I wash, change into my clean clothes, and search for Inek's family.

The six of them are sitting around the kitchen table, finishing breakfast. The affable chatter ceases the instant they notice me. Inek's three younger brothers stare as if they've never seen a girl before. Their mother muses their hair and shoos them out to work.

"Sit, Zosia," she says. "You must be famished." She bustles about, filling a plate for me.

I sit across from Inek, who is beside his father. The resemblance is striking and it's like seeing into Inek's future. Inek's hair is sleep-tousled, but his gaze is hard. I drop mine to the table. I hope I can talk to him in private and explain about those letters.

Mrs. Adamczuk cooks the food by hand. Their kitchen is free of anything more complicated than a manual can opener. She sets a dish full of scrambled eggs in front of me. The smell causes my stomach to growl, and I can't seem to eat fast enough.

"The gossip in the village is at full steam," Mr. Adamczuk says when I finish shoveling eggs into my mouth. "Most of it is pure nonsense, but I'm pretty certain no one has seen your mother, and she's not hiding with one of our neighbors. And the Nazis don't have her."

"That we know," I say. "They could have gotten her while Inek and I were hiding."

"True. Do you have family nearby?"

"No. My parents are from Warsaw, and what's left of their families live there." My father couldn't stand the city. According to my mother, he dragged us all out here for peace, privacy, and the sea. I think about my mother's family. Most of them died in various wars and battles.

"Let's assume she's free," Mr. Adamczuk says. "Do you know where your mother might go?"

I imagine that I'm her and have just escaped from the Nazis. What would I do next? I groan at my idiocy. "She probably went into town to find me. And saw me with the Nazis!"

Mr. Adamczuk says, "You can't know that for sure. But if that's the case, and she didn't witness your escape, she might believe they have you."

I jump to my feet. "I have to go back to Leda."

"No. You will stay here, and I'll go," he says.

Inek straightens. "Her mother or father might be able to find her here." He points to my watch. "There must be some sort of homing device in the strap."

As he explains to his parents about the crab, I'm remembering the others. How they crawled from the piles of dirt. How my father delighted in camouflaging his gadgets, and in fooling the eye.

"Then it is settled," Mrs. Adamczuk says. "If some metal crab can find Zosia, then her family can as well. She will stay here."

But I'm far from feeling settled. Even after Inek and his father go to town just in case my mother is there. I help Mrs. Adamczuk, marveling at their uncluttered and quiet house. And the poor woman has to do all the housework herself! No devices or gadgets to help her. When all this is over, I'll build her an army of helpers.

She seems happy, chatting and paying me more attention than my own mother, asking me questions. But I'm only half-listening. Instead, I imagine that my mother has returned to our house to search for me or to confront the Nazis about her missing daughter.

We're sorting piles of laundry when it hits me. Conservation of mass — the piles of dirt and stone in the barn were much bigger than what could have been dug from the basement workshop. Either my father hid more devices under the dirt, or there was another room under our home.

If there is another workshop, then my mother could be hiding there! Or perhaps my father is there as well, and my mother hasn't been lying to me all these months. The room could also hold those vital war machines my mother talked about. Machines that could help Poland.

By the time Mrs. Adamczuk and I hang all the wet sheets out to dry, I'm determined to return to my house that night and seek out that room.

Inek and his father arrive with the news that no one has seen my mother or any clue as to her whereabouts. The lack of information only increases my desire to go home. I'm well aware Inek and his family will refuse to let me go, or Inek will insist on coming with me. But his family is so… caring. Their house is a home and not a building full of gadgets. They love each other and I will *not* endanger them or bring them any pain. If anything happens to Inek, Mrs. Adamczuk would be devastated.

Once the sun is fully set, I creep downstairs in stocking feet, carrying my boots. I leave a note, thanking them for their hospitality and explaining that I do not want to cause trouble for them. I'm very glad that I never had the chance to talk to Inek in private. It would have just complicated everything, and this way, he'll stay safe.

The back screen door creaks as I open it. I pause, but when the house remains quiet, I slip outside. Pulling on my boots, I shoulder my knapsack and head home. The moonlight is brighter tonight, and I worry my green skirt and light-brown blouse are too visible.

I'm careful to move without causing undue noise so it takes me twice the amount of time to reach the woods around our farm. Then I all but crawl. I stumble over a metal pod and realize it's one of the Nazi's spy owls. Dropping the hand-sized device, I back off. But the thing thumps on the ground—lifeless. Upon closer inspection, I find scorch marks along its body. It was zapped. I glance around but don't spot any of my little crabs. However, moonlight gleams from a few more dead owls.

When I reach the edge of our back field. I stop. Crouching low, I wait and watch as my heart taps a fast beat.

At first, the farm appears deserted, but a light shines from our kitchen window. When I'm sure there is no one lurking around the house, I step from my hiding place.

All of a sudden, an arm wraps around my stomach as a hand clamps over my mouth, muffling my cry of surprise.

"It's me," Inek whispers.

I relax, but he doesn't let go. His chest is pressed against my back.

"I knew you'd try something stupid. I just didn't think you would be *this* stupid." He sighs. "Can you at least answer a question for me before you're caught by the Nazis?"

Curious, I nod, and he removes his hand. "Did you get my letters?"

My heart rips in half as I say, "Yes."

He lets me go and steps away. I shiver as cool air touches my warm back.

"Why didn't you answer them?" he asks.

Glad he couldn't see my face, I close my eyes and say, "Letters are a coward's weapon. If you really wanted to be with me, you would have stood up to my father."

The silence eats at my resolve. I suppress the urge to spin around and tell Inek the truth.

Finally, in a low, flat voice he says, "Good luck with the Nazis."

A slight rustling sound and I know he's gone without having to glance behind me. Instead, I swallow my emotions down and inch closer to my house. Angry voices reach me first. Then the unmistakable thuds of a scuffle are followed by a crash.

Wild, horrible scenarios fill my mind and, after what feels like a thousand hours, I peek in the kitchen window. As I feared, my mother sits on a chair. Her lip is split and bleeding. Bright purple bruises dot her face. Six men—enhanced Nazis—surround her, asking questions about my father, but she keeps quiet. The Nazis stand stiff-limbed and awkward, probably from the encounter with my crabs last night. I recognize Thin-face and Elbow-man, but not the other four. I note

Thin-face's left arm is still immobilized and Elbow-man is balancing all his weight on his right leg.

Thin-face asks my mother a question about my father, but she refuses to answer. He strikes her. I marvel at her strength as I fight the desire to rush to her. Getting caught isn't on my agenda and would only add to her misery. Pushing the fear aside, I concentrate on the reasons that brought me here. I sneak over to the barn and slip inside.

Once I'm certain no one is hiding here, I twist on the bug light. The piles of dirt are smooth. The crabs erased their marks. A few broken ones litter the floor. I touch the face of my watch with my left index finger — the same finger my father used to draw my attention — and whisper, "It's time."

A pulse of light erupts from the face. Bug lights glow from the walls as crabs crawl from the dirt. Then the crabs work together, digging a tunnel into the piles. After a couple meters, they uncover a large metal pipe. I peer inside and see a distant orange glow. Who can resist the light at the end of the tunnel? Not me.

The pipe is more than big enough for me to crawl through. I'm about four meters in when a yelp echoes behind me. My crabs are attacking the Nazis. Good. Except the next curse sounds familiar. Scrambling back, I exit in time to see Inek cornered with his legs covered with crabs.

"No," I say, but they keep climbing. "Stop." They listen, clinging to Inek's trousers. I try, "Come here," and it works. They surround me like soldiers, waiting for orders. Handy. Could I send them after the Nazis holding my mother?

"Thanks," Inek says.

"What are you doing here?" I ask. "I told you —"

"I was halfway home when I figured it out."

"Figured what out?"

"You lied to me. I saw your confusion last night when you were sorting through the rubble of your kitchen. It just took me a while to match it to what you held in your hand. A stack of letters."

"Letters from my father to my mother," I say. "Go home, Inek."

"And that was my other clue. You've been trying so hard to protect me and my family. What better way to send me away than to tell me you don't care for me." He edges closer, careful not to step on the crabs. Who seem to be ignoring him.

"Go home," I say again. "Or I'll…"

"What? Send your little metal army after me?"

"Yes."

"Go ahead."

I point at Inek and say, "Attack." Nothing. I almost laugh at Inek's shocked expression. "En guard." Nothing. "Charge." Nothing.

"You were—"

"Testing to see which commands they obey," I say.

By now he's close enough to touch, and the crabs are still motionless.

"Tell me the truth, Zosia." Inek wraps his arms around my back. "Are you protecting me, or do you really wish me gone?"

"I can't… The Nazis have my mother."

"I'm truly sorry."

"You need to—"

He stops me with a kiss. Heat spreads through me and I'm the one deepening the kiss. Inek pulls me tight against him. Just for a moment, I forget the Nazis and my mother. Forget we are two separate beings.

He's the first to stop and draw back with an impish smile. "I was right."

"Yes, you solved the puzzle. Now go." I shoo.

"Not before *we* help your mother." He presses his lips together, jutting out his chin.

Too stubborn for his own good, fighting with him will just waste more time. "Fine. You can come along. But don't blame me if you get killed." Returning to the pipe, I crawl inside without waiting to see if he follows. My crab army does. Their metal legs clink and clatter behind me.

The tunnel ends at a set of stairs. Bug lights glow as I step down. By the time we reach the bottom, the entire room is lit. It's easily four times the size of the basement workshop.

This must be where my father built his war machines. Lethal-looking devices and gadgets line the shelves, schematics cover the far wall, and prototypes sit in neat rows on the ground. Tools and supplies are scattered as if my father left in a hurry. At the back of the room is a jumble of half-completed farm equipment as if carelessly discarded. It's next to a patch of bumpy ground. I wonder what is hidden beneath. More crabs?

"Wow," Inek says. "If this is what he left behind, imagine what he'll create to fight the Nazis."

I scan the room, searching for a device or weapon that could help free my mother. Finding a promising long-barreled gun, I pick it up and toggle the power button. Nothing happens. It remains dead in my hands. Odd. I walk around the lab, examining the items. Something feels… off.

Part of the far wall slides back, revealing my mother. She covers her gasp of surprise with her hand. Her face resembles raw meat. Before I can react, four Nazis rush in. My metal army scrambles toward them. The men aim their Lugers at Inek, me, and my mother, ordering me to stop the crabs or they will shoot. The crabs halt at my command.

Fear swells. Simple subtraction means two more Nazis are waiting upstairs. Dread churns in my chest.

"Zosia, what are you doing here?" my mother demands.

"Rescuing you," I say.

The Nazis find my answer amusing. The man pointing his Luger at my mother's temple says, "Drop your weapon."

I forgot about the useless device in my hand. Dropping it to the ground, I realize with a heart-lurching certainty that there is no way we can escape. The metal crabs no longer hold the element of surprise, and I won't risk my mother or Inek by using them.

Thin-face strolls around the room, inspecting the weapons. He tries a few of the smaller devices with his right hand. They're all like the long-barreled gun—powerless. He returns. No one has moved or spoken.

"Miss Nowak, your mother was… kind enough to show us your father's secret workshop, but she claims ignorance about what fuels your father's machines. What leaves behind that black oily residue. Perhaps with her daughter's life in jeopardy, she will be more cooperative," Thin-face says.

"I swear, I don't know," my mother cries. "No one knows except Casimir."

Thin-face exchanges a look with Elbow-man. I step forward as the loud report of gunfire fills the room. Inek jerks. A bright red stain spreads on his chest as shock spreads on his face. He crumples to the floor.

I rush over. Kneeling next to him, I press my palm over his wound. "Damn it, Inek. Why couldn't you just go home?"

Dazed, he peers at me for a moment before he smiles. "Because you care."

"Mrs. Nowak," Thin-face says. "One last chance or *Miss* Nowak's next."

"I don't know!"

I stand. "She doesn't. But I do. Let my mother take Inek to the doctor and I'll tell you everything."

"Zosia, no," my mother says. "Our whole country is at stake! *Millions* of lives."

"I don't care," I say.

"I'll let your mother live," Thin-face says. "The boy won't make it to the doctor."

He's right. Inek coughs up blood. Color leaks from his face. Why couldn't my father invent a healing machine? Instead of these machines of war. And click. Two thoughts lock together, and I realize why these weapons seemed wrong. My mind races as I search for a way to use it. My gaze lingers on the crab army built by my father. Built to protect me.

"What is the fuel?" Elbow-man demands.

"It's Baltic Electrons. Also known as Jantar. It's a black oily rock found only on the shores of the Baltic. My father stores it upstairs."

Thin-face taps his Luger on his thigh. "We didn't see it."

"Did you check the attic?" I ask.

"There isn't one."

I shake my head as if amazed by his stupidity. "Haven't you figured it out that my father's all about deceiving the eye? The barn, this workshop…" Thankfully, Mother remains silent.

He gestures with his gun. "Show us."

I hesitate. "Can you give me a moment alone with Inek?"

Thin-face considers. He sends one man to climb the steps to the barn, guarding the dirt pile entrance — my only escape. "One minute."

They pull my mother with them into the other room. I crouch beside Inek. Eyes closed, he's gasping for breath.

I take his hand in mine. "You were right. The first time I read your letters was this morning. I'm sorry."

He squeezes my hand. I lean close and kiss Inek on his cold lips. Then in desperation, I point to the hole in Inek's chest with my left index finger. "Heal him," I order, but my army remains motionless. Think! Father created them to protect and help me. "Fix him," I say and the four closest crabs scramble onto his chest, clicking as more metal gadgets unfurl from their bodies as if they're the Swiss Army knife of crabs.

No time left. I run from the room with my insides turning to ice. I know those metallic creatures can't really fix a living being. Even my father isn't that smart. I probably just increased the speed of his demise. But it's a fairy tale I cling to in order to get through the next ten minutes.

I lead the five Nazis upstairs. We do have an attic. It has multiple entrances—all hidden except one. We squeeze inside the master bedroom's closet, which is bigger than it looks. The cord hanging down from the ceiling appears to be connected to the light bulb, but the switch is located on the wall. Before I yank the cord to lower the ladder, I ask Mother where Father is.

"He's in England," she says.

Thin-face huffs in surprise. "Not in Warsaw?"

"Too risky. He is safe in London, helping our allies."

I meet my mother's gaze. "Those weapons below aren't his inventions, are they?"

"Decoys to make the Nazis believe he was still here."

She's lying. They were too well made to be mere decoys. Her left eye is almost swollen shut by the bruises on her face. Yet there is a defiant hardness in her gaze. My father wouldn't make war machines, but she would. Except she didn't know how to power them.

I tug on the cord, grunting with effort, pretending it won't budge. I rub my arms and ask for help as my finger brushes my wristwatch. One of the younger Nazis yanks the rope with all his strength. The well-oiled door flies open and amber pours out, taking everyone but me by surprise.

Pushing against Thin-face, I grab his Luger and aim it at his heart. He freezes in shock. The young Nazi is buried in mere seconds. Mother wrestles the gun away from Elbow-man then shoots him in the head. I blink in surprise.

More gunfire cuts through the hissing of the amber as another Nazi's forehead explodes. Then the clattering of my army of crabs soon adds to the confusion.

The crabs zap and disarm the last one, but my mother calmly executes him and then Thin-face before I can say stop.

"It's war, Zosia," she says before rushing off to find the man guarding the dirt pile entrance.

She's back by the time I reach our ruined kitchen. Ringed by my crabs, I stand amid the debris, reluctant to see Inek's body, but knowing I should. Mother puts on her apron and bustles about making tea as if this is a normal day.

"How did you know the attic was booby-trapped?" she asks.

I don't answer her. Instead, I ask, "Where is my father?"

"Probably in America by now." She waves her hand dismissively. "The Nazis have no reason to fear him. He ran away like a scared little boy." She huffs. "He asked *me* to abandon *my country*. All so he could build better plows instead of better tanks and airplanes." Her tone is harsh. The image of the dead Nazis floats in my mind.

"He built those crabs," I say in his defense.

She tsks. "Toys really. Mother crab's children he called them."

"They saved me." And were quite handy in neutralizing the enhanced Nazis.

"And we'll use them to bring the bodies to the basement. I'll contact the Polish authorities in the morning. They'll have to take me and my weapons seriously now. Your father wasn't the only creator in the family. The government will move us back to Warsaw, but I'll make sure I bring wagon loads of Jantar along so I can invent more armaments for Poland."

She sounds so rational, yet I'm horrified by her words.

"Zosia, sit. Have some tea." Handing me a cup, she gestures to the ceiling. "I assume the Jantar is hidden in the attic along with the amber?"

I stare at her. She didn't figure out that Jantar is the old Slavic word for amber. And the Greek word for amber is electron so Baltic Electrons are pieces of amber. Easy to find along the Baltic coast, amber fuels my father's machines.

Disgusted by her cold plans, I fetch a clean sheet and go down to the basement labs. My crabs follow me, and I idly wonder how to turn them off.

Inek is lying flat on his back. His skin is gray, and one crab has remained on top of him like a stubborn pet who refuses to leave its dead owner. I shoo it off.

Sitting by Inek's body, I'm too numb to cry. I stare at the dirt floor. It's smooth, except for that patch near the back wall, which is scuffed and lumpy.

Unfolding the sheet, I lay it over Inek, and decide there is nothing holding me here anymore. After he is buried, I'll leave and search for my father in America. Mother can figure out the fuel source on her own.

"Zosia?"

Startled, I jump to my feet. The sheet moves and I back away.

"Still trying to get rid of me?" Inek squirms, uncovering his face. "Shouldn't you have checked my pulse first?"

I rush over and hug him tight as joy fills me.

"Easy." Pain laces his voice.

I relax my grip. "Sorry. I was just… But you were… How?"

He tries to sit up but winces before sinking back. "Those damnable crabs of yours."

I pull the sheet off and inspect his chest. The wound is off-center, about an inch and a half from his heart. The torn flesh has been stitched together with— I laugh. I can't stop the giggles until tears stream along my cheeks.

"Are you going to tell me what's so funny?" Inek asks.

I suck in huge gulps of air to calm my emotions. "The crabs have used fishing line to close the wound."

Inek appreciates the irony. "I wonder what else they did. I passed out soon after they started."

Glancing around, I spot the flattened bullet. I remember Inek was also having trouble breathing after he was shot.

"I think they dug out the bullet and fixed your lung."

"Think?"

"I'm not a surgeon. We should take you to the hospital."

He refuses. I help him upstairs instead. Covering the ruined cushions with the sheet, I settle him onto the couch. My metal army scurries under and over the furniture, waiting for me.

Exclaiming over his recovery, Mother dashes to the kitchen to fetch him tea. Which, it seems to my mother, is the cure for all encounters with Nazis. I realize she gave me tea, but not a hug before. Not once did she ask if I was all right or seek to comfort me.

I sit on the edge of the couch, holding Inek's hand. His family will be so worried about him. Inek is sound asleep by the time Mother returns. She stands on the threshold of the living room with the cup and stares at my crabs with a gleam in her eyes.

"They're mine," I say to her in a low voice. Although I doubt anything less than a thunderclap will wake Inek.

"Don't be silly, Zosia. They can help with the war effort."

"Then make your own. I'm taking Inek home tomorrow and then I'm leaving for America." Where I'll work with Father to create useful gadgets that help people.

"No, you're not." Her stern tone warns that she won't tolerate an argument.

Too bad. She's finally going to get one. "Yes, I am. Did you even consider the danger to me and our neighbors when you decided to trick the Nazis?"

"Of course, it's dangerous. It's war."

An easy excuse. "Why didn't you tell me what you were doing?"

"To keep you safe."

"Wouldn't I have been safer in America with Father?" I demand.

"You belong in Poland."

"And Father agreed to this?" I ask.

She hesitates. "Eventually. He wouldn't agree until those… crabs were ready. I begged him to stay. Pleaded that he should build giant crabs to defend against the Nazis. This is his homeland! But he wouldn't listen. And he refused to tell me about the Jantar. Baltic electrons, pah! What utter nonsense."

Mother clutches the teacup in a tight fist. Her anger still raw even after three months. I remember how eerily calm she was when shooting the Nazis. How she was willing to let Inek die to keep the fuel source a secret. Yes, millions of people in exchange for a single person is logical, yet…

Other missed clues come together. One of them is her statement that the Polish authorities will now take her seriously.

"Where is Father?" I ask.

"I told you—"

"Where in America? It's a big country."

She glances at the floor. "I don't know. He didn't tell me."

"Surely, he sent you letters? Or me? Did you hide them like the ones Inek sent?"

Frowning, she shoots him a disgusted look. "Don't worry, Zosia, you'll soon forget him, and we'll find a… better suitor in Warsaw. We all have to make sacrifices for the war."

I stare at her. When did she turn from patriotic to psychotic? Is that the reason for the inconsistencies in her behavior? "Why did you save Inek's letters if you want me to forget him?"

Her hands twist around the teacup. "The letters reminded me of another… man." Mother's expression softens into… I don't know. I've never seen it before. Maybe love. Regret perhaps.

"Fredek Lisowski and I were to wed in the fall of 1920. He was a soldier and he sent me a letter every week. Fredek was killed in the Battle of Warsaw." Once again, her anger flares. "I met and married your father a year later. His genius attracted me, but his useless devices…" She put the teacup down and wiped her hands on her apron. "I tried to get him to make more useful things like weapons."

"Did you marry him for love or for Poland?"

She won't answer. But deep down I know. With such different views of the world, it must have been difficult for them to be together.

"Why didn't you leave him?" I ask.

"It was my duty to my country. If I had succeeded in changing his mind, we wouldn't be worried about another war. The Nazis would have been terrified of us."

"Why didn't he leave you, then?"

A strange wry smile twists her lips. "He wouldn't leave *you*, Zosia."

Her answer reminds me that she didn't answer my other question. "Has Father sent you any letters?"

"No."

I mull it over. One thing I did know. Father would at least tell Mother where he settled in America. The final clue hits me like a bullet. I stand on weak legs. My mother calls to me as I pass her and stumble down to the basement.

Kneeling by the rough patch of dirt, I cry.

"Zosia," Mother says behind me. "What are you doing?"

I whirl around. "You killed him." It's not a question.

"He was a traitor."

"Are you going to kill me, too?"

"Why would I do that?"

"Because I'm leaving." Fanned out behind her is my crab army. It's almost as if they know they should keep a respectful distance from us.

"Don't be silly. You're staying with me."

"Why do you want me to stay?"

"You're creative and can help me build weapons."

She says nothing about me being her daughter. Nothing about love. Nothing about family. "Did you make that statue of the girl with springs for hair for me?"

Confused, she's slow to answer. "Yes."

"Why did you make it?"

"To keep up the ruse. To make you think your father was still here."

I close my eyes for a moment as pain rolls through me. The statue was part of the deception. Not a gift to comfort me when I was lonely and missing my father. "I'm taking Inek home and then I'm leaving."

"No. You're not. You're going to go to your room. I'll take care of Inek." Her cold tone coats my shattered heart in a layer of ice.

"Like you took care of Father and the Nazis?" I shudder. "No."

When I fail to move, she pulls a Luger from her apron's pocket and aims it at me. "Go to your room. Now."

I gape at her. By the set of her shoulders, I knew she'd kill me for being a traitor. She has only one love. And it's not me or my father. My crabs sense a threat. Silent on the dirt floor, they overwhelm her in mere seconds.

She yells my name, but I turn my back on her.

Her shrieks follow me as I climb the steps to check on Inek.

Like my mother said, it's war.

THE RETURN OF THE DIESEL KID

A Tale of Harbor City Yet to Come

JOHN L. FRENCH

WHEN REPORTS STARTED COMING IN ABOUT A MONKEY RIDING A motorcycle around City Center, Sergeant Shelly Benton of the Harbor City PD suspected there was going to be a problem.

"It can't be," she said when the alert came up on her wrist link.

"Why not, Sarge?" Patrol Officer Seth Avila asked. Cops in Harbor City normally rode solo, but Avila had Benton riding along as part of his rookie review.

"Because it's impossible. Most monkeys are too small to ride motorcycles, unless it's one of those tiny circus things. And besides, its tail would probably get caught in the wheels or something. It's probably a chimpanzee, gorilla, or some kind of an ape."

This did not help Avila, who had a hard time picturing any kind of animal operating a vehicle. He said so to Benton.

"So, what, it's somebody on a motorcycle with an ape in the sidecar?"

"I doubt it. In this town that would be almost normal. You're new in Harbor City, aren't you, Seth?" At his nod, she went on. "It's a strange place. We have costumed crooks who commit gimmick crimes. We have capes and their sidekicks helping us out during the day and masked vigilantes killing bad guys at night. As for apes on bikes, you probably haven't heard about how Captain Simian and his Oranugang threatened to do a number six on City Center unless paid one hundred thousand bananas."

"Bananas? Really?"

"No, Simian meant dollars but if you're gonna walk the walk you have to talk the talk."

"So, what happened?"

"The Raven happened. He swooped in and took 'em out. The orangutans wound up in the Harbor City Zoo. As for Captain Simian, who knows? He hasn't been seen since."

"So, Sarge, you're saying…"

"There's probably an ape on a motorcycle somewhere in the business district."

"Shouldn't we call in a cape to help?"

Benton shook her head. "What for? It's just an ape on a bike. Besides, the only one of 'em fast enough to catch 'em is Hermod, and nobody's seen him for weeks. Punch it, Seth, and let's see if we can catch it."

Avila agreed and hit his lights and siren. Catching a monkey on a motorcycle would score him high marks on his performance eval.

Other police officers had the same idea. Who would not want to catch or even see a monkey on a bike? And so the city center was flooded with patrol cars, all looking for the same thing.

They found it, or rather them. It was not a monkey on a motorcycle, it was several chimps on several motorcycles, including one who had a pink poodle in a sidecar. All of them attracted the attention of at least one patrol officer and led them north and away from the business and financial district.

As the senior officer involved in the pursuit, Sergeant Benton took charge. She ordered barriers and roadblocks designed to corral the apes.

It worked. The apes were funneled into a series of one-way streets, the last of which was a dead end in the warehouse district. Once trapped, the riders stopped and just sat on their bikes.

Armed with tasers, beanbags guns, tranq rifles, and other less-than-lethal weapons, the officers slowly closed on their quarry, none of which responded to their approach.

"They're not moving, Sarge."

"I can see that, Seth. That's strange, even for Harbor City. Okay, everybody, stop where you are. Seth, beanbag the closest one."

Avila did, expecting his target to howl, shriek, or turn and charge when struck. Instead, when it was hit, it did nothing but *clang*.

Clang? Benton thought. Animals don't *clang*. Then it hit her. *Oh crap, it's him. He's back.* Then the pink poodle started a countdown. "Ten, nine, eight …"

"Everybody, move back, now!" Benton shouted. The officers quickly obeyed as the poodle continued, "…three, two, one."

The explosions when they came were unremarkable, just strong enough to destroy the mechanical apes and the motorcycles they were riding. But then again, Mike Kanick had never been in the game to hurt or kill people. He was in it for the fun and the money.

"We've been suckered," Benton said to no one in particular as she and her fellow officers watched things burn. She opened her wrist link. "This is unit 5801 with a signal 33. All units converge on City Center, with special emphasis on banks, shops, and jewelry stores. The Diesel Kid is back in town."

The Diesel Kid, aka Mike Kanick. It was not his real name. No one on the wrong side of the law *ever* used their real name. Why make things easy for those on the right side? No, the Kid picked that name because it sounded like, well, you know.

The Kid liked machines, he always had. He had an affinity for them. He loved their sounds and smells. So, when he decided that crime was more fun than playing it straight, he went the gimmick route and used the things he loved.

At first, he made machines that would open secure doors and crack safes. Locks and tumblers were no match for him. Then he pulled his first big gimmick. He designed and sold safes. So good were these safes that many businesses purchased and installed them. Within six months, one out of every ten safes in Harbor City was a Kanick Safe. A month after that, Mike sent out a signal. The safes "woke up," walked out of their stores, businesses, and shops, and delivered their contents to him.

He was caught, of course. Several alert police officers and night security guards simply followed the wayward safes to his office. Mike was arrested and convicted. He did a few years then wrangled a job in the prison machine shop. Most people believed that it was impossible to secretly build an autogyro in prison. Mike proved them wrong.

Over the next decade, Mike pulled his crimes using machines large and small. Because he favored the use of the internal combustion engine, he picked up the moniker "The Diesel Kid." He was arrested several times and escaped just as many. He always planned his escapes before committing his crimes, because he knew that you get away with every crime except the last one.

And now, after a three-year absence, he was back. His return was announced by the smell of diesel fumes and the *clank, clank* of heavy machinery. From a warehouse not too far from City Center, giants emerged. They were almost two stories high, and if WWII army tanks had long arms instead of guns and short legs instead of treads, they would have looked like these mechanical beasts. There were ten of them and they walked straight for the business district, targeting banks, art galleries, auction houses, and jewelry stories. There was nothing gentle about them, this was smash-and-grab on a grand scale. And the police were helpless.

The things were bulletproof, explosive proof, and shielded against electric shock. Obstacles put in their way were thrown aside or crushed, including police cars, fire trucks, and an urban assault vehicle on loan from the U.S. Army. The Diesel Kid had built and planned well and had waited for just the right time. When he learned the cape Kratos, who was known for his strength, had been killed and that the speedster Hermod had not been seen in weeks, he knew it was time, for only strength or speed was likely to stop him.

Or, just maybe, chance.

About the time the auto-apes exploded, Victoria Conrad arrived an hour early for school. She was a senior on the varsity track and field team. They had a track meet that weekend and she wanted to get in some early morning laps before class started.

Victoria was "Vicky" to her friends and "Connie" or just "Con" to her boyfriend Trey Mercer. Trey had graduated the year before. He had majored in Shop and now worked as a mechanic in his father's garage. Knowing Vicky was going to run laps, he decided to come out and watch her before going to work.

There were just the two of them, Trey in his coveralls and Vicky in her track uniform. They kissed briefly, then he went to sit in the front row of the stands and she took her place at the starting block.

"Count me down, Trey," she shouted.

"Okay, Con, from ten, nine, eight..."

No one knows the when or why of how the hero mutation expresses itself. Some say that it is the result of great stress. Others say it's a genetically timed response. Most feel that it is simply a matter of… chance.

Chance it was for Victoria Conrad. Or maybe it was the kiss, that had been known to happen. When Trey started his countdown, she readied her run. At "five, four, three…" she felt an adrenaline surge. When she heard, "one. Go!" Vicky started running and in less time it than it took Trey to blink, she was three-quarters around the track.

When she realized what was happening, Vicky began a controlled slowdown. It came easy to her, as if she had been doing it all her life. By the time she stopped, she was at the start line where she was met by Trey.

"Con, what just happened?"

"I don't know, I just started running and everything seemed to slow dow… oh crap, I'm a cape."

"You are. You're a cape! Con, that's wonderful!"

"No, it isn't," she said, almost in tears. "Capes can't do sports. It's not allowed. Unfair competition and all that crap. It means I'm off the team—no track meets, no scholarships, no college, no future."

Vicky started to cry, then shake. Smart boyfriend that he was, Trey put his arms around her and said nothing, just comforted her by his presence and with his hug. He kept hugging her even when shaking became vibration, a very fast vibration. He tried to pull away, found that he couldn't, that he was vibrating with her.

"Con, slow down. You're scaring me. Deep breaths, in and out."

Vicky listened to Trey, started controlling her breathing, and was quickly back to normal. Well, not normal, not anymore, but she did stop shaking.

"That was weird," he said. "It was like everything had stopped but you and me."

"That's what it was like when I was running." Vicky paused. "Say, you don't think…"

"I don't think, that's why Mom says I'm a mechanic like Dad."

"No, I mean, maybe my shaking turned on *your* hero mutation."

"Holding you usually does turn me on, but not today. I was too worried about you. Do you think so, about the mutation?"

"Only one way to find out. Take your place in the blocks and let's race."

The two took their positions. Vicky counted down from five. At, "one. Go," they both took off. Vicky lapped Trey twice before he could run five meters.

"Well, I don't have the mutation," Trey said once Vicky slowed to a stop. He looked around. "People are starting to come to school, Con. We'd better talk about this somewhere else."

"Sure, but there's something I want to try. Take my hand and be ready."

"Ready for what?"

"Ready to run."

Holding tightly to Trey's hand, Vicky started slowly, then ran faster and faster until time seemed to slow. She and Trey went twice around the track then through the parking lot to his father's garage. There they stopped.

"What I wonder," said Trey, who had minored in physics, "is why our clothes didn't burn off from the friction."

"You'd like that, wouldn't you?" Vicky asked with a smile. As Trey blushed, she said, "I can share my speed with you so I guess I share it with our clothes as well, or anything else I touch. Now, what are we, or rather, what am I going to do about this speed problem of mine?"

Before Trey could answer, both their wrist links sounded an alert.

TO ALL HARBOR CITY RESIDENTS. AVOID CITY CENTER. MECHANICAL BOTS ARE WREAKING HAVOC AS THEY RANSACK STORES, SHOPS, AND BANKS. AGAIN, AVOID CITY CENTER.

The news reports that followed detailed the damage and how the police and what capes who had arrived on the scene were helpless against the mechanical monsters. They were concentrating their efforts on saving people and evacuating the district. One reporter bemoaned the loss of Kratos and Hermod, "for only great speed or great strength can stop these Frankenstein-like creations. Without them, there may be no choice but to bring in the destructive power of the military."

"I think that answers your question, Con," Trey said.

"What question? Oh no, you mean that I should… but how? All I could do is run around them real fast. I wouldn't know how to stop them."

"But I do. I'm a mechanic, remember? Not only can I fix machines, I also take them apart."

Vicky found herself going into speed mode, vibrating in place while her mind rapidly went through all possible solutions to the problem. When she stopped, she said, "You're right. Let's do this before I change my mind." It was something she'd been wanting and waiting to say to Trey but under entirely different circumstances.

Trey took another look at the video feed from City Center. "Let me get my tools. I'm gonna need the big wrenches."

Sergeant Shelly Benton was at the command post with Lawman Noah Stein of the Costumed Crimes Division, Chief Greta Duke of Patrol, and Captain Anthony Hartman who headed up Tactical Ops. They were discussing how the metal behemoths might be stopped and were at the point of paroling one or two of the least mad scientists they had under lockup when the air shimmered and a blur resolved itself into a pair of young people, a girl in a track uniform and a boy in mechanic overalls.

Oh, what fresh hell is this? Benton thought before asking, "Who the hell are you?"

"She's your new speedster and I'm her sidekick. No, make that her alfred. Now, where's the nearest bot?"

"Are you two even registered?" Captain Hartman asked harshly, mentally figuring the size of the jackpot they'd be in if they sent two teenagers to their doom.

"No, sir," Vicky replied. "I just got my power this morning."

"Oh, for Christ's…" Hartman's exclamation was cut short by Lawman Stein. Stein was more familiar with the more colorful parts of Harbor City's world of capes and crooks and knew that nothing was going to stop this… Track Star and her alfred.

"Two blocks down and hang a left. There's one cleaning out the McPhail Federal Saving Bank. Just be careful. Remember, neither of you is registered, which means you're not covered by city insurance."

"To hell with that," Chief Duke said. "I know there's no stopping you kids. I certainly couldn't be stopped at your age. So, if you're crazy enough to go against these things, I'm crazy enough to deputize you for the duration of this crisis. You'll be covered but, as Noah said, please be careful."

The two teens blurred then ran two blocks down and turned left. Seeing the mechanical bot a block away, Vicky stopped because talking wasn't possible while she ran. "So, what's the plan?"

"You circle it while I figure out how to take it apart. Then I take it apart."

"Good plan."

And they were off.

At the speed she was traveling, the bot appeared to be moving very, very slowly. Vicky ran around it, giving her boyfriend time to find its weak points. Then, because her brain was working as fast as her body, she found one on her own, or rather, remembered one from the old comic books, when capes and masks were still the stuff of fiction.

She started circling the bot faster and faster, putting it in the center of a mini-tornado. Subjected to extreme winds inside the funnel, the bot broke apart and collapsed.

To Vicky and Trey, the collapse of the bot occurred in very slow motion, so they easily avoided the flying parts. Once it was completely down, Vicky stopped.

"I guess you didn't need me after all," a somewhat upset Trey said.

"Silly, I'll always need you. And right now, you're needed here, to learn what you can from this thing. I'm gonna go tornado the rest."

"Go, just be care..." Before Trey could finish, Vicky was gone.

Even not knowing where the other bots were, finding them was easy. Vicky ran at speed up one street and down the other, following the signs of devastation and destruction. On finding a bot, she did to it what she had done to the first, then ran after the next one, and the next one. Soon, all that was left of the mechanical bots were piles of debris.

After the destruction of Bot-1, as it came to be called, Sergeant Benton and Lawman Stein caught up to Trey.

"Where's Track Star?" Stein asked.

So, she's got a name now, Trey thought before answering. Pointing, he said, "She went that-a-way, Lawman," and went back to his examination of the remains of Bot-1.

"Well," Benton said, "I hope she left one intact."

A shimmer, a blur, then Vicky, now Track Star, appeared. "No, I didn't. Should I have?"

Stein answered. "We were hoping to follow it back to the Diesel Kid."

His examination over, Trey stood and said, "You won't have to." He pointed to the main part of the bot. "Look here. It's an empty compartment. I figured that the loot was initially dumped into it. When the compartment was full, it was discharged. Equipped with some means of movement, it sped off to this Diesel Kid while the bot continued on, its further action a cover for the compartment bot's escape."

Captain Hartman arrived on the scene and had heard this last part. "That's all well and good," he said, "but it still doesn't tell us where they went."

"No," offered Trey, "but I'm sure you have drone surveillance of the whole thing. Just look for ten separate movements all converging on the same location."

"That would take forever," Hartman complained.

"Not if you have someone who could help you watch the video in super fast-forward. Right, Track Star?"

Vicky smiled, approving of her cape name. "Good idea, and you thought you weren't going to be any help."

Track Star, nee Victoria Conrad, held hands with Lawman Stein and Chief Duke while the three of the watched the video and tracked the compartment bots to, where else, a warehouse on the waterfront. Captain Hartman and Sergeant Benton led the Quick Response Team's raid of that warehouse.

"How did you find me this time?" the Kid asked, already planning his next escape and caper. The more he could get them to tell him, the easier both would be.

"Let's just say, Mike Kanick," Shelly Benton said, as she slapped cuffs on his wrists and shackles on his legs, "that you were brought down by a track star and a real mechanic."

So, Harbor City had its new speedster, albeit a part-time one who still had to finish high school. The Mercer Garage saw an increase in business as police officers in the know brought their personal and assigned vehicles in for maintenance. And with his pending trial and expected conviction, the state penitentiary made itself ready for the return of the Diesel Kid.

Hyena Brings Death

Bernie Mojzes

Hyena circles the smoking wreckage, wary of any movement within the cockpit, of any flicker of flame from under the crumpled nose of the biplane. There is none—no ragged breath from the figure slumped over the instrument panel, and though the cooling engine billows clouds of burnt oil into the cold desert night, there's no telltale scent of spilled petrol in the air.

Hyena cracks open the rumpled fuselage with a crowbar. Inside are valves and pistons, tubes and wires. There is no one around, so Hyena unwraps her *tagelmust,* the long, indigo scarf that covers her head and face. Better to keep the precious fabric clean than waste water washing it, especially when it comes to engine grease, which, she learned long ago, never comes out.

Hyena works with practiced ease, even in the dark, stripping the engine of its parts. She drains the oil pan into a clay jug and siphons petrol into glass bottles set (carefully) in a wooden crate, before loading them into her truck.

Sadly, the propeller is damaged beyond repair. Maybe next time, but luck hasn't been with Hyena when it comes to propellers; more often than not, these machines tend to kiss the ground nose first.

Hyena climbs the fuselage and examines the pilot. The blood is sticky-wet on his face and on the instrument panel, but it no longer flows. In the moonlight, it looks like wet ink. The pilot is a slight man, maybe half a hand taller than Hyena, she estimates, and not too much heavier. Hyena grips the leather of his jacket and heaves, pulling him half out of the cockpit, flopping him over the side and letting gravity drag him to the soft Sahara sands, where her sisters and brothers cackle with anticipation of the feast.

The stick is broken, snapped where the pilot's body slammed into it on impact, and one end has smashed the altimeter.

Hyena leaves the stick and the altimeter and takes the rest: compass, airspeed indicator, rudder controls. The connecting cables. She uncouples the Lewis gun from atop the upper wing and stores it safely away, along with its ammunition.

Oh, but there's more, and Hyena wonders that there was anything left for her to salvage at all. Four twenty-pound bombs are stored under the pilot's seat, having miraculously survived the impact. She packs them carefully in buckets of sand and loads them into her truck.

The moon is low in the sky when Hyena is done. She wipes the grease and blood from her hands, and then puts the veil back on, wrapped around her head and neck and over her face. Hyena climbs into her truck, and leaves the rest, the shell of the aeroplane and the pilot, for other scavengers.

In the old stories, Hyena brings death into the world.

The world was young, then, and a very different place: green and verdant, and people and animals lived happy and healthy lives in the shadow of heaven. When you grew old, you had only to climb the rope that bound Earth to Heaven, and you would be restored.

One day, while Hyena was climbing to Heaven, she grew hungry. But there was nothing to eat, nothing but the rope that she climbed.

"Just one bite," she thought, "to ease my hunger."

And then, "Just one more bite."

When the rope snapped and Hyena fell back to the Earth, she was still hungry, and Heaven drifted off into the sky, far away and unreachable.

Now the Earth is dry and brown, a place of shifting sands and loyalties, of thirst and starvation, of war and murder and insufficient resources.

This is how Hyena brought death to the world.

Hyena has been doing this for some time: collecting, taking what people no longer need, what's been thrown out, lost, or misplaced.

Scavenging. Her truck she found half-buried after a sandstorm. The truck had belonged to two Frenchmen. She found them the following day, not far off, by following the vultures.

She lives through luck, and so what if that luck is someone else's misfortune? The Frenchmen died, the vultures lived, and Hyena got a truck.

The sun is rising behind her as she drives, hazy through the dust her tires kick into the air. It is a long way to her den in the Aïr Mountains, and she has much to do.

There is another version of Hyena's story, but it isn't one that's often told. It's a tale of hunger, of a world where the people and animals lived and bred and kept living, until they had eaten everything green and growing, leaving nothing but sand and dust. And still they lived on, stick thin, with jutting ribs and spines and hollow cheeks and stomachs.

Do you remember that time?

Hyena does.

It was in the land they call Tripolitania that Hyena saw her first flying machine. Men came from the north across the sea to wage war against the Turks, who had come from the east where the sun lives to wage war against everybody else, and war is always a fertile field for a scavenger.

The flying machines of the Italians flew low and slow and had the wings of birds. Hyena was impressed but couldn't think that they might be of any use to her, any more than a bird on the wing was of any use. But then she saw the man within, so far away that he looked like a beetle, reach out and drop something, deep behind the Turkish front lines.

Where the thing fell, there was a roar and a flash of light, and when the wind blew the dust away all that remained on the ground were the dead and the dying.

Hyena has a set of wings from that aeroplane, deceptively called *Taube*, or "dove," in her den. She mounted them to a framework of wood and aluminum and bone that mimicked the machine she'd seen flying. But she's since realized that it's completely inadequate for her needs. For what she has planned.

That was just a few short years ago, and several wars have come and gone and come again. Plenty more salvage available to make her improvements.

Hyena has kept her den hidden for centuries, a matter that has only become difficult in recent years, since she found her truck and needed to make her den accessible to something with wheels. Now that her plans are nearing fruition, it's even harder. But it won't matter soon, because she's almost done.

The problem with the flying machines of the Europeans is that they are focused on the Earth. Like eagles or vultures, they look for their prey on the ground.

Not Hyena. Hyena's looking up, at the ones who betrayed her. Betrayed *them all*. If Hyena's going to go to war, it'll be the one war worth having.

The machine that hulks in her den is huge, cobbled together from *Taubes* and Avro 504s and a variety of Nieumans, from B.E.8s and Morane-Saulniers. Pieces of automobiles—Renault and Rolls Royce—and Triumph motorcycles. Parts are parts, as long as they can be made to fit. And Hyena is oh-so-good at finding how to make them fit. The wings are stacked six high, with a dozen engines suspended from them. Cables made of wire and camel gut and Frenchman tendons provide support and manipulate the flaps and rudders.

There is only one vital piece missing (though there is always room for improvement) —the propeller for the largest engine, the one seated in the nose of the aircraft. She'd built it out of the bones of innumerable things, engines from aeroplanes, trucks, and even a Decauville loco-motive that she had found sacrificed in Morocco. It would be enough, she knew, to take her far beyond the reach of any other aircraft. Knew it in her bones.

And then... then she'll show Heaven what it means to bring death.

Sometimes you have to make your own luck, and Hyena needs a propeller. That's what drew her deep into Egypt, to Beni Suef, where the British have set up operations.

It's a moonless night, and Hyena nearly laughs out loud with the ease with which she evades the guards and slips through the barbed wire.

It is well past midnight when she acts. The man walks with the swagger of a pilot as he exits the officer's lounge, smelling of leather and whiskey. His skin is pale in the darkness, and he stiffens at the hot touch of Hyena's teeth against his neck, pressed against both carotids, which provides her the opportunity to take the pistol from his side and re-wrap her veil before she lets him see her.

Hyena's English isn't very good—of all the tongues she's consumed, only one of the Frenchmen and a Moroccan trader had any English (if she feasts on this one, it will solve her problem, but too late) —but she makes herself understood: she needs a propeller. A big one. The biggest. He's going to help her get it out of camp.

The British pilot laughs. "The *biggest* propeller, eh? Well, then, you'll want one off a Handley Page, then."

"Yes."

"Well, that's not here, then, innit? This is Africa."

Hyena shrugs. Yes, this is Africa. It has always been Africa, long before the other places had names.

"Well, if you think the RFC is going waste their *good* planes on bloody Africa, you're touched." The pilot looks down at the pistol and sags in defeat. "Their good pilots, either."

"Where?"

"France. Belgium. England, if you want one fresh from the factory."

Hyena shakes her head. "Too far. Too long. What is here?"

"You're out of your bloody mind, you know, if you think they're going to let you just walk out with a propeller over your shoulder."

Hyena grins behind her *tagelmust* and presses the gun against his ribs. "We are not walking."

The choices, it turns out, are pretty slim indeed. There are two B.E.2c's, a B.E.2e, a French Morane-Saulnier L, an F.E.2b, and a couple older Aircos that the pilot describes as "practically useless death traps."

They take the F.E.2b, rather than the newer B.E.2e, because Hyena likes the propeller. It's not as big as she'd hoped, but it has *four blades!* All the other propellers she's collected only have two. It seats two as well, which is convenient. The pilot directs her to the front cockpit as he climbs into the rear.

"Unless you want to try your hand, in which case, I'll just bugger off to bed."

There aren't any controls in the front cockpit, but there is a pair of machine guns. Hyena's not comfortable with the pilot behind her, but she's the one with the gun, so she nods and climbs in.

The engine sputters and the propeller spins. There's a rush of air that steals their words, and the aeroplane begins to move.

Hyena's breath catches. She is going to fly. And she is afraid. For the first time in many centuries, she is afraid. But there's no time for that. There's a bump as the wheels lift off the ground and come back down, and Hyena tastes blood. Another bump, but she's smart enough to keep her tongue in her mouth this time.

They're in the air before the guards realize, and out of range before they can react.

They're in the air for half an hour before a tap on the shoulder startles Hyena. She's just been glorying in the feeling of being airborne, of the cold wind washing over her, overwhelmed by the sheer magnitude of the *noise*! Between the wind and the engine and the propeller, she can't hear herself think, so she'd stopped thinking. She's thinking now, though, almost panicked, she's on her feet and spinning around with the pistol in her hand.

The pilot raised both his hands, placating, then reaches forward to grasp something, which he pulls to his ear. Then he points to Hyena, and toward the front of her cockpit. Oh. That strange tube. Of course. Hyena had seen them in other dual-cockpitted aeroplanes she'd salvaged, but never understood their use. She'd never imagined flying would be so loud. Fighting sudden vertigo, Hyena finds her seat and manages to pull the speaking tube to her ear.

"First time flying?" the pilot asks, his voice strangely intimate over the noise.

Hyena nods, even though she knows he can't see her. "In an aeroplane, yes." There's another tap on her shoulder, and when she turns, the pilot mimes moving the tube to his mouth. She mimics him and repeats herself. She's not sure he can hear her. The wind tears the words from her breath. And it's not like falling is really much like flying, after all.

Another tap on her shoulder, and she remembers to put the tube to her ear.

"There's nothing like it, flying. It's like you're free, for the first time in your life. No chores, no cares, no nagging Mum or bullying maths professor. It's almost enough to forget what you're really up here to do." He points to the machine gun mounted next to Hyena. "Almost."

"Once, all this was a garden," Hyena says into the speaking tube. "A garden given us by the gods, to live in forever."

"Eden," the pilot says.

"Nothing is good forever," Hyena says. "We lived and ate and loved. We grew numerous, and still lived, and still loved, and still ate, until there was nothing left to eat."

"Well, that's a bit of bad luck, innit?"

"No." Hyena feels her teeth grind. "Not luck. Bad design. When the garden dried up and the suffering began, the gods said it was our fault for being greedy. All we ever wanted was what they promised. When Hyena brought death to the world, they acted like it was a bad thing."

The pilot starts to say something, hesitates. Continues.

"I've seen enough death to know, there's no such thing as a good death."

"That is because you never saw what it was like before."

It's colder up here than Hyena expected, and she wishes she had something warmer than her robes, something that would cut the wind. Now she understands why the pilots wear thick leather jackets in the desert sun.

She should have had the British pilot give her his jacket. There's so much she doesn't know, so much to learn. She should have watched more carefully as he guided the aeroplane into the sky, but she was too excited, too exhilarated, and, she has to admit, too frightened to do more than watch the ground fall away into shadow.

Hyena is certain that the machine she has constructed will work, but until now, she hadn't even considered that actually flying it would be any more complex than driving her truck, which had been significantly simpler than convincing a camel to walk. Now, she's not so sure. Even creatures born for the skies take a tumble the first few times they try out their wings, and she has only one chance to get this right.

"You're lucky, here," the pilot says, startling her.

"I've always had luck," Hyena says.

"No, I mean the war. It's not so bad here, not like back home. Not to say that what's happening here is *good* in any way, but it's not the fucking bloodbath it is in Europe."

There's a bitterness in his voice that Hyena doesn't expect. "War is war," she says.

"Not like this. It's never been like this before."

The pilot is quiet for a time.

"I was sent here before the worst of it. Obsolete equipment, second-rate pilots, might as well send them off to Africa, right? I've got three brothers, in the Infantry. Had three brothers. All three of them killed the same day, along with sixty thousand others. Gassed in a muddy trench in France, or shot if they tried to run. It's like some kind of invocation. If we sacrifice enough, if we bleed *enough*, God will grant us victory."

"The gods don't care how much we bleed, as long as their bellies are full. That is why I need a propeller."

The pilot's silence is a question.

"I am flying to Heaven, to bring them what we have."

The pilot snorts. "On Heaven as it is on Earth. A taste of their own medicine."

"Yes."

The pilot is quiet then, and other than the roar of the engine and the rushing of the wind, there is silence.

It's nearly two hours before Hyena sees the marker she left to show where she hid her truck and signals it's time to land. The landing is a lot harder than the takeoff, because the pilot is only human, and humans are stupidly night-blind, and because sand makes a terrible runway. But Hyena knows better than to let her tongue protrude between her teeth this time.

When the aeroplane skids to a halt and the engine dies, the propeller slows and finally stops, still intact. Hyena stands and turns to put her hands on the pilot's shoulders. She looks him in the eye. "You are not second-rate."

Hyena fetches her tools, and together, they remove the propeller and carry it to the truck. As they work, Hyena explains which parts she wants to take, since he seems cooperative.

"Why not take the whole bloody thing?" the pilot asks.

Hyena tilts her head.

"Unbolt the wings, strap them to the roof. This bit—" he raps on the fuselage with his knuckles "—will fit in back of the truck since the landing gear's snapped off."

"Yes." Hyena nods. It would work. She has a pulley, and she has a second pair of hands, for once.

The sky grows pale as they load the truck. It just barely fits; the guns need to be unbolted from the frame, and Hyena has to shift several crates into the cockpits of the plane and abandon a stack of rubber tires. The sun has peeked over the horizon as they worked, and the desert has begun to heat up.

The pilot wipes his forehead with the back of his hand. "So, what now?" he asks.

"For you?" Hyena shrugs. "You can stay here and maybe someone will come. I cannot say who they will be."

"Lovely."

The rising sun tinges the pilot's hair with reds and oranges, or maybe that is just the color of his hair. She has heard of such things, among the northerners. In the light, she can see the man's pale face is littered with auburn dots. His nose is absurdly small, like a button, slightly upturned.

"Or you can come with me, and I can leave you when we stop to refuel. There will be people there, but I cannot say who they will be."

"One of the oases we've been bombing, no doubt." The pilot snorts something vaguely like a laugh. "Or that we're about to bomb. I'm probably better off just walking out into the desert."

Hyena can't help but grin. Custom prohibits letting the *tagelmust* drop so that a stranger can see your face, but custom also prohibits women from wearing the veil at all, and if Hyena cared about men's customs, she wouldn't be who she is. And the pilot needs to see her face before he answers her next question.

She unwraps the veil, revealing her face, her neck, her head, revealing black lips in a black muzzle, pale gray hair striped with black, straight and wild like bristles. When she smiles, she shows her teeth. Strong teeth that can grind bone to powder.

The pilot's breath catches, and he swallows.

Hyena's grin shows her tongue, pink against black. "Or, you can come with me."

The pilot's cheek twitches. He tilts his head, eyes flickering toward the brightening sky. "And attack Heaven."

Hyena's grin grows wider.

"Yes," says the pilot. "I think I just might."

In the thousands of years that she's had one, Hyena has never brought a man to her den. She's never brought anyone. Not alive, at least.

It didn't matter, she supposed. It's not like she expected to come back to it, after this.

Still, if she'd known she was having company, she'd have cleaned up a little.

The pilot steps gingerly over bones—bones of animals (and what is man but an animal?) and bones of machines. His nose wrinkles, and Hyena bites back an angry comment. It's not his fault that he's only human, after all. But he doesn't balk at the work, and he seems properly appreciative of her masterpiece.

"You don't seriously expect that thing to fly."

Hyena grins at him, her widest grin, full of the future, and he shudders.

"I should have walked into the bloody desert," he says, as he reaches for a wrench to start disassembling the F.E.8.

The sun is still high in the sky when they collapse, exhausted, onto the pile of rags that Hyena hastily gathered for their bed, fragments of cloth and silk, whatever she thinks might feel good to her guest. His hide, after all, is far too thin to be comfortable in her nest of bones. They're both asleep before either can say a word to the other.

At some point, though, they're not asleep, not entirely, and the pilot's confident hands turn out to be good for more than coaxing an aeroplane into the sky.

It takes a few weeks to integrate the F.E.8 into Hyena's machine. Some of it needs to be completely reimagined. Now that she has experienced flight herself, she has a better understanding of how the wind flows. (Is there wind in Heaven? And between Earth and Heaven? It's been so long, she doesn't remember.)

It's far too late for doubts, but they plague her anyway. It's the pilot's fault. She had no doubts before he appeared; now his contributions to her work have made her machine better, stronger, faster, and all she can think of is how spectacularly they can fail.

She doesn't want him to die, that's the problem. (They all die, now, sooner or later. That was the gift she'd given them, long ago. The lesser evil.) It seems too soon, though, too young. But the machine is complete.

Hyena grins when the pilot sits back on his heels and says, "That's it, then. It's done. It's bloody done." But the hopelessness that tinges what he says next strikes her: "Bloody fucking hell."

"You don't have to come," she says. "You can take the truck."

"And go where?"

"Anywhere."

He laughs, and there is so much in the sound that Hyena doesn't understand, so much contradiction. "And let you bullocks up all our hard work? I don't think so. Question is, where are you going to find a runway long enough to get this thing off the ground? And how are you going to get it there?"

So she shows him. They'll need to carry the aeroplane there in pieces and reassemble it. The path is steep but manageable, and Hyena has already constructed a system of pulleys and cables with a petrol generator to power it. Four days it'll take them, she thinks, maybe three with his help, and he nods.

And then she shows him the runway—it's two hundred meters long, almost straight down, off the side of the mountain. Jagged rocks and boulders litter the base of the cliff.

"On second thought, I'll take the truck."

But he doesn't, not yet. Instead, he examines the rockface, estimates its pitch and the size and location of the many outcroppings. He describes a simple anemometer to measure the wind, which Hyena builds. When he's done his measurements and calculations, he presents Hyena with a diagram. It's a ramp that extends ten meters out over the cliff and has a 15-degree inclined slope.

"That should clear the outcroppings for at least the first fifty meters. If you haven't managed to get any lift by then, well, the rest won't matter. It'd be better if it was longer, but we don't have a way to make that structurally sound."

Hyena shrugs, and they start to build. It doesn't have to be too sturdy; both of them know it will only be used once, and if it tumbles down after, it won't matter. She'll either be long gone before it reaches the ground, or she won't, in which case, it's unlikely to matter too much.It occurs to Hyena that if they expect the ramp to collapse, maybe they could direct the direction of the collapse. She adds to the diagram, her lines not nearly so precise as the pilot's: a pair of hinges, rollers in tracks down either side. The pulley system could be re-engineered to thrust the ramp out, over the cliff, once the weight of the aeroplane was fully centered on it. Another trigger would lift a flap to catch the plane's wheels, preventing the ramp from sliding out from under the plane when it started moving.

"Like a slingshot," the pilot says, admiring. "This might actually work. I mean, not the flying to heaven bit, that's just straight-out daft, but in terms of getting this monstrosity off the ground."

Of course, the aeroplane will need some structural modifications to support the added stress, which will delay her departure. A few more days, another week. Hyena is surprised how much she treasures each of these extra days and nights, each hour of this last reprieve, before they each go off to their separate dooms.

They make love, that last day, long and slow, as if every moment could be immortalized in memory. But it won't; that's something Hyena is sure of. Memory is even less reliable than life. Bodies are killed, or break down slowly, and memory can't survive that. He'll forget it all once he's back with his own people, back in his old life. As if death needed anything to speed up the loss. If Hyena cared, it would break her heart. This. This is why she's never brought anyone to her den. This is why, for centuries, for millennia, for as long as she can remember, she's been alone.

She helps him pack the truck. There's all kinds of salvage that they both know she'll never need again, that he can sell or trade to start a new life, if he's lucky. Only enough petrol for a quarter tank, after the aeroplane is fully fueled. That'll get him into town. After that, it's not her responsibility.

She can see him, watching her as she climbs the path, until the path takes her around a bend, and he's gone.

She hugs his leather jacket to her. It still smells of him. She had made herself a flight jacket of goatskin, but he'd just laughed at her. "You look ridiculous. You'll never make it to heaven dressed like that."

She waits there, out of his sight, until she hears the engine of the truck start. Then she continues her climb.

It seems to take longer than it should, and yet her arrival at the plateau on which her plane waits comes unexpectedly. The entire mechanism she's constructed depends on perfect timing, every piece of it, from the synchronized pattern of the pistons to the firing of the Lewis guns, to the triggering of the launch ramp. She could write a book about time and mechanics, and another about time and memory, both true and both contradictory, if she had time. It would be inconvenient if she got them tangled while she was in the air.

She checks the aeroplane's systems: petrol and oil tanks full, the rudders and flaps all operational. She checks all her (their) screws and bolts, double-checks the mechanics of the sliding ramp. She crank-starts the engines, one by one, and starts the generator, checking that the belt that will power her launch is turning correctly.

After that, there's no more putting it off. Besides, it's nearly midday, when the trip will be shortest.

She climbs up into the plane and settles into the pilot's cockpit. One last check of the instruments, of the bombs under her seat. The rest of the bombs are in the other cockpit, out of her reach, as are the observers' guns. The guns are useless, and she probably should have removed them to save their weight. The bombs, those she'll use last, burying the nose of the plane in whatever she needs to destroy when everything else is exhausted.

The hand on her shoulder surprises her; she spins, teeth bared and hackles up.

"You're in my chair," the pilot shouts over the sound of the engines. He's wearing her goatskin flight jacket.

And Hyena laughs through her sudden grin.

The ramp works as planned. With the breaks disengaged and engines at full, the aeroplane rumbles forward, up to and onto the ramp. There's no way to hear the click of the trigger, the snap of the flaps at the back of the ramp lifting, the screech of rubber and rope catching, the scrape of wood sliding over rock, but Hyena feels it, in her heart if not her body. The ramp slides forward, collapsing into its tracks and rolling out. At the end of the tracks, the ramp stops, the front end drops and the back end rises up, slingshotting them forward before it breaks off entirely and begins to tumble down the side of the mountain.

Their momentum carries them forward for a few seconds before gravity's call can no longer be denied. The nose drops, and the base of the cliff rushes toward them.

Hyena has survived long falls before, recovering slowly over centuries with gifts of food and water from her sisters. The last time, she wasn't packed in a machine with dozens of bombs and nearly ten thousand pounds of petrol. Well, she hadn't expected to live through this adventure, she just wishes the pilot had taken the truck and gone.

The air screams around them. The aeroplane jerks and shudders as an outcropping catches the landing gear and tears it away, and the nose tips toward the mountain, briefly, but the pilot is *not* second-rate, not at all, and a moment later the world turns abruptly. The ground disappears, and Hyena looks out across an endless sky.

There's a tap on her shoulder, and the pilot holds up his speaking tube. She puts hers against her ear.

"Bit of a nail-biter there for a minute," he says, which must be an idiom she's unaware of. "Where now?"

Hyena grins at him and points straight up.

"Aeroplanes don't work that way," he says.

"This one will." She's sure of it.

After a moment, the pilot smiles at her. He nods and turns the aeroplane toward the midday sun. The engines roar as they rise. The air grows cold and dark and thin, and the stars come out to play with the sun. Hyena wraps her arms around the pilot's leather jacket and doesn't look back.

ABOUT THE AUTHORS

David Lee Summers became a steampunk in 1987 when he used a nineteenth century telescope on Nantucket to examine the evolution of distant pulsating stars. Since that time, he has published a dozen novels and numerous short stories and poems spanning a wide range of the imagination. *Owl Dance, Lightning Wolves, The Brazen Shark,* and *Owl Riders* comprise the Clockwork Legion steampunk series. His other novels include *The Astronomer's Crypt, Vampires of the Scarlet Order* and *Firebrandt's Legacy.* His latest novella is a World War II-era cryptid tale called *Breaking the Code.*

David's short stories have appeared in such magazines and anthologies as *Realms of Fantasy, Cemetery Dance, Straight Outta Tombstone, Gaslight and Grimm,* and *After Punk.* He's been twice nominated for the Science Fiction Poetry Association's Rhysling Award.

In addition to writing, David has edited the science fiction anthologies: *A Kepler's Dozen, Kepler's Cowboys,* and *Maximum Velocity: The Best of the Full-Throttle Space Tales.* When not working with the written word, David operates telescopes at Kitt Peak National Observatory. Learn more about David at www.davidleesummers.com.

Aaron Rosenberg is the best-selling, award-winning author of nearly fifty novels, including the DuckBob SF comedy series, the Relicant Chronicles epic fantasy series, the Areyat Islands fantasy pirate mystery series, the *Dread Remora* space-opera series, and, with David Niall Wilson, the *O.C.L.T.* occult thriller series. His tie-in work contains novels for *Star Trek, Warhammer, World of WarCraft, Stargate: Atlantis,*

Shadowrun, Mutants & Masterminds, and *Eureka* and short stories for *The X-Files, World of Darkness, Crusader Kings II, Deadlands, Master of Orion,* and *Europa Universalis IV.* He has written children's books (including the original series STEM Squad and Pete and Penny's Pizza Puzzles, the award-winning *Bandslam: The Junior Novel* and the #1 best-selling *42: The Jackie Robinson Story*), educational books on a variety of topics, and over 70 roleplaying games (including the original games *Asylum, Spookshow,* and *Chosen,* work for White Wolf, Wizards of the Coast, Fantasy Flight, Pinnacle, and many others, the Origins Award-winning *Gamemastering Secrets,* and the Gold ENnie-winning *Lure of the Lich Lord*). He is a founding member of Crazy 8 Press. Aaron lives in New York with his family. You can follow him online at gryphonrose.com, on Facebook at facebook.com/gryphonrose, and on Twitter @gryphonrose.

John L. French is a retired crime scene supervisor with forty years' experience. He has seen more than his share of murders, shootings, and serious assaults. As a break from the realities of his job, he started writing science fiction, pulp, horror, fantasy, and, of course, crime fiction.

John's first story "Past Sins" was published in Hardboiled Magazine and was cited as one of the best Hardboiled stories of 1993. More crime fiction followed, appearing in Alfred Hitchcock's Mystery Magazine, the Fading Shadows magazines, and in collections by Barnes and Noble. Association with writers like James Chambers and the late, great C.J. Henderson led him to try horror fiction and to a still growing fascination with zombies and other undead things. His first horror story "The Right Solution" appeared in Marietta Publishing's *Lin Carter's Anton Zarnak.* Other horror stories followed in anthologies such as *The Dead Walk* and *Dark Furies,* both published by Die Monster Die books. It was in *Dark Furies* that his character Bianca Jones made her literary debut in "21 Doors," a story based on an old Baltimore legend and a creepy game his daughter used to play with her friends.

John's first book was *The Devil of Harbor City,* a novel done in the old pulp style. *Past Sins* and *Here There Be Monsters* followed. John was also consulting editor for Chelsea House's *Criminal Investigation* series. His other books include *The Assassins' Ball* (written with Patrick Thomas), *Souls on Fire, The Nightmare Strikes, Monsters Among Us, The Last Redhead, the Magic of Simon Tombs,* and *The Santa Heist* (written with

Patrick Thomas). John is the editor of *To Hell in a Fast Car*, *Mermaids 13*, C. J. Henderson's *Challenge of the Unknown*, *Camelot 13* (with Patrick Thomas), and (with Greg Schauer) *With Great Power …*

You can find John on Facebook or you can email him at him at jfrenchfam@aol.com.

Heather E. Hutsell is the authoress of over twenty titles, including the steampunk mystery series *The Case Files*, short story compilations *The Doll Collection* Volumes 1 & 2, and an epic poem, *The Merry Widow of Frankenstein*. Her other works include fantasy, romantic horror, absurdist fiction, dystopia, and fairytales gone awry. Her most recent publications are the paranormal novella *Nevermore, Inc.*, and *366 Tales: Stories Year Round*, a collection of flash fiction. Heather has also written two historical documentary series for Lionheart Productions, LLC, contributed numerous articles to OneUnitedLanaster.com, and has stories in three anthologies put out by Crazy 8 Press. You can learn more about her projects at www.heatherehutsell.com.

Award-winning author, editor, and publisher **Danielle Ackley-McPhail** has worked both sides of the publishing industry for longer than she cares to admit. In 2014 she joined forces with Mike McPhail and Greg Schauer to form eSpec Books (www.especbooks.com).

Her published works include eight novels, *Yesterday's Dreams, Tomorrow's Memories, Today's Promise, The Halfling's Court, The Redcaps' Queen, Daire's Devils, The Play of Light,* and *Baba Ali and the Clockwork Djinn,* written with Day Al-Mohamed. She is also the author of the solo collections *Eternal Wanderings, A Legacy of Stars, Consigned to the Sea, Flash in the Can, Transcendence, The Kindly Ones, Dawns a New Day, The Fox's Fire, Between Darkness and Light,* and the non-fiction writers' guides *The Literary Handyman, More Tips from the Handyman,* and *LH: Build-A-Book Workshop.* She is the senior editor of the *Bad-Ass Faeries* anthology series, *Gaslight & Grimm, Side of Good/Side of Evil, After Punk,* and *Footprints in the Stars.* Her short stories are included in numerous other anthologies and collections. She is a full member of the Science Fiction and Fantasy Writers Association.

In addition to her literary acclaim, she crafts and sells original costume horns under the moniker The Hornie Lady Custom Costume Horns, and homemade flavor-infused candied ginger under the brand of Ginger KICK! at literary conventions, on commission, and wholesale.

Danielle lives in New Jersey with husband and fellow writer Mike McPhail and four extremely spoiled cats.

Ken Schrader writes Science Fiction, Fantasy, Weird Westerns, and anything else he can get away with. He's a shameless Geek, a fan of the Oxford comma, and he makes housing decisions based upon the space available for bookshelves.

He sings out loud when there's no one around, enjoys a good grilling session, and loves a powerful drum beat. He can also procrastinate so well you'd think it was a superpower.

He lives in Michigan, and despite the seasonal allergies, he always enjoys mowing the lawn.

Misty Massey is the author of the *Mad Kestrel* series of rollicking fantasy adventures on the high seas. She is an editor for several small presses, and an instructor for the Speculative Fiction Academy (https://www.speculativefictionacademy.com/) When she's not writing or editing, Misty appears on the Authors & Dragons podcast sister show, Calamity Janes, as the cheerful, sundrenched cleric, Malibu. She's a sucker for ginger snaps, African coffee, and anything sparkly. You can keep up with Misty at mistymassey.com and on Facebook and Twitter.

James Chambers received the Bram Stoker Award® for the graphic novel, *Kolchak the Night Stalker: The Forgotten Lore of Edgar Allan Poe* and is a four-time Bram Stoker Award nominee. He is the author of the short story collections *On the Night Border* and *On the Hierophant Road*, which received a starred review from *Booklist*, which called it "…satisfyingly unsettling"; and the novella collection, *The Engines of Sacrifice*, described as "…chillingly evocative…" in a *Publisher's Weekly* starred review. He has written the novellas, *Three Chords of Chaos*, *Kolchak and the Night Stalkers: The Faceless God*, and many others, including the Corpse Fauna cycle: *The Dead Bear Witness, Tears of Blood, The Dead in Their Masses*, and *The Eyes of the Dead*. He also writes the Machinations Sundry series of steampunk stories. He edited the Bram Stoker Award-nominated anthology, *Under Twin Suns: Alternate Histories of the Yellow Sign* and co-edited *A New York State of Fright* and *Even in the Grave*, an anthology of ghost stories. His website is: www.jameschambersonline.com.

Derek Tyler Attico is a science fiction author, essayist, and photographer. He is a winner of the Excellence in Playwriting Award from the Dramatist Guild of America and a two-time winner of the Star Trek Strange New Worlds short story contest. Derek is also a contributing freelance writer to the *Star Trek Adventures* role-playing game from Modiphius Entertainment, and a game designer for the upcoming Renegade Legion RPG. With a degree in English and History, Derek is an advocate of the arts, human rights, and inclusion.

When **Maria V. Snyder** was younger, she aspired to be a storm chaser in the American Midwest so she attended Pennsylvania State University and earned a Bachelor of Science degree in Meteorology. Much to her chagrin, forecasting the weather wasn't in her skill set so she spent a number of years as an environmental meteorologist, which is not exciting...at all. Bored at work and needing a creative outlet, she started writing fantasy and science fiction stories. Twenty-two novels and numerous short stories later, Maria's learned a thing or three about writing. She's been on the *New York Times* bestseller list, won a dozen awards, and has earned her Masters of Arts degree in Writing from Seton Hill University, where she is now a faculty member for their MFA program.

Maria's favorite color is red. She loves dogs, but is allergic, instead she has a big black tom cat named...Kitty (apparently naming cats isn't in her skill set either). Maria also has a husband and two grown children who are an inspiration for her writing when they aren't being a distraction. Note: She mentions her cat before her family. When she's not writing, she's either playing pickleball, traveling, taking pictures, or zonked out on the couch due to all of the above. Being a writer, though is a ton of fun. Where else can you take fencing lessons, learn how to ride a horse, study marital arts, learn how to pick a lock, take glass blowing classes and attend Astronomy Camp and call it research? Maria will be the first one to tell you it's not working as a meteorologist. Maria welcomes readers to learn more about her and her books at https://www.MariaVSnyder.com.

Much to his embarrassment, **Bernie Mojzes** has outlived Lord Byron, Percy Shelley, Janice Joplin and the Red Baron, without even once having been shot down over Morlancourt Ridge. Having failed to achieve a glorious martyrdom, he has instead turned his hand to the penning of paltry prose (a rather wretched example of which you currently hold in your hands), in the pathetic hope that he shall here find the notoriety that has thus far proven elusive. His work has appeared in a number of anthologies and magazines, including *Bad-Ass Faeries II* and *III, Gaslight & Grimm, Betwixt Magazine, Daily Science Fiction,* and *What Lies Beneath*. In his copious free time, he published and co-edited *Unlikely Story* (www.unlikely-story.com) and the ever-timely *Clowns: The Unlikely Coulrophobia Remix*, as well as editing *The Flesh Made Word* for Circlet Press. Should Pity or perhaps a Perverse Curiosity move you to seek him out, he can be found at http://www.kappamaki.com.

Yes... Our Circus.
Yes... Our Monkeys.

A. L. Kaplan
Alicia M Rabb
Allison E. Kaese
Alp Beck
Andee Bowden
Andrew Hatchell
Andrew Kaplan
Anonymous Readers
Anthony R. Cardno
Aramanth
Ashley Grant
Asp Zelazny
Barb Moermond
Becky B
Bess Turner
Beth Kee
Beth Lobdell
Beth Rimmels
Beth Sparks-Jacques
Bill Kohn
Bodge Inglee Richards
Brendan Lonehawk
Brian D Lambert
Brooks Moses
Brynn
Buddy Deal

C.A. Rowland
Carl W Bishop
Carol J. Guess
Carol Mammano
Chad Bowden
Charissa D. Jones
Charity Myhre
Charlee Roth
Cheri Kannarr
Christine Norris
Christopher Hykes
Christopher J. Burke
Cindy Joy
CJ Frost
Colleen Feeney
Craig & René Arnush
Cristov Russell
Cynthia Radthorne
Dale A Russell
Dana Fraedrich
Danielle Ackley-McPhail
David Goldstein
David Zurek
Dayton Shaw
Deborah A. Flores
Debra Lieven

Doc Coleman
Don Crossman
Donna Marie Hogg
Doug Williams
Douglas G. Yeager
Douglas Yeager
Ef Deal
Elaine Tindill-Rohr
Elaine Yang
Ellery Rhodes
Elyse M Grasso
Emma Lombard
Eric Schumacher
Eron Wyngarde
Gary Phillips
Gavin
Gayle Homes Martin
Ginger Devaney
Greg Levick
Hadrosaur Productions
Heather L.P. Estep
Heidi B Pilewski
Helen Walter
Hiram G Wells
Ian Harvey
Isaac 'Will It Work' Dansicker
Jaap van Poelgeest
Jack Deal
Jacob H Joseph
Janet Worley
Janito V. F. Filho
Jason
Jeanne Talbourdet
Jeff Young
Jenn Long
Jennifer Eaton
Jennifer L. Pierce
Jeremy Bottroff
Jess
Jessa Willson
Jessi Sindel

Jessica Lewis
Joanne Burrows
Joe Monson
John L. French
John Shrek Walters
John Stuart
John Wilson
Jon W. Quigley
Jonathan Mendonca
Jonathan Roth
Jordan G Ritchie
Josh McGinnis
Julian White
June L. Chase
June L. Chase
Kal Powell
Kat James
Kathryn Black
Katie French
Kelly A. Durkee-Erwin
Kelly Pierce
Kerry aka Trouble
Kestrel von Nerdenheimer
Kierin Fox
Krinsky
Kristiina Mannermaa
Krystal Bohannan
KT Magrowski
Kurt Beyerl
Kyro Dean
Larien
Laura Pesula
Linda Pierce
Lisa Kruse
Lloyd Lively
Lorraine J. Anderson
Louise Lowenspets
Lynda McCann
Mad Madeline
Madame Askew
Madeleine Holly-Rosing

maileguy
Margaret Bumby
Margaret M. St. John
Mari Hersh-Tudor
Maria V. Arnold
Marie Devey
Marilyn Bennett
Marissa C.
Mark Carter
Mark Newman
Martin Oe.
Mary-Michelle Moore
Matt & Liz Aronoff
Maureen Lewis
Mel Follmer
Melody Huckins
Michael Barbour
Michael Fedrowitz
Michele Hall
Michelle LaCrosse
Mike Smith
Morgan Hazelwood
Museworthy Inc.
Natasha Hubbard
Neil Ottenstein
Nellie B
No Name
Oliver James Minall
Otter Libris
Patrick Thomas
Paul Mojzes
Paul Ryan
Paul van Oven
Phil Huffsmith
Phil Pearson
pjk
prophet
PunkARTchick "Ruthenia"
Rachel
Raphael Bressel
Rhonda Goodman-Gaghan

Rich Walker
Richard Novak
Richard O'Shea
RKBookman
Robert C Flipse
Robert Claney
Robert Dahlen
Robin Schwarz
Russell Dennis Trimble
Sally W
Sanan Kolva
Sara E. Ontiveros
Sarah Olliso Flores
Scantrontb
Scott Schaper
Sebastian Ernst
Shawnee M
Shervyn
Sheryl R. Hayes
Sioux McGill
Sonya Mota
Stace Johnson
Stacy K Waddington
Steph Parker
Stephanie Lucas
Stephen Ballentine
Stephen Buchanan
Stuart Chaplin
Susan J. Voss
Susan R Grossman
Tasha Turner
Taylor Hunter
tchwrtr
Tess DeGroot
The Creative Fund by BackerKit
Thomas Karwacki
Tim DuBois
Timothy Ryan Scully
Tina M Noe Good
Tom Tiernan
Tracy 'Rayhne" Fretwell

Valerie Bello
Vicki Hsu
Walter J. Montie

white beard geek
William J. Jackson